PRAISE FOR

women on the verge of a nervous breakthrough

"Ruth Pennebaker's prose is sharp enough to do Dorothy Parker proud."   —Robert Leleux, author of *The Memoirs of a Beautiful Boy*

"Everyone who's ever had a mother or a daughter—or been a mother or a daughter—will be saying 'Yes!' all the way through Ruth Pennebaker's marvelous first novel about three generations of related women living together. There is angst and wit with a Texas twang as life unfolds in this story set down squarely in the time we are living in now."

—Margo Howard, author of *Ann Landers in Her Own Words: Personal Letters to Her Daughter* and the *Dear Margo* column at wowOwow.com

"Ruth Pennebaker has hit the trifecta with *Women on the Verge of a Nervous Breakthrough*, an irresistible comic novel that is breezily hilarious, thought provoking, and, ultimately, tender and heart tugging. From [a] sullen teenager to [a] neurotic divorcée to an elderly woman who's lost her savings in the recession, these women are vibrant with life, conflict, and high spirits."

—Sarah Bird, author of *The Gap Year*

women
on the
verge of a
nervous
breakthrough

ruth pennebaker

BERKLEY BOOKS, NEW YORK

THE BERKLEY PUBLISHING GROUP
Published by the Penguin Group
Penguin Group (USA) Inc.
375 Hudson Street, New York, New York 10014, USA
Penguin Group (Canada), 90 Eglinton Avenue East, Suite 700, Toronto, Ontario M4P 2Y3, Canada
(a division of Pearson Penguin Canada Inc.)
Penguin Books Ltd., 80 Strand, London WC2R 0RL, England
Penguin Group Ireland, 25 St. Stephen's Green, Dublin 2, Ireland (a division of Penguin Books Ltd.)
Penguin Group (Australia), 250 Camberwell Road, Camberwell, Victoria 3124, Australia
(a division of Pearson Australia Group Pty. Ltd.)
Penguin Books India Pvt. Ltd., 11 Community Centre, Panchsheel Park, New Delhi—110 017, India
Penguin Group (NZ), 67 Apollo Drive, Rosedale, North Shore 0632, New Zealand
(a division of Pearson New Zealand Ltd.)
Penguin Books (South Africa) (Pty.) Ltd., 24 Sturdee Avenue, Rosebank, Johannesburg 2196,
South Africa

Penguin Books Ltd., Registered Offices: 80 Strand, London WC2R 0RL, England

This book is an original publication of The Berkley Publishing Group.

This is a work of fiction. Names, characters, places, and incidents either are the product of the author's imagination or are used fictitiously, and any resemblance to actual persons, living or dead, business establishments, events, or locales is entirely coincidental. The publisher does not have any control over and does not assume responsibility for author or third-party websites or their content.

PRINTING HISTORY
Berkley trade paperback edition / January 2011

Library of Congress Cataloging-in-Publication Data

Pennebaker, Ruth.
    Women on the verge of a nervous breakthrough / Ruth Pennebaker.
        p.   cm.
    ISBN 978-0-425-23856-1
    1. Middle-aged women—Fiction.   2. Divorced women—Fiction.   3. Single women—Fiction.
4. Austin (Tex.)—Fiction.   5. Domestic fiction.   I. Title.
    PS3566.E4765W66   2011
    813'.54—dc22
                                2010023023

PRINTED IN THE UNITED STATES OF AMERICA

10   9   8   7   6   5   4   3   2   1

For Teal

acknowledgments

I'm fortunate to have wonderfully astute and opinionated writer friends like Joyce Saenz Harris and Sophia Dembling, who read my manuscript and offered their thoughts on it. Thanks to both of them.

Deirdre Mullane, my agent, brought tremendous enthusiasm and intelligence to the project, and I'm very grateful for her representation.

Then there's my husband, who has an incredible sense of narrative and freely offers his advice on my writing. I always appreciate his criticisms in the long run, since I know he's often right—even though it kills me to admit it.

Finally, Carol Dawson is a writer's best friend. Her ideas and criticisms added immeasurably to this novel.

chapter 1

"I don't want you to get upset when I tell you this," Richard said.

He was breathing heavily into the phone.

"Upset about what?" Joanie asked.

"You already sound upset, Joanie. Maybe I should tell you later."

"Upset about *what?*"

"Will you calm down?"

"I hate it," Joanie said, "when somebody starts a conversation like this. *Don't take this the wrong way. Don't get upset. Nothing personal, but* . . . You always know it's going to end badly."

Silence. Joanie examined her nails and listened to Richard's breathing. She could wait. Hell, she could wait forever. She was getting good at that. The person who controls the silence controls the conversation. She had read that somewhere.

"Upset about what?" she asked again. Her voice was light, casual. It sounded good. What was the word? Oh, yes. *Insouciant*.

"Well," Richard said, "B.J. is pregnant. I thought you should know."

"D.J.? Who's that?"

"*B*.J., Joanie. You know who she is. We've been living together for three months now."

"Oh. Really? That little teenager?"

"She's twenty-nine, Joanie. She'll be thirty by the time the baby is—"

"You motherfucking asshole!" Joanie screamed. She slammed down the phone.

People were always yelling in this house.

Ivy had distinctly heard her forty-nine-year-old daughter screaming. She'd heard the word *asshole*, along with other even more unsavory terms. Ivy's own mother, dead for some thirty years and not particularly mourned, would have washed her daughter's mouth out with soap if she'd ever heard her utter words of that ilk. "Didn't I bring you up better than that?" her mother would have asked, her eyes narrowing, her lips pursed.

But this was the twenty-first century and nobody's mouth got washed out with soap anymore, as Ivy frequently reminded herself. Besides, she was living at her daughter's house, trying to be helpful and unobtrusive and not at all critical. It wasn't her place to find fault.

Ivy peered into the shadowy living room. Her daughter was slumped on the couch, arms crossed, remote control clutched to her chest. The stark light from the TV illuminated her face. Either the TV shadows were moving or her daughter's facial muscles were running amok, twitching like a furious cartoon character's. She looked ready to pull out a shotgun and unload it.

"Roxanne," Ivy said. "Did I hear you yelling?"

"I have no idea what you heard, Mother," Joanie said sullenly.

"Well, maybe the yelling came from the TV," Ivy said helpfully. "What are you watching?"

Joanie raised the remote control and turned off the TV with a sharp snap, leaving the room in shadows.

"I'm not watching anything," she said.

"Would you like some hot tea?" Ivy asked.

"I hate tea, Mother. You know that."

"Well," Ivy said. "That's right. You always hated tea. Your brother was the one who loved it." She lingered in the doorway, thinking for a few more seconds. "Do you want to talk?"

Joanie pulled a sofa cushion up to her chest and wrapped her arms around it.

"No," she said. "Thank you, Mother. I'd just like to be alone."

"And then," Joanie said, "he has the fucking nerve to tell me he and that little albino are having a baby."

"She's an albino?" Mary Margaret said. "You never told me that."

Joanie heaved a sigh, settling into the couch with the phone at her ear. She'd better watch out. Her mother was probably still lurking around, trying to eavesdrop. Always ready to criticize—the way she had been Joanie's whole life.

"Well, maybe not *technically* an albino," she said in a lower voice. "But very pale. Washed-out looking."

"Does she have pink eyes?"

"Mary Margaret, this is *serious*. Caroline will probably have a nervous breakdown when she hears about this pregnancy—"

"You haven't told her yet?"

"No! Of course I haven't. You're the first person I've talked to."

"So," Mary Margaret said, "how is Caroline these days?" Caroline was Joanie's daughter.

"How is any fifteen-year-old girl? I don't know. She won't tell me. She hates me. Every night, by the time I get home from work, she's in her room with the door locked."

"She used to be such a sweet girl."

"She's still a sweet girl," Joanie said quickly, even though "sweet" wasn't exactly the word that described Caroline these days. Other *s* words would be more appropriate: sulky, stubborn, sardonic, scornful, secretive, spiteful.

"And she probably doesn't hate you," Mary Margaret said after too long a pause.

"She acts like she hates me. You should see the way she rolls her eyes every time I say something."

"She shouldn't do that. It's rude."

"Teenagers are supposed to be rude, Mary Margaret. That's how they prove their independence."

"God! Spare me. Now you're sounding like a therapist."

Mary Margaret had never been in therapy. She'd grown up on a ranch in West Texas, where people believed you should shut up and stop whining and get over your problems. Life was supposed to be hard. And unfair! So what?

"I know Caroline doesn't hate me," Joanie said slowly. "Not really. But she *thinks* she hates me. That's worse."

"How do you know what she thinks?"

"I'm her mother, Mary Margaret. I can tell."

chapter 2

"Your father called me with some news," Joanie said to Caroline the next morning as she drove her to school.

"Why d'you call him my father?" Caroline asked. She pulled her long, straight hair back over her shoulders. It needed to be cut, but she kept ignoring Joanie's occasional hints about getting "just a trim" and her hair kept growing. Right now, it looked like limp, wet yarn.

"What else would I call him?"

"*Richard*. Isn't that his name?"

Joanie braked at the stoplight and stared straight ahead. Next to her, Caroline was bent over her cell phone, typing in a message. Texting, that's what they called it. Caroline was always texting or reading messages, staring at that little rectangle of light like the meaning of life was going to appear there. The rest of the world—unimportant, boring, filled with loser adults like Joanie—dropped away.

"All right. *Richard*. I just wanted to make it clear who I was talking about—"

"It's clear. Why would I be confused about that?"

More texting, with greater intensity. What was Caroline typing now? *I hate my mother*, no doubt. But they probably had a code for it—like that joke Joanie had once read, about comedians who were so familiar with one another's routines that they simply called out the numbers of their jokes and everybody laughed.

Number One: I hate my mother.

Number Two: My mother is a bitch.

Number Three: God! You should see the pathetic outfit she's wearing today! I don't want to be caught dead with her.

"Caroline," Joanie said. "It isn't helpful when you use that tone of voice with me."

More texting; furiously intense texting. Which number was she writing now? Joanie had read that texting while driving was very dangerous. Well, trying to read your teenage daughter's texting while you were driving was even more dangerous. Joanie was going to wrap her car around a tree any minute now. Good. Maybe it would destroy that nasty little cell phone Joanie was paying a monthly fortune for. Joanie and Caroline would walk away from the wreck, unhurt and thrilled to be alive. Profoundly shaken by the experience, they would once again be close and happy, the way they used to be. Things like that happened. Not often enough. But sometimes.

"Caroline," Joanie said. "Listen to me."

"I'm listening."

"Your father—I mean, *Richard*—and his girlfriend—"

"Girlfriend? What girlfriend?"

"Oh, you know. That one he's been with for a few months."
Be positive, Joanie told herself. Do not, under any circumstances, undermine your child's other parent by your tone of
voice or the content of your words. That is unfair to your child
and to the mature relationship you are trying to build with
your former spouse. "B.J. The—the *blonde*."

"Oh. Yeah. Her." Caroline shrugged. She looked straight
ahead. At least she wasn't texting any longer.

"Well," Joanie said, not entirely trusting her voice. "I have
some news about them. Richard and B.J. are going to have a
baby."

Caroline's head bent over farther, toward her lap. She stared
at her cell phone still clutched in her hands. She didn't say
anything, didn't text. But Joanie could see a telltale blush
spreading up her neck. Caroline had thin, almost transparent,
skin—like a baby bird before it grew feathers. You could always read her emotions just below the surface.

"Honey, I know you're upset by this," Joanie said. "It's a
surprise. It's—"

"I'm not upset."

"—it's just a *shock*, that's all. You weren't expecting this,
and—"

"Why don't you ever listen to me, Mother?" Caroline's voice
was harsh, laden with sarcasm, the way it always was when she
called Joanie *Mother*, instead of Mom. "I am not upset."

Joanie edged the car into the circular drive in front of Caroline's high school. She put the gear in park and turned to
Caroline, just as her daughter slipped out and slammed the

car door. Caroline's thin face was pale and set. It had sharpened and changed in ways that were almost unrecognizable to Joanie, who sometimes searched it to see the solemn, sweet girl Caroline used to be.

Joanie watched for a few more seconds, as Caroline disappeared into a crowd of students. Behind her, someone honked. She put the car back into gear and drove toward downtown. She didn't need to be late for work again.

"I need your ideas," Zoe said. She took off her Euro-chic glasses, with their straight, black tops and clear rims, her eyes roaming feverishly around the table. "You are all creative people. I need you to *create*."

Silence. Eight pairs of eyes, including Joanie's, stared back at Zoe.

"This could be a big account," Zoe said. "The biggest one our agency has ever landed. But nobody's going to give it to us. Do you understand that? We have to be *hungry* for it."

Joanie stared at her pen, twirling it around in her fingers. At fraught times like this, she feared for Zoe's mental health. Since Zoe—the agency's latest creative director, preceded by two rumored nervous breakdowns and one Xanax overdose—was her supervisor, it also made her fear for her own sanity. She frowned and tried to look properly intense. Hungry. Hell, yes, she was hungry. It was almost lunchtime.

"I hear you saying you want us to create," said Tanya. She took off her glasses, too, and narrowed her eyes. "This is a big account."

"A very big account," Zoe said.

"A very big account," Tanya said.

"We can't afford to be small thinkers," Zoe said. Her fingers arched upward toward her face, vibrating in the air. "We have to reach inside ourselves—"

"Think outside the box," Tanya said.

"—demand more of ourselves," Zoe continued, looking irritated at being interrupted with a shopworn cliché when she was building into a high-stakes management crescendo. "You wouldn't be here if you weren't talented and driven. You're the best creative team I've ever worked with. *All* of you.

"I know I'm asking for a lot. But I have faith in you. I have faith in us."

"I think we all understand that," Tanya said. She was in her thirties and was an expert in "messaging strategies," she had told Joanie. She had offered to help Joanie with her own messaging ability, but so far, Joanie hadn't taken her up on it. "We're ready for this."

"High fives!" Zoe announced. She went around the table, slapping hands with her coworkers. When she reached Joanie, Joanie tried to slap back with enthusiasm and high spirits and bravado. But for some reason, she just felt silly.

"So," Bruce said, craning his neck into Joanie's office doorway, "what did you think about the big meeting? Kind of like a pep rally, huh?"

Joanie smiled pleasantly, noncommittally. "It was interesting."

"You free for lunch?" Bruce asked.

"Uh—no. I've got plans already. Sorry." Joanie swept her arm up in front of her face and squinted at her watch, trying not to look too obvious. "Oops. I'm late."

"Another time, maybe," Bruce said.

He waved at Joanie as she rushed past him. He looked a little forlorn, standing there in the doorway, his striped shirt a bit rumpled, his graying brown hair a little disheveled. For a few seconds, Joanie felt a twinge of empathy for him. It was hard to be middle-aged in a youth-worshiping industry navigated by children in their twenties and thirties. She knew that; felt it all the time.

"He's not a bad person. Bruce, I mean," she told her friend Mary Margaret over lunch.

"Who? Oh, that old guy?" Mary Margaret said. She blew heartily on her miso soup, sending a couple of green onions sailing through the air in Joanie's direction.

"He's not that old. In his late fifties, maybe."

"Married?"

"Divorced, I think." Bruce didn't wear a wedding ring. Joanie wished she would stop noticing things like that. It made her feel she wasn't a highly serious career woman, committed only to her work and to rocketing her way to success.

"Good-looking?"

"Well, yeah, sort of. Kind of cute."

Mary Margaret shrugged dismissively. She could talk endlessly about men, as long as they were good-looking, sexy—and unavailable. Like her current boyfriend of three years, Marc, who would never leave his wife. He was handsome, admittedly, but Joanie always suspected his lack of attainability made him even more attractive to Mary Margaret.

"The trouble is," Joanie added quickly, before Mary Margaret could bring up her latest bereft and lonely weekend spent watching HBO reruns, waxing her legs, and sneaking cigarettes out of her freezer, where she hid them from Marc, who disapproved of smoking, even in absentia, "Bruce is burned out. He has a terrible attitude about work. Everybody knows he should have quit the business years ago."

Mary Margaret shrugged, as she bit into her sushi. But Joanie didn't go on. She didn't say what she was thinking, which was that she didn't feel she could afford to be too close to someone with a bad attitude like Bruce's. Joanie was too new, untested. She needed the job too badly.

She didn't want to think she was that kind of person—calculating. For most of her life, she'd considered herself to be openhearted and generous. But that had been in her old life, before the divorce, when she didn't have to support herself, didn't have a future to worry about. Was being open and generous a luxury she couldn't afford now? Was it easier to be a good person when you didn't have as much to lose?

Mary Margaret was the kind of friend she laughed and gossiped and drank with, though. She wouldn't be interested in Joanie's doubts about herself. You had different friends for different facets of your life, Joanie supposed. There were friends you talked to and friends you listened to. It was a rare friendship that combined both.

Besides, Mary Margaret especially wouldn't find Joanie's platonic interactions with Bruce very interesting. She knew Joanie had given up on sex since her divorce. Joanie didn't want sex, didn't need it, had sworn a blood oath to keep to herself for the rest of her life—probably. She was temporarily deranged and just needed a vibrator, Mary Margaret said. But Joanie knew better.

"How was your weekend?" Joanie asked Mary Margaret.

"It was hell," Mary Margaret said. "Pure hell." She dabbed her face with a napkin and started to explain. Joanie tried to look interested while she guardedly peered at her watch. Clearly, their lunch was going to run long.

Only six months ago, when Ivy's stock portfolio had plummeted along with the rest of the country's and she'd come to live with Joanie and Caroline, Joanie had tried to comfort herself with bright plans for their lives together.

Admittedly, she and her mother had never gotten along. But now, she and Ivy and Caroline had the wonderful opportunity to get to know one another. They would talk and laugh at dinner, exchanging gossip and secrets, telling one another things only another woman could understand. Caroline would learn about another, older, generation, while Ivy would benefit from being around someone young and energetic and modern. They would both come to a greater appreciation of Joanie of course: Joanie, the middle generation, the glue in the household, the center of it all.

God Almighty, had she been deluded! Either that or temporarily insane. Joanie wished she were still insane, though. She'd be a lot happier.

Night after night, sharing dinner with her mother and daughter, Joanie thought about Jean-Paul Sartre, of all people. In college, she had read one of his most depressing plays,

No Exit. The play had three characters who drove one another crazy. It ended with the realization that hell is other people.

Who ever said, Joanie thought now, that a liberal arts education was a waste of time? Jean-Paul would be right at home at her table, night after night after night.

"That girl doesn't eat enough," Ivy was saying, pointing to Caroline. "She's too skinny."

Caroline ignored her grandmother and glared at Joanie instead.

"Don't call her *that girl*, Mother," Joanie said. "Her name is Caroline. She's your granddaughter."

"I know who she is," Ivy said placidly. "She's still too skinny."

"Make her stop talking about me," Caroline hissed to Joanie.

"It's rude to comment on other people's weight, Mother," Joanie said.

"She's spoiled, too," Ivy said. "You haven't been enough of a disciplinarian, Roxanne."

"Why does she keep calling you *Roxanne*?" Caroline asked.

"Hey! I've got a really great idea," Joanie said brightly. "Why don't the two of you talk to each other? You're sitting at the same table, aren't you?"

"Not by choice," Caroline said.

Ivy belched loudly. Ten years ago, as a fastidious aging woman, she would have been mortified by the sound. Right now, she looked relieved and cheerful. She belched again. It was a monster burp, long and loud and deep. A fraternity boy would have been proud.

"Oh, God." Caroline groaned. "That is dis*gusting*."

"Will you please pass the macaroni, Mother?" Joanie asked.

Ivy passed the macaroni. She dabbed her mouth with a napkin very daintily, her record-setting belches forgotten. "That is excellent macaroni, Roxanne. Did you use my recipe?"

"No, Mother. It comes from that take-out place. I don't like to cook—"

"No," Ivy said, shaking her head. "You never did."

"Besides," Joanie said, "I don't have the *time* to cook every night."

"I believe I always cooked homemade meals," Ivy said. "Every night."

"You didn't work outside the home, Mother. You were a housewife."

"You can get some easy recipes on the Internet, Roxanne."

"Grandma knows about the Internet?" Caroline asked.

"No, she's just talking," Joanie said. "She doesn't know what she's saying."

"Will you please stop talking about me as if I weren't here?" Ivy said. "I know all about the Internet. I know how to Goggle."

"It's *Google*, Mother."

"I have lots of homework," Caroline said. "May I be excused?"

"I Goggle all kinds of things while you're at work," Ivy said. "I read the most interesting article recently. It's about the intermingling of the races. People shouldn't do that. It's not good for bloodlines. It weakens people. Do you want to see the article?"

"I don't think so, Mother," Joanie said.

"Is Grandma a racist?" Caroline asked.

"Caroline," Joanie said, "didn't you say you had lots of homework?"

Ivy belched again, looking even more contented.

Joanie stared at the store-bought macaroni, watching the orange cheese congeal. Sartre had been right, but Joanie could be even more specific: Hell was three generations of women living under the same roof.

Every night after dinner Ivy could hear the doors slamming. The girl—what was her name? Oh, yes, Caroline—screamed a lot, too. There was a lot of tension in the house. Ivy could feel it. Tension was very bad for families. That was why Roxanne looked so angry and tired all the time and the girl was too skinny.

When Ivy had been Roxanne's age, she had run a calmer household. All those women's libbers made fun of housewives, but what did they know? Ivy had had a very happy marriage, even if she and her husband, John, hadn't had very much in common. John liked to come home and watch TV and drink a beer. He was always tired after work. All he wanted to do was sit in his easy chair and take naps after dinner.

Sometimes, Ivy asked him about his day at work. She had read in those women's magazines she used to buy at the grocery store that you should be interested in your husband's job. Or, if you weren't interested, you should pretend to be. John always said nothing worth mentioning happened at work. He was an accountant. Accountants didn't like to talk. But that was all right.

Ivy and John—well, let's be honest, it was mostly Ivy—had

brought up two lovely children. Roxanne had never given them any trouble. She had been pretty and agreeable. In fact, she had been much more agreeable as a child and teenager than she was right now. Given her age, she might be going through the Change. Ivy needed to remember to ask her about that.

Ivy loved the name Roxanne. It sounded so exotic—like a character in a novel or a romantic poem. (She wished her parents had called her Roxanne, instead of naming her for a common houseplant.) John had insisted on giving Roxanne the middle name Joan, after an aunt who had gotten hit by a Greyhound bus and died when she was just twenty-six. Joan was a very ordinary name, Ivy had always thought. But it would do as a middle name, which would eventually be left behind when her daughter married.

When Roxanne went off to college, she came home at Thanksgiving and announced she was now calling herself "Joanie." Joanie fit her better, she'd explained. She'd never felt comfortable as a Roxanne. She'd lifted her chin when she'd said that, staring at them through her new, long bangs, as if she dared them to object.

John had looked up from his mashed potatoes and gravy and nodded approvingly. But Ivy had been deeply dismayed. For a while, just to be agreeable, she had tried to call her daughter Joanie. But she often forgot about it. Roxanne was too beautiful a name to be wasted and forgotten and replaced by an homage to a woman who hadn't had the sense to get out of the way of a bus.

In her magazines, Ivy had always read, too, that you shouldn't have a favorite child. That was very damaging to the child you didn't love as much. She had tried as hard as she could not to show that her son, David, was her favorite child. From the moment he was born, though, something about him touched Ivy in a way that Roxanne—or John—never could. It was wrong to feel that way. She had prayed about it some-times, but God hadn't seen fit to answer her. Some things you were left to struggle with on your own.

Looking back, she'd had a very good life. She could under-stand that now, especially when she looked at her daughter, who was so miserable and skittish. Ivy had been perfectly content till the evening eight years ago when John fell asleep in front of the TV and never woke up.

He was cold by the time she realized there was something wrong. She called 911 and sat down next to him, waiting for the paramedics. She pushed the hair back from his forehead, smoothing it. He looked very peaceful. She sat there, trying to recall the last words they had spoken to each other. What could they have been? Even now, all these years later, after she had racked her mind again and again, she still couldn't remember.

But they had been kind words, she was sure of that. They hadn't had much to talk about, had often seemed to forget about each other for long periods of time. But they had always been kind when they spoke, like strangers who were polite every time they met.

"What in the hell did you think you were doing, Joanie?"

"Stop screaming at me, Richard. We're not married anymore."

A short silence on the line, then, "All right. Why did you have to tell Caroline about B.J. and me having a baby? I wanted to tell her myself." Richard spoke in a much more reasonable, measured tone. He sounded hurt.

That was a good question. Joanie had wondered why she was telling Caroline the news the moment she opened her damn big mouth earlier in the day.

She could give Richard a whole list of excuses: He hadn't told her *not* to tell Caroline, had he? (True.) It was a mother-daughter matter. (A big lie.) Joanie hadn't intended to say anything. It had just happened. (Not true enough.)

"I'm sorry," Joanie said, realizing exactly why she'd broken the news to Caroline. She was sick of being belittled and blamed for everything in her daughter's life. God, couldn't she do *any*thing right?

It had been so easy, so familiar, to bring up news about Richard that would upset Caroline. Once again, she and Caroline would be on the same side, huddled together and battling the rest of the world—which included Richard and his sorry ilk.

"I know I shouldn't have done it," she said. "I just did. I'm really sorry."

The line fell quiet again, but this time it was a companionable silence. Companionable silences between the two of them were rare these days. Most of the time, Joanie dug into Richard with claws she'd never known she had, scraping and scratching till she drew blood. She wanted him to suffer. Some days, she realized she could have slashed his throat and watched him, impassively, as he bled to death. Who knew she was capable of such hatred and vitriol? It had surprised her again and again, till there were no surprises left.

"I know," Richard said. He sighed. "It's kind of awkward for me, too. I hadn't planned on this."

So he hadn't planned on it? Well, wasn't that a shame, Joanie thought with a certain grim satisfaction.

Richard would be fifty-three by the time the baby was born. Fifty-three with a newborn and a girlfriend who was barely old enough to vote. So much for the easy, free, exciting bachelor's life he had hoped for.

Shortly after Richard left her, when she'd been devastated and depressed, Joanie had read armfuls of books about divorce, male menopause, midlife crises. According to therapists' anecdotes and studies, the partners who left marriages usually ended up unhappy. For the most part, they expected to be immediately and everlastingly blissful after dumping their spouses. But they weren't. They were left with the same problems they'd always had. Nothing had been solved; just the bedroom scenery had changed.

That had been a small, stray bit of comfort on those nights she cried till her eyes were red and crusted shut and her nostrils were raw. Now, it seemed, it had come true.

It didn't make her feel good or smug, though, dammit. That was the fucking problem with life. When you finally got what you wanted, when you were finally proved right, it didn't make you happy the way you expected it to. You just felt empty for some reason. Empty and vaguely sorry for the blind, brutal ways people tried to make themselves happy and failed.

"Will you talk to Caroline?" Richard asked. "She won't take my phone calls."

"Oh, sure. Glad to. She hasn't yelled at me in hours. You know how I hate being ignored like this."

~~~~~

Tap, tap, tap on her bedroom door.

"Just a minute," Caroline said, speaking sharply.

The doorknob turned anyway. And her mother wondered why she kept her door locked all the time? Because she had no privacy whatsoever. That's why.

Caroline pulled out her phone and bent over it. When her mother got on her nerves—which happened about forty-three times an hour—she always pretended to text. That way, she didn't have to look at her mother. She could pretend to be busy and preoccupied. Ha. She usually just wrote messages to herself like, "I hate my goddamned life" or "I wish I could fucking die," followed by several lines of exclamation marks, depending on how bad her mood was.

Everybody in high school went around texting all the time. That was because they had lots of friends and extremely exciting lives. Unlike Caroline, who only had one friend—Sondra—and a life that was so pitiful and boring that she might as well have been in a coma most of the time. Even if she'd had lots of friends, she wouldn't have had anything to text about.

More doorknob racket. Her mother was going to unhinge the door if she didn't stop it. Then she'd have to get a new door and she'd blame Caroline for it. She'd probably dock her allowance or take away her phone. Bitch.

"Caroline! Will you please unlock this door? You know I've told you to—"

Caroline yanked the door open, and Joanie almost fell into her room. The door smashed into the wall and bounced off.

"Roxanne!" Ivy screamed from her room. "Are you all right?"

"We're fine, Mother!" Joanie yelled back. She'd fallen out of her left shoe, stumbling into the room, and she wiggled her foot back into it. She ran her fingers through her short, curly hair and sighed. "Can we talk?" she asked Caroline.

Her mother looked tired and old, Caroline noticed. She had dark circles under her eyes and her mouth drooped at the corners. Her whole face seemed to be falling in the direction of her awful round-toed shoes.

And what was Joanie so nervous about, anyway? She was rubbing her hands together like she wanted to start a fire with them. Most days, Caroline couldn't stand to look at her mother. Just the sight of Joanie—trying too hard, always staring at her, thinking too long before she said anything, hovering like a needy, apologetic vulture—enraged her.

"Sure," Caroline said.

"Can I sit down?" Joanie asked. She looked at Caroline's unmade bed, then at the desk chair that had a good three-feet-deep pile of clothes strewn on top of it. She was making a mental note, Caroline could tell, about the room's messiness. But she'd save it till later.

"Be my guest."

Joanie sank down on the bed, too close to Caroline, who moved up against the wall and threw her head back. She stared at the ceiling fan, trying to cross her eyes.

"Caroline, stop that!"

Caroline uncrossed her eyes. The truth was, she hated crossing her eyes. But she knew her mother hated it even more, so she could never resist doing it. It was fortunate that Joanie watched her all the time like a human guard dog, or her eyes would probably get stuck and then her life would be even worse than it already was.

In the background, above the slap of the ceiling fan, she

could hear her mother speaking in her irritating, determinedly hopeful voice. Something about how she shouldn't have told Caroline about her father and B.J.'s baby, that he wanted to tell her the news himself, yak, yak, blah, blah, blah, how she knew it was hard on Caroline to hear something like this, yammer, yammer, yammer, baby, divorce, other boring shit.

What was she going to do? Talk forever?

Caroline closed her now uncrossed eyes and thought about Henry's face—how, later in the day, a slight black stubble crept up his cheeks. She would love to rub her hand across his roughened cheek and pull his head toward her and kiss those lips that were so luscious they were almost bruised and—

"What are you smiling about, honey?" Joanie asked.

Caroline snapped her head back up straight, like she'd just been startled out of a deep sleep. For once, she stared right into her mother's eyes—searching, faded, curiously sweet—and didn't look away immediately.

"You looked so happy," Joanie said tentatively.

Happy, Caroline thought. Her mother had no idea how happy. She could never understand the warm rush that coursed through Caroline's body when she thought of Henry. Or the icy slap of the occasionally troubling, depressing realization that Henry was totally unaware of her existence, except as an occasional, desperate source of help with his Spanish homework.

Caroline stared for a few seconds at Joanie's face, feeling a twinge of pity for her mother. Joanie's life was so sad and hopeless and empty. She was almost *fifty*. What did she have to look forward to? Getting as old and decrepit and creaky as Grandma, belching at the dinner table, smelly, forgetful, gray-haired, wrinkled. Joanie had some new job that she babbled about, but Caroline usually didn't bother to listen, and she had a few boring friends, and a car that was leaking black smoke and rattling, and some of the saddest-looking old-lady clothes Caroline had ever seen.

She smiled, suddenly, generously, at Joanie, who smiled back delightedly.

Joanie bent toward her and hugged her. Caroline tried not to stiffen and even managed to pat Joanie on the back a couple of times. She sniffed the air, trying to place her mother's perfume, vowing that she would never wear anything that cloying and floral, no matter how old and desperate she got.

"I love you so much, Caroline," Joanie said. She kissed Caroline's cheek and squeezed her hard. Joanie knew it was time for her to leave, but she just wanted it all to last a few seconds longer.

chapter 3
~~~~~~~~~~~

Caroline hated being an only child.

Even her best friend Sondra was better off. Sondra had an older brother named Sean who'd gotten kicked out of the University of Mississippi when he was a freshman. "For drinking too much!" Sondra had told Caroline, her eyes wide with horror. "Drinking! Everybody at Ole Miss drinks. It's kind of like people go there to major in it. How could you get thrown out of there for *drinking*?"

Sondra blamed her parents' overprotectiveness on Sean's dismal collegiate record. They were afraid she'd turn out the same way he had. Sean was now a parking-lot attendant at a downtown lot, where he spent his spare time studying to become a magician. Sometimes, he gave Sondra and Caroline a parking space at half price. But when that happened, they had to stay and watch him do card tricks for a few minutes. He wasn't very good.

"Turn over that card," he'd tell them, pointing to a card on the small table in his kiosk. "It's an ace of spades."

Caroline's stomach always tightened when this happened. It was never an ace of spades. But sometimes it was a two or three of another suit. "That was pretty close," she once told Sean. That didn't make him feel any better. Sometimes, he flung the cards down on the wooden floor, yelling and swearing. Last week, he'd set his magic book on fire in the middle of the parking lot, added a little bourbon to the flame, then stomped it out.

"Sean has undiagnosed ADD," Sondra said later. "That's why he's no good at magic. I wish he'd go back to premed."

But Caroline saw a different side to all of this—this whole business of having a sibling, older or younger, successful or not. You got to share your parents with somebody else, instead of facing the blinding glare of their attention all on your own. It had been bad enough when it was just her and her parents. But now she had both of them straining to be the better, more favored parent—along with Ivy, who was always examining her for signs that she might have an eating disorder or have joined a satanic cult, and B.J., who seemed to want to be her friend or something.

Half the time, Caroline felt overwhelmed by their attention. The other half, she felt neglected in their crazy adult world, with her mother trying to be a success in the advertising industry, her father acting like a bachelor contestant on one of those reality shows, and her mother and grandmother screaming at each other or simmering with tension over the latest dish Joanie had managed to overcook or serve icy and semidefrosted.

When Caroline was younger, when Joanie and Richard were still married and happy—or at least pretending to be—it had been better. Caroline had been the kind of daughter who was well mannered and dutiful and had easily made high grades. Back then, she had lots of friends and she hadn't been nearly as shy or awkward as she was now. Richard went to work every day and Joanie stayed at home, taking up one hobby after another, and turning up at Caroline's school to be a room mother or Girl Scout Brownie leader. It was a normal life. Caroline had been happy then. But she hadn't thought about it much till it was over.

Richard had moved out two years ago, shortly after Caroline's thirteenth birthday. Caroline had awakened early that morning. It was funny how she had known something was wrong, felt like something strange and quiet and poisonous was in the air—but maybe she had just made that up later to make herself feel better. She had been standing in the kitchen, drinking orange juice straight from the plastic container, when she heard an odd noise from the living room. It sounded like somebody crying. But that couldn't be right. Caroline was the only one in the family who ever cried.

She'd walked quietly, barefoot, and peered into the living room. All the shades were still down and it was dark. Joanie, who always opened the shades first thing in the morning to let in the light, was lying on the couch. She was still in her bathrobe. When she saw Caroline, she struggled to her feet and opened up her arms.

"We're going to be all right," she'd said fiercely into

Caroline's hair as she hugged her. "We're going to be fine." Joanie had pulled back and looked into Caroline's face, smoothing Caroline's straight hair and trying to smile. Then her face began to dissolve, just like an old TV commercial Caroline had once seen for a headache remedy where a tablet begins to fizz and then liquefies. That had been her mother's face, melting right in front of her eyes.

Caroline had wrapped her arms around Joanie's neck and Joanie had sobbed like a small child. They had stood there, in the living room, for a long time while Joanie cried and Caroline patted her back and wondered when it had happened that she had grown taller than her mother.

For weeks after Richard left, Caroline and her mother lived like two creatures in a cave. That's what it felt like, anyway. The shades stayed drawn and the house was dark. Joanie usually slept on the couch. She didn't comb her hair, except when Caroline nagged her about it, or put on makeup. She just cried and lay on the couch, staring at the new flat-screen TV Richard had bought just a few weeks before. Joanie had never watched TV much. But now, she seemed hypnotized by it, even by the loud commercials about constipation and impotence.

At first, Caroline had been afraid her mother would kill herself. Joanie showed all the classic signs of depression, according to the Internet: She didn't sleep much, didn't eat, had no energy, stared, cried, didn't bathe enough.

"You're not going to kill yourself, are you, Mom?" she'd finally asked one day. It was in mid-August, shortly before school was about to start, when she'd have to leave her mother alone.

Joanie sat straight up and raked her hair back, looking surprised. Looking—for the first time in weeks—alive.

"Of course not," she said. "My God, Caroline. Of course not." She stood up and walked toward Caroline, gripping her daughter's shoulders and peering into her face. Joanie's eyes were red-ringed and swollen, but focused after so many weeks of listless staring. "I would never, ever kill myself. I can promise you that. *Never.*"

Joanie cupped Caroline's chin in her hand. "Do you understand me? That is not an option—"

"I just wanted to ask," Caroline said. "You know—to know . . . what was going on."

Joanie pulled Caroline into a damp, suffocating hug. Once again, she spoke into Caroline's hair, her breath warm against Caroline's skull. "I am so, so sorry, honey. My God. Oh, Caroline. I haven't even been thinking about what you've been going through. I've just been thinking about myself the whole time—"

"It's okay," Caroline kept murmuring. She felt relieved, lighter. Somewhere in her, a hope was stirring that maybe their lives would go back to normal. Joanie was going to be all right. Maybe Richard would be coming back. He'd called Caroline repeatedly over the weeks, but she wouldn't answer the phone when she saw his number. Maybe she should now. Maybe she should let him know it was time for him to come back home.

When Caroline thought about it later, she realized her question to Joanie had been a point when everything changed.

Afterward, she finally began to talk to her father and see him—and quickly recognized that he wasn't coming back, ever, no matter how much she wanted their old life back.

But at least Joanie was getting better, as if Caroline's question had been a sharp slap to her face that had jolted her back to the world. She turned off the TV and began sleeping in her own bed again. She took a shower every morning and changed her clothes and started cooking bad—but determinedly nutritious—dinners. She still didn't eat much and her clothes hung too loosely on her body. But the shadows around her eyes receded and she began to make plans and look for a job. She even joined that crazy divorcée group, where all the dumped women in town showed up to talk about how much they hated men.

What was so odd about this time were Caroline's own raw feelings. She continued to distrust her father. But that made sense, didn't it? After all, he'd left her and her mother. But what was strange were her emotions toward her mother.

For months, she'd been some kind of nursemaid, hovering over her mother, concerned about her, protective, worried sick. But once she'd asked her mother about committing suicide, once her mother had begun to get better, Caroline's feelings changed toward her. Something inside her grew hard.

The better her mother got, the more furious Caroline was with her. It made no sense at all to Caroline, but most of the time she couldn't explain her own feelings, even to herself. She was just angry at her mother, hating and despising her at times. It didn't matter why. It was exactly like Richard's leaving: It just was.

chapter 4

It was a pretty morning outside, with a blue sky and soft gusts of warm wind, but Ivy had work to do. She sat down at the family computer in a cluttered nook in the hall and typed in her name and password: ISH1933 (for her full name, Ivy Sledge Horton, and the year of her birth). Then she sipped her hot tea and waited for the computer to warm up.

The computer, which was oversized and scuffed up and colored an institutional gray, made groaning noises and thudded and whirred like an old vacuum cleaner. Ivy wished Roxanne would replace it with something newer. It was important to stay up to date with technology. Otherwise, you'd get left behind while the rest of the world moved forward.

Ivy had learned that more than a year ago when she and her neighbor Myra Hawkes had taken the class High Tech for Modern Seniors at the county library in their small West Texas town. The course had been taught by a young man named Barry who had a ponytail and a bad case of acne. When Myra saw his ponytail, she wanted to drop out of the class. She couldn't stand men with long hair. But Ivy had talked her into staying. Even Jesus and most of his apostles had worn their hair long, she had explained to Myra.

To her surprise, Ivy loved working on the computer from the very first day at the library. She had always been a quick typist and sat up straight, with her fingers poised at the keyboard. She wasn't like some of the other old people in the class who complained about the modern world and resisted change. Like Betsy Ledbetter, for example, whom Ivy had always secretly loathed. Betsy had never learned to type. She had been too busy entertaining and gadding around town in some convertible or another as if she thought she were Isadora Duncan.

Ivy had always wanted to suggest that Betsy wear a long scarf when she drove her convertible. She knew this was uncharitable and unchristian, but Ivy had always struggled with her meaner impulses. The fact was, a lethal scarf at an earlier point in Betsy's life, when she'd been beautiful and flamboyant and snobbish, would have served her right. Ivy had never forgotten that Betsy had blackballed her from the Junior League because she hadn't dressed stylishly.

But that was then and this was now. Betsy's husband, Ike, who had once been an oil tycoon, had died suddenly. (A heart attack? Aneurysm? These days, it was hard to keep all the causes of death separate.) Ike had left Betsy with a big, gaudy mansion and an ocean of debt. Also, although Ivy hated to listen to vicious gossip, several paternity suits had swirled around his depleted estate shortly after his funeral.

Well. It was odd, wasn't it, how life caught up with people? Betsy now lived in a small apartment on the edge of town. She hadn't aged well, in Ivy's opinion. She still dyed her hair an awful pale orange (like a Creamsicle) and wore too much makeup (uneven penciled-in eyebrows and obvious spots of rouge).

And there she and Ivy were, taking a class at the local library and learning to use the computer. Ivy couldn't help but notice that she was the star pupil in the class, whom Barry often pointed at admiringly ("Look at how fast Ivy's taking to the computer!"), while Betsy, poor thing, stared at the computer screen with her glasses slipping down her nose and her overly long fingernails making a racket on the keys. Yes, life did catch up with you sometimes.

Finally, the computer was warmed up. Ivy began an Internet search. Today, she was reading about the causes of the Great Depression. People were too ignorant about history these days. They went around talking about how the country was "only" going through a recession. To Ivy, who'd already lost much of the money she and John had saved, this recent recession was more dangerous than people knew. They were crazy if they weren't scared.

The minute their teacher, Senora Schmidt, left the room, Henry swiveled in his chair and smiled at Caroline.

"Hey. Can you tell me something?" he asked her.

Henry had liquid brown eyes and pearly, even teeth. Hollywood teeth, anchorman teeth. They looked even whiter next to his tanned face. Caroline stared at him dreamily, drinking him in, trying not to be too obvious.

"Sure," Caroline said. She sat up straighter, hoping that would make her breasts look bigger. Sometimes, fifteen-year-olds got boob jobs, especially if they lived in New York or California and had mothers who were more understanding and glamorous than Joanie. They went to a plastic surgeon and came back to school and immediately became popular. Caroline tried to imagine her skinny little pipe cleaner body enhanced by great big breasts, so that she looked like the letter *P*. She'd wear tight shirts all the time.

"Those verbs for *to be*," Henry said. "You know?"

"*Estar* and *ser*," Caroline said. "You mean the infinitives?"

"Yeah," Henry said. "The infinitives. What's the difference between them? I don't get it."

Senora Schmidt had explained the difference between the two infinitives just yesterday, scrawling notes all over the chalkboard. Had Henry missed the class? No, he'd been there. Caroline had spent the entire hour gazing at the back of his head, watching how his neck—with its downy black hair—receded into his shirt collar. Still, she'd managed to pick up the differences in the infinitives. It wasn't that hard. Maybe Henry just hadn't been paying attention. Maybe he'd been distracted by Caroline's intense staring at the back of his neck. People could feel it when someone was staring at them. It could ruin their concentration. Henry might fail Spanish because of her. Maybe Caroline should fail it, too. That way, they'd be in class together next year.

"*Ser* is supposed to be permanent, like your name or something," Caroline said. "*Estar* is more temporary—like the weather or how you're feeling."

Henry nodded, his eyes shifting around the room. Three or four other students had whipped out their cell phones and were busily texting into them. Someone else tossed a spit wad that arced high into the air and landed on the floor a few feet away. The boys talked in a low rumble and the girls giggled. It was an honors class, so it was more serious than most. Caroline always wondered what ordinary classes were like. Her mother wouldn't let her take them, though. She said Caroline was too smart to waste her time. Her mother didn't understand anything. Caroline's whole life was a waste of time, except for brief, tiny moments like this when she felt alive.

The door opened with a whoosh and Senora Schmidt stepped back into the room, walking rapidly. She propped herself up on her desk, facing the class.

"*Quien puede explicar la diferencia entre ser y estar?*" she asked.

Henry's hand shot up into the air. The answer he gave, in his smooth baritone and halting Spanish, was brilliant. Just brilliant.

Dear David, Ivy wrote to her son on the computer.

Are you and Stella doing well? How is the children's school year going? I haven't seen them in so long! Please send me some photographs when you have time.

Are you still as busy as you were at work?

Ivy sat back and stared at the computer screen. She wanted to make sure she didn't have any typos or misspellings. She always read and reread her emails to David before she sent them.

For years, she had telephoned David and Stella every Sunday afternoon. When John was alive, they had done it together, both of them on separate extensions at their home. But John had never said much. Men of his generation didn't talk, as a rule. They left that to women.

Stella was a very smart, very attractive woman David had met in New York, where he was a lawyer. She had been a paralegal at his firm. She had long, dark hair and a thin face, and her family lived in upstate New York.

Ivy had only met Stella's family once, at David and Stella's wedding in Buffalo. They had thin faces, too. They had been very polite, but formal. David said that New Yorkers weren't as friendly as Texans. He made it sound as if being friendly wasn't really a good thing. Ivy had wanted to ask him about that, but she hadn't had the opportunity. It was like everything else about David—the way he talked, dressed, ate, fixed his hair, the facial expressions he made: everything about him, everything that was dear and familiar to Ivy, had changed after he left home to go to college, then to law school, on the East Coast.

David had changed, and she and John hadn't. Their not changing was like being friendly. It wasn't good, but she didn't know why. She wanted to ask what was wrong with them, what was wrong with being friendly and having supper at five o'clock and holding hands while they prayed before a meal. She wanted to ask, but there was never time. No, that wasn't quite true. There may not have been time, but she wouldn't have asked, anyway. The time for asking David questions like that had passed, folded away somewhere and forgotten, like clothes he'd outgrown.

So Ivy and John had called every week for years. Their conversations with David—and sometimes, Stella—grew shorter. David always sounded rushed and impatient. He was busy at work. Ivy understood that. You had to work hard to be successful. She was proud to have a son who was so successful, a partner in a big New York law firm. Didn't she talk about him a lot to her friends? Yes, she did.

But she just wished she could understand how she fit in his life now. She had thought it would be different, after John died. Surely David would want her to come and live closer to him and his two children—those grandchildren, Daniel and Judith, whom she hardly knew. He would understand how lonely she was.

Thinking about this, she could feel the grief rising in her. *This will do no good,* she told herself. *Stop it, immediately.*

She took a deep breath and let it out slowly. Breathing like that was good. She had just read about it on the Internet in the health section of a website. She imagined she was in a beautiful, peaceful place, where she felt loved and taken care of, where the sun was warm instead of scorching, and her skin wasn't wrinkled and pouchy and dotted with age spots. She opened her eyes and saw her unfinished email staring at her.

We are all doing very well in Austin, she wrote. Roxanne has a job. Caroline is in the tenth grade in high school. I am keeping busy.

Busy. Ivy hated that word. Everyone was busy these days. How are you? *Busy,* they'd all answer, sighing and rolling their eyes, as if saying that one word took every spare second they had.

It would never do to say you weren't busy, that your days passed as slowly and as uneventfully as a dripping faucet, that you were sad and lonely and you watched life speeding past you from a faraway window; relentless, oblivious, indifferent. What was going on outside that window wasn't yours any longer, belonged to someone else younger and healthier.

Love to you, Stella, and the children, she wrote. Mom.

"We spoke," Caroline announced, "in Spanish class." She pulled a book out of her locker, slammed the door shut, and turned around to face Sondra.

"What happened?" Sondra asked. She jolted forward a little, pushed by a passing group of people in the hallway. That happened a lot to Sondra. People didn't ever seem to notice her. She was even more invisible than Caroline. "What did he say? How long did you talk to him?"

Sometimes Caroline, who had a good mind for math, tried to estimate how many people could truly be seen in high school. Ten percent, maybe? The jocks, the superachievers, the popular kids, the rich kids, the kids with famous parents. A year ago, Caroline had broken her arm—and for a little while, people had noticed her when she was wearing a cast. Total strangers had come up and offered to autograph it. She still had the cast at home, split apart and on her desk, with all the autographs and bright, squiggly drawings on it. Maybe she should tape it together and wear it on her other arm.

"Oh, he just asked me about the assignment," Caroline said.

Nobody else would have been impressed by this information, except for Sondra. Together—which they almost always were—they looked like Mutt and Jeff, Caroline's father had said once. "They're cartoon characters," he explained, when Caroline looked blank. "One was tall and thin, the other short and fat." He grinned when he said it, but Caroline hadn't found it funny. She started stooping over even more. It was bad enough being built like one of those flamingos people put in their front yards. But, clearly, being with Sondra made her appear even taller. Terrific. No wonder she'd never had a boyfriend in her whole life.

"What did you tell him?" Sondra asked. She pushed her bangs away from her forehead, a couple of strands sticking to a big pimple. She was the only person on earth—with the exception of Caroline's mother—who thought Caroline's boring, tedious life was at all interesting.

"Just—well, nothing," Caroline said, a little annoyed. The only thing worse than being ignored was having someone pay too much attention to her. "Verb forms. Infinitives."

"That's great." Even speaking with Caroline, Sondra's voice usually hovered at a whisper. *What did you say?* people—parents, especially—were always asking her. But most of the time, they acted like she hadn't said anything.

Sondra and Caroline pushed their way through the hall, then through some double doors onto an outdoor patio.

"Did you bring the cigarettes?" Caroline asked.

"Yeah." Sondra nodded. "They're in my car."

They wound their way through the groups of students, buzzing like busy insects, screeching with laughter, calling out to one another. "Dude!" one boy screamed at someone else.

He was in Caroline's algebra class and he'd gotten a failure notice last week. "Dude!" he called out again, stepping right in front of Caroline and Sondra and not even looking at them or saying excuse me.

"People are so rude here," Sondra said. She was quoting Caroline, who had said exactly the same thing last week, when a blonde in a sundress and flip-flops had stepped on her foot, laughing and talking on her cell phone. Her name was Zee. She and Caroline had been friends years ago, when they were in grade school. They hadn't spoken since middle school, when Zee had become pretty and well liked and Caroline hadn't. Zee usually wore small stiletto heels, which would have hurt more. The flip-flops had been a lucky break.

"Sometimes," Caroline said grudgingly. She wished Sondra wouldn't quote her. Couldn't she think of anything to say on her own? *Shut up,* a second voice chimed in. *She's your best friend. Why are you being mean to her?*

Those voices—sometimes Caroline listened to them at war with each other for minutes at a time, like a Ping-Pong match that never ended. She might be bipolar. She needed therapy. She needed drugs to improve her personality.

"Shit! I forgot to lock the car!" Sondra said, as they crossed the parking lot. "I hope nobody broke in." She opened the driver's-side door, which always screeched loudly, like a cat in pain, and crawled behind the wheel. Caroline followed, easing into the passenger's seat, after she removed a wadded-up paper towel and a blackened banana peel, throwing them on the floor on top of several old newspapers.

Sondra rolled down the window and craned her neck around the car. Mounds of old, folded clothes she was supposed to take to Goodwill three months ago lined the back-seat, spilling over onto the floor. "I don't think anything's missing," she said.

Please. Who would want to break into Sondra's car? It was an '84 Toyota Corolla—older than they were—with a front fender held on by masking tape, a rusty hood, a back left tire that was almost always semiflat, and torn plastic upholstery that smelled like the old fruitcake that had liquefied in the car one summer. Sometimes, when your foot stuck to the floor, you'd find a piece of green candied fruit at the bottom of your shoe. Homeless people had higher standards than Sondra had. Starving Third World people, gypsies, roving bands of chimpanzees wouldn't have gone near her car.

"Where are the cigarettes?" Caroline reminded her.

Sondra leaned over and opened the car pocket. It flew open, spilling a few papers and loose debris on Caroline's lap. "They're in here, somewhere," Sondra said. She brushed her bangs back again, her forehead shiny with sweat. Her hands, riffling through the papers, were chubby like Sondra herself.

"Here," Sondra said, handing a bent menthol to Caroline. She picked up a small orange lighter on the dashboard and struggled with it. Finally, a tiny flame appeared. Caroline inhaled and watched the cigarette tip begin to burn. She rolled down the car window and exhaled smoke out the window.

The two girls sat, staring straight ahead, smoking determinedly. Caroline still hated it. It tasted vile. She'd read that it took some people longer to get hooked on smoking. She must be one of those people. She was slow at everything. She and Sondra had been smoking a cigarette a day for the past month and she still wasn't addicted. She didn't have any bad habits at all, except for biting her nails and being mean to the two people who liked her the most. How could you be fascinating or bewitching if you didn't have any bad habits?

"That was so good," Sondra said a few minutes later, stubbing out her cigarette—only halfway smoked—in the ashtray. She coughed. "I've been thinking about having one all day. It's so relaxing." When Caroline didn't say anything, Sondra repeated herself. "So relaxing."

"My father and his girlfriend," Caroline said, inhaling stubbornly so she would finish the cigarette all the way to the end, even if it killed her, "are going to have a baby." She exhaled a stream of white smoke and watched as it clouded the car.

Sondra glanced at her, unsure. Some kind of reaction was expected from her, she knew. But she couldn't tell how Caroline felt.

"I think it's gross," Caroline said, prompting her.

"Ick. Me, too."

"That means they've been having sex," Caroline added, screwing up her face and trying not to imagine it. "Everybody in the world is having sex. Except for you and me and my mother."

"And your grandmother," Sondra pointed out.

Caroline elbowed her. "Sondra, that is disgusting." She screeched, then started to laugh, at first halfheartedly, then with delighted yelps. Sondra, pleased to have caused the amusement, joined in. The two girls cackled and held their stomachs till their muscles ached. For the first time that day, for the first time in ages, Caroline felt relaxed and happy.

A passerby might have thought the two girls, both in the

lighthearted, sunny days of youth, were sharing a memory of the fun they'd had at school that day. He might have even envied them for being young and happy and carefree. But they might as well enjoy themselves while they could, he would have thought, since life became so much grimmer and more difficult the older you got.

"Disgusting!" Caroline said again, and the two girls burst into fresh laughter.

"Does anyone else have something to share?" Denise asked.

Joanie cleared her throat. "Well," she said, looking at her hands (when was she going to stop biting her nails and grow up?), "my ex-husband and his girlfriend—"

"Which girlfriend?" Nadine asked.

She always interrupted, no matter how many times Denise gently reminded her that each woman in the divorcée support group should be allowed to speak without someone else jumping in and hijacking the conversation. But that was Nadine, they had all learned. She jumped and hijacked a lot.

"B.J.," Joanie said.

"That really young one?" Nadine asked. "Is he still with her? *God.*" She crossed her arms in front of her chest and looked deeply, fervently annoyed.

"They always go after young ones," Sharon said. "They're scared to death of getting old and dying. That's why."

Sharon was a little older than Joanie, tall and rangy as a clothespin. She'd recently spent her fiftieth birthday in Hawaii with friends, even though she couldn't afford it.

It was important, Denise always told them, to take care of themselves. But maybe Sharon shouldn't have spent so much money on a big trip, where she got badly sunburned the first day and completely wasted every night on piña coladas with extra rum. Three weeks later, her face was still peeling; half red, half white.

Sharon's experience should teach them something, Denise had said. We should take care of ourselves, but our actions had consequences. They all needed to remember that.

Sharon had nodded when Denise said that. "I didn't even get laid once," she'd reported bitterly. "And that was the whole purpose of the trip."

"I believe Joanie was speaking," Denise said now. She smiled encouragingly at Joanie.

"Richard and B.J.," Joanie said, "are having a baby."

The room erupted in jeers.

"That is gro*tesque*," Nadine hissed. "God! Hasn't anybody heard of birth control?"

"A baby? Are they nuts?"

"That is so typical—"

"When are men going to grow up and take responsibility for—"

"—doesn't he know how much this will hurt—"

"Are you kidding? They don't care about things like that—"

Joanie sat there, listening to the chorus go on without her.

For almost two years, she'd been comforted, supported—almost absorbed—by this divorcée group. She'd spewed out bitterness, rage, despair, had sobbed till her abdomen stiffened and ached, and her eyes were raw. She'd always considered herself to be a private person, but this group had seen her at her worst and had gathered her up and held her close when she felt worthless and lost.

Hell, she'd still be lying on her bathroom floor, nearly catatonic, screaming into an unwashed towel and counting the tiles, if it weren't for these women.

But now, hearing their rising outrage, she felt curiously detached and calm. Maybe she had outgrown this group, moved beyond most of the women here. Maybe it was time for her to leave, gracefully. Wasn't it time for her to get on with her life and leave all the sadness and rage behind?

"How do you feel about the baby, Joanie?" Denise asked. She pushed her tumbleweed hair back and smiled her Mother Earth smile.

Around her, the voices subsided. Everyone looked at Joanie and waited.

Joanie drew in a deep breath. "I'm mostly worried about Caroline," she began. "But, aside from that—I'm all right with this. I'm fine."

Then she stopped and stared at her lap. Her throat had closed and she couldn't talk. For a few long seconds, she stared helplessly at her fingers writhing against the material of her blue jeans, scratching hard against her legs.

You liar, she told herself. *You pathetic little liar, you god-damned fool. You aren't fine with this. You aren't fine with anything. You just thought you were. Aren't you ever fucking going to learn anything?*

A wave of sorrow ripped through her so powerfully that she snapped her head back and burst into loud, angry sobs. She leaned over and buried her head in her hands, raking her fingers through her hair and shaking all over.

Where in the hell was that noise coming from, she wondered. That sound, like a wounded animal howling. Where was it coming from—and wouldn't it ever stop?

"Caroline," Ivy said. "Have I talked to you about God?"

Caroline stared back at Ivy, who sat, perched and expectant, on the chair across from her in the dining room. They were having dinner together, since Joanie had her dopey meetings on Thursdays. Ivy had cooked roast beef. In the best tradition of midwestern cooking, it was brown and overcooked and tough.

It occurred to Caroline that, if there were a God, she wouldn't be living in the same house with her mother and grandmother. Also, if she had to live with them, at least one of them would know how to cook decently. Ivy was—amazingly—an even worse cook than Joanie. Had some kind of bad-cooking gene gotten passed down from mother to daughter in their family? If so, Caroline never wanted to try to cook.

On the other hand, God might exist, but he was punishing Caroline.

Not that she believed in God.

"I don't have time right now, Grandma," Caroline said, standing up. "I've got to study." Her grandmother looked up at her expectantly. "Thanks for dinner," Caroline added unconvincingly, trying to ignore her still-full plate. "It was delicious."

"I pray for you every day, Caroline," Ivy said. "Do you know that? I pray for your mother, too."

"What do you pray for?" Caroline asked, a little bit intrigued. She was going to be sixteen in July. Maybe Ivy could start praying for her to get a new red BMW convertible. If

God could deliver on something like that, Caroline might start going to church occasionally. It wouldn't hurt.

Besides, it wasn't like Ivy had much to do, anyway—aside from reading racist sites on the Internet. She might as well be praying for something good. Maybe God listened to people like Ivy, who were going to be dropping dead soon. Caroline wondered how God felt about boob jobs. She could always go to a religious plastic surgeon, if necessary. A Southern Baptist.

Ivy smiled, feeling pleased by her granddaughter's openness to the Lord. Every time she mentioned God around Roxanne, her daughter rolled her eyes. It was probably too late for Roxanne, anyway, after all her years of agnosticism and swearing and divorce and her recent dreadful tendency toward alcoholism, which Ivy had begun to notice and comment on. But a child! That was different. Children were always hungry for religion when you approached them the right way.

"I pray for grace," Ivy said. "I pray that you will come to know the Lord. I pray that you will become a good, strong Christian woman like me."

"Grandma, I'm really busy," Caroline said. "I've got to do my homework now."

"I'm here anytime you want to talk," Ivy said. She tried to smile encouragingly. Clearly, the girl had been scared off religion by Roxanne. "We can pray together anytime you feel like it. Or go to church, if you'd like."

"I'll think about it, Grandma." Caroline slung her backpack over her shoulder and trudged to her room. What she really needed was a suitcase, so she could run away from here. Her home had become a nuthouse.

~~~~~~~~

Joanie stirred her drink with a straw and watched the ice cubes bob up and down. This was her second drink—a double bourbon on the rocks—and she couldn't even feel it. All right, so she was drinking too much right now. Obviously. Ivy, a teetotaler, had been hinting for years that Joanie was an alcoholic. That would make her happy. Her daughter had messed up again.

"Are you all right?" Nadine asked.

Joanie shrugged. She knew she looked like hell. Tiny bloodshot eyes, scarlet nose, cheeks smeared with mascara, damp blouse. "Compared to what?" she asked. She looked up at the waitress, who had a pierced nostril and hair as red as iodine, and pointed to her glass. "Another one, please."

"Me, too," Nadine said.

The waitress nodded and disappeared, leaving a suffocating fog of perfume in her wake. She looked happy and wholesome, in spite of her Goth accoutrements. She was young. She would learn. Life sucked.

"What really bothers me," Joanie said, "isn't that I'm feeling so upset about Richard and B.J. It's just that—"

"It took you by surprise," Nadine said.

"It took me by surprise," Joanie echoed. "I thought I was okay." She sighed. "Does that happen to you?"

"Nope." Nadine shook her head. She screwed up her freckled face, which always seemed a little sweaty, even when it was cool outside. "I never think I'm doing okay."

"Maybe that's better," Joanie said. "You don't fool yourself."

Nadine shrugged. "I don't know. I'd like to fool myself into thinking I'm happy sometimes."

"Here you are, ladies," the waitress said. She placed napkins and fresh drinks in front of the two women. Her name, according to her nameplate, was Babette.

"Cheers," Joanie said, touching Nadine's glass.

The two women often went out for drinks after their weekly group meetings. Most of the time, they were accompanied by another group member, Lori. But Lori's babysitter had run off with the drummer in a locally prominent rock band and had given up babysitting Lori's—and everybody else's—kids. Lori had phoned Denise to say she couldn't come back till she found a new babysitter. She also sent word that all the group members were to avoid patronizing the band The Fried Roosters out of solidarity with her dilemma.

When they met in the group, Nadine was outspoken, even raucous. Around Joanie and Lori, she was quieter and more uncertain.

It was college, she had once told Joanie, blushing furiously as she talked. She'd never gone to college, not even for a semester. It was hard for her that everyone else—each group member—was a college graduate. And they had good jobs that required dressing up. Nadine, who worked in a day care called Tremendous Tots, always wore play clothes and sweats, like the children.

That had been a striking moment for Joanie. College had been so long ago for her. She never thought about it these days. Everyone she knew had gone to college. She couldn't imagine what it was like to be outside that defining circle—

even if she hadn't realized it was there. She thought about casually filling out employment applications, always having a degree to list, never thinking about its meaning. What must it be like not to have that?

"I do think you're doing better," Nadine said. "Most of the time, anyway."

"That's what I thought, too," Joanie said glumly. She took a swizzle stick and stabbed it through her cocktail napkin. "What about you?"

"I'm the same," Nadine said. "Feels like I'm always going to be the same."

Nadine had once shown Joanie a picture of her ex-husband, Roy. He had curly dark hair and a cocky grin. He was a contractor for some of the enormous, grotesque houses people were building on the lakes around town. Eighteen months ago, he'd told Nadine he was in love with one of the women whose house he was building—the Tuscan-style house he'd talked about incessantly, with the six bedrooms, seven baths, three wet bars, oval turquoise pool and smaller, matching oval Jacuzzi. The water in the pools reminded him of jewelry he'd once seen in Santa Fe. His new girlfriend's name was Jacqueline, pronounced the French way, he'd said.

Nadine usually called Roy "that goddamned little prick" and Jacqueline "that two-bit slut with the phony French name." Nadine was "stuck" in the anger phase of the grieving process, their group leader, Denise, had once announced. That's why she had such vivid dreams of Roy being dismembered by a herd of jackals in Africa, then having his bones picked apart by hordes of vultures, then finally being ground into the dirt by a passing convoy of jeeps carrying illegal arms to guerrilla groups. If Nadine could just work through her anger, Denise had said, then she could move on to other, more evolved stages of grief—like bargaining and depression and acceptance.

Denise, with her intense, earnest manner and surefire formulas for success, had meant well. As usual.

But Joanie had watched Nadine pinken with embarrassment as Denise spoke about her. Why was Denise so sure of what Nadine should be feeling? Joanie had wondered. What did she know about Nadine and her life? Maybe anger was the only thing holding her together, so she wouldn't reel out of control, spewing little pieces of herself all over the walls. Maybe it always would be. People used different things to hold themselves together. Roy might look, in his photo, like an arrogant guy whose actions weren't very surprising. But he had taken Nadine from an unhappy family and made her feel safe and loved for twelve years. Why wouldn't she be angry about losing him? Why couldn't she stay angry? What was so wrong with that?

In Joanie's opinion, Denise made what she called the "grieving process" sound like an escalator. First floor, denial. Second floor, anger. Keep moving. Stop stalling. Get to the top, where there was a big sale on peace of mind and resolution and evolved personhood. But it wasn't always that easy or predictable.

"I miss Lori," Nadine said now. "You know what? Lori's the first black friend I ever had." She stopped abruptly. "I mean, not intentionally," she added, searching Joanie's face quickly. "I've just never had black friends before. It just happened that way. Don't tell Lori I said that."

"I won't," Joanie said, thinking that Nadine was her first friend who'd never gone to college.

It was funny how you wandered through life, seeing only

people like yourself. Then something like divorce and betrayal and heartbreak whacked you over the head, and people like yourself became a different, wider group.

Beethoven's Fifth Symphony began to play on Caroline's cell phone. She looked up from her bed, where she'd thrown herself. Everything was dark in her room. Caroline liked it that way. In fact, she wished it were even darker.

In the little cell phone display square, she could see her father's picture. He'd put it on her cell phone, along with the Beethoven that played when he called her.

"Beethoven is my favorite composer," he'd said at the time, even though Caroline had never heard him listen to Beethoven before. "When you hear it, you'll know it's me."

Caroline rolled over on her back. Now what? She didn't want to talk to her father. But if she didn't answer the phone, then he'd complain to Joanie, who would come barreling into her room for another one of those vile mother-daughter talks she was always insisting on. Like Caroline didn't have other things on her mind.

"Hello?"

"Hello! How's my wonderful daughter today?"

Caroline sighed. When was he going to get over all this enthusiastic, I'm-such-a-great-father bullshit? She couldn't stand it when he talked like this. Like he'd just had forty cups of coffee and his eyes were bulging out.

"Who is this?" Caroline asked. She crossed her eyes, just to keep in practice.

"It's me. Your dad." Richard cleared his throat. "Didn't you hear the Beethoven, honey?"

"Oh. Yeah. I guess. I forgot that was yours."

A short, hurt pause. Caroline could see Richard's face, struggling, trying to figure out what to say next. Just like Joanie did most of the time. It served him right. He wasn't here. He had a new home. A new girlfriend. And they were about to have a new kid. He wouldn't be interested in Caroline, the old kid. He was just pretending.

"Well . . . I'm calling about this weekend, Caroline. B.J. and I are really looking forward to having you at the house."

Caroline sighed again, louder this time. She listened to the crackling silence on the line.

"Me, too," she said finally.

"Great!" Richard said heartily. He sounded relieved. He'd done his fatherly duty and now he was dying to hang up. "I—we'll pick you up Friday afternoon. Okay, honey? At five."

Caroline hung up. She pulled a few strands of hair through her fingers and examined her split ends in the darkness. She gritted her teeth. She tried to relax her jaw, which felt tight and sore from all the tension in her life.

She didn't want to spend the weekend with her father and B.J. She knew they didn't really want her, either. It didn't matter what her father said. He was lying to make himself feel good—like he was a really great father. And B.J.—she knew B.J. didn't like her. Caroline was just part of the package that came along with Richard. They would be nice and smile at her and ask her what she wanted to do, but it wouldn't mean anything. It was all a big show.

But she didn't have any alternatives. She didn't want to hang around with her mother and grandmother, either. She didn't want to do anything. She just wanted to disappear. Like now. It was so dark inside her room she could hardly see herself. She liked it like that, when she was invisible. It felt right.

chapter 5

Looking back, Joanie now understood that she'd led a pretty easy, uncomplicated life. Till a couple of years ago, anyway.

Growing up, she had been smart, attractive, reasonably self-assured. Like other middle-class children, she had floated unthinkingly from high school to college in the late 1970s. She'd majored first in French, then comparative lit, then sociology, psych, history, American studies, art history, and finally, liberal arts by the time she got her bachelor's degree.

In college, she'd dated three boys, lost her virginity in a motel room in a seedy complex that had been destroyed two years later, and climbed an oak tree to protest rampant gentrification of poor, underserved neighborhoods in Austin. (She'd been a little relieved when the police hauled her out of the tree and threatened to arrest her; once she'd climbed up the tree, she'd realized she had no idea how to climb down. "Go back to your side of town, hon," the police officer had told her. "Don't you get it? People on the east side have bigger problems than cuttin' down a few trees.")

After graduation, she'd taught in a Montessori school, then worked for a florist. She inherited a few thousand dollars when her grandmother died and was just about to leave for Europe when she met Richard. He came into the florist's shop to order flowers to send to his mother. A big bouquet for Mother's Day.

"Roses—and something else," he said. He drummed his fingers on the counter silently and looked up at Joanie. "Any ideas?"

He smiled and his eyes crinkled. They were nice, warm brown eyes, almost golden at the edges. "Baby's breath," she said.

"Baby's breath," he echoed. "That's good."

They were married a few months later. They had been married for seventeen years when Richard decided his life was too predictable and boring. He wanted something else, something more, something that didn't include Joanie. He would try to be a good father to Caroline, though. That was important to him.

"You met him when he was buying flowers for his mother?" Nadine had asked in Joanie's divorcée support group. Back then, Nadine was still making lots of jokes about running over her husband in her pickup truck, then circling the block to make sure he was dead.

Joanie nodded.

"That should have been a good sign," Nadine observed. "Men who like their mothers, I mean."

Well, it hadn't been. As Joanie had learned when she began to date Richard, he'd been buying a particularly large bouquet for Mother's Day because his father had just left his mother so he could have a more exciting life.

It was funny. You heard that kind of story when you were young and it was just an anecdote about somebody's old, weird father going through a midlife crisis. It didn't have anything to do with you, even after you married the weird father's son.

But then the son had turned into his father—all those years later, at almost exactly the same age. "It was like he had an alarm clock ticking inside him," Joanie had told Mary Margaret. "All of a sudden, it went off."

She should have known, she should have been smarter, warier, et cetera. But she hadn't been. Joanie had had an easy, uncomplicated life till it turned into something entirely different and everything around her changed. She sometimes thought that maybe Richard hadn't been the only one with the internal alarm clock, undetected till its noise raised the dead.

"I don't believe in good signs anymore," she'd told her support group. They'd all nodded back at her, Nadine in particular.

chapter 6

~~~~~

Caroline was deeply messed up and neurotic. She knew
that. She was pretty sure she had multiple personality
disorder. MPD, people called it. It was incurable. You walked
around with one personality and then—*bam!* You were somebody else. It was kind of like being possessed by demons, except you didn't have to be religious or believe in the devil to
have it happen to you.

Personality changes happened to Caroline on a daily basis.
Like today. She woke up in a pretty good mood. She even
hummed while she brushed her teeth.

Then she looked in the mirror and started to feel worse.
She hated the way she looked—her green eyes with the stubby
lashes, her flat nose, her freckles, her pale skin. She'd peered
down the front of her T-shirt to do her usual morning check

to see whether her breasts had grown any overnight. Well of course they hadn't. They were still totally flat, except for her nipples, which stuck out like little pink knobs on her chest.

She stepped in the shower. That was the only place on earth she ever had any privacy. Sometimes, she cried there, just to get it over with. She usually stayed there till the water turned cold. Then she turned it off and pulled a towel around her.

After the shower, she'd pull out a top and blue jeans. Then she'd wrap a jacket around herself and go to the kitchen. Joanie would start hounding her to eat breakfast. "At least some toast, honey," she'd say. "It's good for you."

The sound of her mother's voice—pleading and bossy at the same time—would set Caroline's teeth on edge. She'd feel some kind of ridiculous fury rise up in her, scalding the back of her throat. Caroline didn't even question it any longer. It was an automatic reaction, like Pavlov's drooling dogs, set off by Joanie or Richard or Ivy. The girl who'd been crying in the shower vanished, replaced by this angry shrew.

"I need to go into therapy," she'd told Joanie last week when they were driving to school.

Joanie had turned to look at her and had almost run into the curb. "What for, Caroline?" she'd asked. "Are you all right?"

Caroline had stayed very still, holding her arms in front of her, breathing as quietly as she could, desperate to leave the car. Why had she been stupid enough to say anything? She'd started to change again—into the thin, quiet girl who hovered in the school hallways, never talking, never laughing, never being noticed by anyone but her only friend.

"Of course I'm all right," she'd said.

~~~~~~

Joanie pushed a DVD into her computer and sat back to watch. It was Day Two of the agency's drive to land the big new account. One of Joanie's tasks was to research the company and evaluate its previous advertising.

The truth was, she had no idea what she was doing. She hoped nobody knew that. She hadn't researched or written anything since she was in college—back when people actually walked to the library to read books. These days, they just sat at their desks and typed in words at some kind of lightning speed that astonished her. The "kids" she worked with— the account executives and creatives in their twenties and thirties—played the computer like virtuoso musicians, making it flash from one screen to the next, always searching for something new and better. She could hardly see their fingers move, could only hear the soft, rapid bursts of the computer keys.

How did they do it? She had no idea. She had poky, minimal computer skills. (Thank God Ivy had insisted she learn to type one summer when she was a teenager.) She knew how to Google, but big deal. Even her mother knew how to Google.

She peered into her reading glasses. They were jaunty and angular, brightly striped. She'd bought them on a desperate whim, hoping to make herself look hip. They didn't work, though. They made her look like an ordinary, nearsighted middle-aged woman who was trying to look hip.

Joanie typed *Frontier Motors Austin Texas* into the search box and hit ENTER.

"How's it going?" a voice asked—Zoe, her supervisor. Joanie could tell from the hoarse, exhausted voice even before she looked up. Zoe was a wreck these days.

"Fine!" Joanie said brightly. "I'm really enjoying this."

Zoe collapsed onto the chair next to Joanie's desk. She stuck her long legs out in front of her and began to wiggle her feet around nervously. She wore towering stiletto heels like all the other girls—well, *young women*. Did they think it gave them authority or made them sexier? She supposed so. Joanie wore flats or fat, low heels. If she wore stilettos, she'd probably take a dive, claw the air, and end up sprawled on the floor with her front teeth knocked out. She didn't think that would be authoritative or sexy.

"I just got an email from Frontier Motors," Zoe said. She fanned her face with the piece of paper, then grabbed it with both hands to read. "Oh, fucking piece of shit!"

"What?" Joanie asked.

"They spelled my name with an umlaut," Zoe said. "I hate that." She glared at the paper, then began to read, her head bobbing nervously back and forth. "Okay, they're expecting us to make a presentation next month . . . three other groups are competing . . . if we have any questions, call or write."

Zoe laid the paper on Joanie's desk and stared up at the ceiling. "I have a really good gut instinct about this client," she said, speaking to the sagging tiles overhead. "I think we're a really good fit. Have you looked at the advertising they've used in the past?"

"Well, no, I was just about to—" Joanie began.

"Check it out," Zoe said. "God, it's *miserable*. Horses . . . cowboys . . . trucks . . . the open range. You know, the usual dumbass shit people come up with about Texas. I mean, a herd of three-legged jackals could have come up with something better than this."

Zoe suddenly jumped to her feet, teetering on her heels and looming over Joanie. "I also feel very good that we have you working on this, Joanie. I had a really good gut instinct about you, too. It wasn't easy to—well, you know—get everybody on board with it. With hiring you, I mean."

"It wasn't?" Joanie asked faintly. She felt her stomach sinking.

"Oh, you know. Your lack of experience. All that time at home, doing nothing," Zoe said. She shook her head and exhaled noisily. "People just don't understand—when they don't have the kind of instinct about other people that I have. It's hard to explain something you just *feel*. You know what I mean?"

"Well . . . yes."

"I had to fight for you," Zoe said proudly. "I just think older—I mean, *mature*—women are undervalued in our society." She smiled down at Joanie, brushing a hand across her shoulder. "I have complete confidence in you."

She pivoted out of Joanie's office like an Alpine athlete on stilts, stalking through the office.

Joanie sat and stared at her computer screen. It had gone blank.

Ivy was spending far too much time around the house, puttering and getting bored, Joanie had said, getting bossy about the whole thing. Her mother needed to get out more.

So Ivy had gotten out that morning. For a half hour or so, she'd wandered around the neighborhood, trying to peer into the windows of houses without looking like she was being nosy (that would be rude). She had always enjoyed looking in houses, trying to imagine how other people lived.

Finally, she came across a store. In the polished front windows, mannequins modeled elegant knit ensembles, waving to one another, smiling, preening. They looked carefree and expensively chic. How nice. Maybe Ivy would go shopping. She hadn't bought anything new in years, since she didn't have any money. But that was all right. She could still look, couldn't she? She pushed the front door open and a bell shrilled.

"May I help you?" the saleswoman asked. Her gaze slid down Ivy's arm like an icy rivulet, stopping disapprovingly at Ivy's feet. Ivy was wearing a five-year-old, peach-colored sweat suit, rumpled but clean. Her loafers were scuffed, but she had read somewhere that loafers were timeless.

"No, thank you. I'm just browsing." Ivy straightened her posture and approached the nearest hanging rack. While the saleswoman watched, she determinedly and slowly worked her way through the hangers, pausing to look at each of the jackets as if she couldn't decide which one she liked the best. They were outrageously expensive—more than a thousand dollars apiece. Not classic styles, either, which was what Ivy had bought upon occasion, back when she used to have a little money. They were the kind of extravagant, lightning-fast fashion that would be swept out into the trash bins in a month or two.

"Are you looking for yourself?"

Ivy glanced at the woman. She was tall and thin, likely an anorexic. About Roxanne's age, but trying hard not to show it.

"Not necessarily," Ivy said.

"These are really for a younger demographic," the woman added pointedly.

Ivy could feel her face flush. She felt deeply uncomfortable. Why had she come into this haughty store in the first place? She couldn't afford anything here—but she was too stubborn to let a middle-aged anorexic chase her out. Once, snobbish saleswomen had made her feel terrible and apologetic about herself. But not now. She was too old to be intimidated.

Still. She had come here before lunch because she was lonely and bored and needed to get out of the house. Now, she was only feeling worse about everything. These days, she often had the feeling she didn't belong anywhere.

She turned at the back of the store, past a lavish mirror framed with gold scallops, into the accessories department. Scarves and jewelry were draped over foam faces with big, blue eyes. Ivy lingered over the scarves, fingering their soft silkiness, admiring their lush colors.

Behind her, the saleswoman had stopped to speak to another customer, a well-dressed woman who wore skinny leather boots and an impatient expression. The saleswoman's face and voice had changed, becoming warm and effusive, intimate even. She laughed and gestured as she spoke, looking eager to please.

Ivy's mother had always taught her that life wasn't fair and she should never expect it to be. That wasn't a bad philosophy to live by, Ivy had found. Very little in life had disappointed her, since she had never expected much.

But maybe she'd expected a little more when she'd grown older. She had never lived an extravagant life. She'd always clipped coupons and bought things on sale. Wasn't that all so she could be taken care of when she was old? Her golden years, they were called.

The economy's plunge in 2008 had shorn the top half off her savings. At first, she watched it all nervously on the Internet. She called David, asking what she should do. Nothing, he said. Just wait. Be patient. Finally, she had stopped watching the collapse of her and John's life savings. She couldn't bear to watch.

Life isn't fair, her mother had said. As always, her grim view of life had been essentially correct.

But ever since Ivy lost so much of her money and came to live in her daughter's house, she occasionally tried to readjust the unfairness of life. Sometimes, she did things just to make herself feel better, less helpless, to try to even the balance in the world. They were petty, awful actions she didn't approve of, but she did them, nevertheless, and she didn't feel guilty. In fact, they brought a small, ridiculous smile to her face.

She turned her back, then bent over and tucked an iridescent blue green scarf into her purse. Casually, slowly, she straightened up and stowed her purse under her arm. For a few more minutes, she remained in the store, moving from rack to rack. The saleswoman talked and laughed more to the woman in the boots. She didn't even glance up when Ivy left the store and the bell tinkled behind her.

Shit. The bathroom roll had run out of paper.

Joanie took the last bedraggled piece and patted her wet face with it. She was sitting on the toilet, staring at the stall door with the sign advising employees to wash their hands, trying not to cry anymore. She dug her compact out of her purse, opened it, and stared at her face. Yech. She looked like one of those tornado survivors she'd seen on TV the night before—dazed, bereft, leaking tears and snot, hypnotized by the wreckage around her.

"This was where my bedroom used to be," the woman had told the TV cameras. She pointed toward the shards of her life—a ripped pillow, a splintered bed board, tattered pieces of clothing, all on the ravaged earth where she used to live an orderly life. It was all unrecognizable to her, a dream of another, earlier life that had passed from existence.

Good grief, Joanie told herself. Enough of the self-pity. Any minute now, she'd be comparing herself to a Katrina survivor, clinging to the top floor of her flooded house, every bit of her life in ruins, begging to be saved. Didn't she have any *perspective*? Evidently not. She was becoming a full-blown narcissist.

Denise kept telling the members of the divorcée group that they needed to complete their mourning process. Well, great idea, fine, high fives all around. But why did it have to take so damn long? Just when Joanie had been sure she was feeling a little better, that she could handle Richard and the albino having a baby together with poise and aplomb—that she could rise above it, like Jackie Kennedy or Princess Grace, looking down on it benevolently—she'd had that full-throttle breakdown last week at the end of the group meeting. She'd completely fallen apart, like a bowl of half-firmed Jell-O, liquid and solid, but mostly liquid, sticky and brightly colored. A real, howling mess; a support-group emergency.

Hell, she'd thought she was one of the group leaders, for God's sake. A real success story and source of inspiration others could learn from, a woman who was "getting on with her life." A survivor, a beacon of hope. But oh, no. Instead, she'd become a divorcée horror story, a cautionary lesson for one of Denise's other groups. She could see and hear Denise talking about her—anonymously of course, but what difference did that make?

"A woman in one of my other groups," Denise would say, eyeing the group intently, "seemed to be doing quite well. She'd gotten a new job. She was starting to feel better, getting her life back into balance."

"But then," Denise would add, after a dramatic pause, making sure everybody was hooked and receptive to the horror to follow, "her husband and his new girlfriend got pregnant." She would stare at the group, at their worried, tearstained, hopeless faces. "And she just—fell apart."

How many of those life lessons had Joanie and the other group members heard in the months they'd been together? Dozens. They were all parables for the same lesson Denise kept beating into them week after week like they were a masochistic percussion section. *You have to grieve. You have to take your time. Forget your false confidence; it will ruin you. Slow you down in the long run. Expect to fail a hundred times before you succeed. Be patient with yourself.* Blah, blah, blah.

Oh—and that was the worst thing about Denise's neverending, melodramatic homilies: She was right most of the time. Joanie just hated it when annoying people were right.

But why couldn't she pick up the pace and start feeling better *now*? Why did things have to take time? Joanie was going to be fifty next month. Did she have to wait till she was a hobbling geriatric case, poised over the grave, to feel better?

And her job—well, that was the real kicker. At least, Joanie had thought, she'd been able to get a pretty good job fairly quickly. She'd been proud of that. It was proof she wasn't a total loser, even if Richard evidently thought so.

Joanie had pulled together a brisk, dress-for-success outfit. She'd crafted a decent-looking resume out of very little substance (e.g., volunteer work teaching English to Spanish-speaking immigrants; room mother in elementary and middle school classes; leader of her daughter's Odyssey of the Mind group—a highly dysfunctional group of kids and parents who came together so the kids could learn to be creative thinkers, supposedly. Although she'd seen no need to mention that or the screaming matches or ultimatums or door-slamming that ensued, that had set the stage for a disaster of a presentation that hadn't even won an honorable mention, even in a feel-good era when kids got blue ribbons for just showing up).

She'd applied for three jobs, gotten interviews at two of them, landed an offer within three weeks. She was a success at something, she'd told herself. She could get interesting, paying work. She was a "mature woman." Maybe that was an advantage in the workplace—even if it was, clearly, a disadvantage in marriage. Mature women didn't have PMS, pregnancy scares, insanely jealous boyfriends hanging around. They were calmer, more stable, seasoned.

Deep inside, she'd hoped and believed that Zoe—although a bit eccentric and borderline crazy and frighteningly fragile and high-strung—had recognized something in her. Some hidden talent and drive, something of value in her. But she hadn't.

It was bad enough to hear that others hadn't wanted to hire her and that Zoe had had to fight for her. (Joanie could imagine the discussions. "But, Zoe. This woman graduated from college twenty-five years ago and she hasn't done *any*thing since then." Or, "We've never hired anybody who had *room mother* on her resume.")

What was worst of all to Joanie was that Zoe hadn't seen anything special in her. She had instead glommed on to Joanie as some kind of sad cliché. A shopworn, middle-aged housewife whose husband had dumped her. A feminist cause to be championed. A little social experiment in doing good.

Joanie had nothing against doing good and helping the challenged and making life more equitable. She just rebelled at being the object of such good intentions. She didn't want the help; she didn't deserve it. She'd wasted too much of her life already, chasing fads and hobbies like so many butterflies, frittering away days and weeks and years. She hadn't been luckless; she'd been thriftless with her life. It had been her own fault.

Sure, she wanted a second chance. Of course she did. But she didn't want somebody else's second chance. It just didn't seem right. It was insulting, when you got right down to it.

She flushed the toilet, washed her hands and face, and marched outside.

"I will have a tuna fish sandwich, please," Ivy said to the waitress.

"Whole wheat or white?" The waitress leaned her head back and yawned loudly without covering her mouth.

That was the kind of rude behavior that was typical these

days, in Ivy's opinion. Sometimes she complained to Roxanne about it. Roxanne told her the world was changing. Ivy shouldn't get concerned about manners when people were gunning each other down in traffic for not moving fast enough. Now, *that* was a problem—all these Second Amendment nuts. And the death penalty. Did Ivy know that the state of Texas executed more death row inmates than any other state? Well, she should think about that, for a change. Not manners.

"Whole wheat, please," Ivy said. Her mother had always insisted on good manners. It made for a more civil society, she said. You could always tell a person's breeding by his manners.

"Drink?" the waitress asked. She appeared to be a Mexican, even though this wasn't a Mexican restaurant. Ivy rejected such establishments on grounds of questionable hygiene. Hispanic, Roxanne always corrected her. *They're Hispanic or Latino these days, Mother. Not Mexicans.*

"Water, please."

"What kind?"

"Excuse me?" Ivy asked. Maybe this young woman's English wasn't that good. People in Washington, D.C., were building a fence so people who didn't speak English couldn't get into the country. Ivy thought that was a good idea. It wasn't racist, as Roxanne always insisted. It was a way of holding on to what you had.

"What kind of water, ma'am? Tap?"

"Yes. Just water," Ivy said, speaking slowly, trying to be kind. That's right. Even though she'd never been to Mexico, she had heard that people there couldn't drink water from the tap. No wonder this young woman was surprised. No one had told her that in America it was safe to drink tap water. How sad.

The young woman brought back a glass of water with crushed ice in it, just the way Ivy liked it. She was pretty, with long black hair and thick curly eyelashes, and she wasn't too dark.

"Thank you," Ivy said formally. The young woman, whose nameplate read LUPE, smiled at Ivy. She had attractive, almost completely straight teeth. Ivy smiled back at her.

Usually, Ivy didn't eat out at lunch. She didn't do much of anything, and that was getting to be a problem. She woke early in the morning, when the first bare light of dawn touched the trees and grass outside her window. Another day, she always thought to herself. Another day she should be grateful for, she should thank God for.

But why? The doubt had hit her sharply, like a blow. She had always been good at gratitude, had found it in the most barren places. Like West Texas, where the wind blew red dust into the houses and the spindly trees snapped and the sun was harsh and unforgiving. In the years she'd lived there, with John, with their two children, she'd always managed— somehow!—to find gratitude in the overlooked cracks of life.

She had a roof over her head; a strong, solid house; a faithful, uncomplaining husband; two healthy children; friends. Of course she'd had her complaints, like everybody else. Money was never plentiful. But she had grown up during the Great Depression and World War II. She knew how to make do. She boned chickens and boiled broth from their bones, she hoarded little pieces of soap to shape into larger pieces, she saved bits of string, even though she'd forgotten why, exactly, she needed so much string.

The years and decades had passed, and she no longer pined

for the many things she'd missed when she was newly married—excitement, harmless teenage flirtations, the frivolity of an occasional new colorful dress just because she wanted it, having a husband who shared her interest in reading and small-town theater. That was good. It was better not to miss the many things that she couldn't have, anyway. Better to look at what she had—all the blessings of a stocked freezer in the garage, central air and heat, a steady companion in the evenings, a well-tended neighborhood, a savings account that grew slowly and steadily (before it evaporated).

You could always long for what you didn't have. Or you could be grateful for what you did have. It was a choice. People today didn't realize that.

"Here you go, ma'am," Lupe said, sliding the sandwich in front of Ivy.

"Your English is very good," Ivy said. "You don't even have an accent." Oh, dear. Did that sound offensive? "Where are you from?" Ivy asked quickly.

"Dallas." If Lupe was offended, she didn't act like it. She flashed Ivy another bright smile and refilled her water.

Ivy sat and chewed on her tuna fish sandwich, which had a little too much mayonnaise on it, to be frank. Around her, other patrons crowded the small tables with the bright cloths thrown over them. This was a very popular restaurant, Roxanne had told her. The local newspaper had rated it as one of the city's unsung treasures. And if Ivy wanted to eat there, she should go early.

In fact, it had been Roxanne's idea that Ivy needed to get out more. Their house was centrally located, close to lots of good places to eat and shop, she'd said. There was no reason for Ivy to sit around the house, watching TV and reading stories on the computer about how the Earth was about to end in a fiery explosion, when God had finally had enough of the human race's selfishness and irreverence. She needed to get out a little and explore the city. It would make her feel better.

Ivy patted her mouth with the napkin and asked Lupe for the check. More than seven dollars for a tuna fish sandwich and tap water! Ivy slowly counted out her money, leaving a five and three ones on the table. She left a good tip—more than 10 percent.

She waved at Lupe as she left, pushing open the door and walking out into the bright sunshine. It was the beginning of another long afternoon. But at least she'd gotten out, for once. And she had a new scarf.

"This is all so new to me—the workplace, the people," Joanie said. "Sometimes, I just don't think I'm up to it. Zoe reminded me of that."

"Zoe's a moron," Bruce said, cutting into an enchilada with his fork. "Her idea of management is to make everyone who works for her as hysterical and neurotic as she is."

"She's succeeding, then," Joanie said. "I'm a wreck."

She had run into Bruce as she left the restroom, trying to escape to her tiny office to hide before anybody saw her. When Bruce asked her how she was, she'd pasted on a big, phony smile and told him she was fine, just great, really.

"You don't look fine," he'd said. "You look like hell. Let's go to lunch."

So they had. It had been a strange lunch at a noisy downtown Tex-Mex restaurant, full of long silences and awkward chatter, but somehow, she hadn't minded it. It was nice to sit with someone from work and not have to pretend, for once.

"This new account—Frontier Motors—" Joanie began.

"Zoe's staking her career on getting it," Bruce said.

"Do we have a chance?" Joanie asked.

Bruce shrugged. "Well, there are lots of other incompetent agencies out there. Maybe we've got a shot."

"You think our agency's incompetent?" Joanie asked.

"No," Bruce said. "Not exactly. Just dysfunctional. Like any other business. Or family." He shrugged. "I've been there eighteen years. Creative directors come and go. They'll probably have to carry Zoe out in a body bag. Prepare yourself. She's not going to go peacefully."

"You sound so cynical," Joanie said.

"You've been at home too long, Joanie. Welcome to the workplace."

chapter 7
~~~~~~~

"Can you drive me to Dad's house?" Caroline asked Joanie early Friday evening. Her mother was sitting at the computer, glaring at the screen.

Joanie frowned. "I thought they were picking you up."

"They were," Caroline said. "But B.J.'s car broke down. They have to take it to the shop."

Joanie sighed. "When do you need to go?"

"Half an hour," Caroline said.

Her mother sighed again. Ever since she'd gotten a job, she was really becoming a drama queen. Like it was a very big deal to drive her only child a couple of miles. Like she was so busy doing extremely important things.

"This wouldn't be a problem," Caroline pointed out helpfully, "if I had my own car."

"Yes, it would. You still don't have a driver's license."

"I will in July."

Joanie stayed silent. She clicked a few computer keys, still looking cranky and out of sorts. She used to have a decent disposition. But ever since the divorce and Grandma's moving in, she had become very moody and passive-aggressive, in Caroline's opinion.

"Can I get a car for my sixteenth birthday?" Caroline asked. "It's the only thing I want for my birthday. You don't have to get me anything else." She'd been waiting for months to bring up the subject to her mother. Right now was as good a time as any, she guessed.

"Caroline," Joanie said evenly. "Do you know what I'm doing?"

Caroline looked over her mother's shoulder to the computer screen. "Paying bills."

Joanie sat back in her chair and crossed her arms. "Yes," she said. "And you know what? We don't have much money."

"So?"

"So," Joanie said, trying to control her voice, trying to remain calm, even though she didn't feel calm, not at all, "we don't have the money to get you a car."

"But, Mom! Everybody in high school has a car—"

"Everybody minus one," Joanie said, smiling a little, knowing it was a cheap shot she just couldn't resist. Somewhere, in the dim reaches of her mind, this remark echoed. Somebody had once said that to her. Oh, yes. Ivy. Had her own mother smiled in the same way, knowing her remark was going to provoke and infuriate? Probably.

"That's not funny!" Caroline screamed. She stalked to her room and slammed the door.

Joanie stayed at the computer and gritted her teeth. For once, she didn't care, didn't go running after Caroline to apologize and grovel for forgiveness. If Caroline wanted to carry on like that, so be it. It had been a long, hard day, and Joanie was achingly bone-tired. She didn't need any more drama in her life.

Joanie pulled into Richard's condominium complex and stopped the car. It was a new "green" area in south Austin, home to the hip zip code. She didn't like the complex. Too much metal, too many hard angles, too much brightly colored stucco. Like Richard, it was trying too hard to be cool.

She stared at the second floor, where Richard's unit was. She knew which window was his. Did she see somebody's face there? She couldn't tell. She didn't want to stare. She just wanted to leave, immediately, get out, drive away. Funny that it was painful, even though she didn't like the condos. You couldn't have paid her to live here. She wouldn't have been caught dead here. But it was where her ex-husband was living with his new girlfriend and their future child. Where he'd made a new home for himself.

"Good-bye," Caroline said. "Thanks, Mom." She leaned over and kissed her mother's cheek.

"You're welcome," Joanie said. Her voice caught a little, but she tried to flash a big smile at Caroline. No need for her to know—well, anything.

Joanie turned off the radio as she drove home, over the bridge and onto the tree-lined streets close to her house. The air rushed into her lowered windows, moist and fresh. She talked to Richard a few times a week, emailed him occasionally, mostly about Caroline. That was okay. She had gotten used to that kind of contact with him, as long as he wasn't dropping bombshells like his guess-what-we're-pregnant, ain't-that-swell phone call.

But she tried not to see him much. Even now—after she'd finally realized that she'd only cared about him, had never really loved him in the way she heard love being talked about, moaned about, obsessed over among her friends in the support group—she didn't want to see him. It still hurt. If she hadn't really loved him, what had she been doing with her life all those years?

And even if she hadn't loved him that much, he'd still rejected her, humiliated her. She wasn't interesting or important enough to stay with. She was someone who could be flung away. What had Dorothy Parker said? *He will flick you from his sleeve.* Something like that. Joanie had been inconsequential to Richard, someone who could be flicked.

Richard wasn't a stranger or a mere acquaintance. He was someone who had known her for more than twenty years, had chosen her, told her he loved her, married her, awakened in the same bed with her, made love to her, whispered in her ear, laughed with her, comforted her when she cried. But, in the end, it hadn't mattered. He had known her, but he hadn't cared about her. In the end, she'd been negligible, flickable, something to be discarded.

She knew he'd dated, had been seen with other women around town. She'd even met B.J. a few weeks ago. It had been awkward. But for some reason, she hadn't taken it too seriously. B.J. was so young and pale, a whisper of a young woman, a girl, really. She'd be gone soon, like the others, and Joanie would never see her again. Because, she'd told herself and her support group, Richard didn't want to commit to anybody. He just wanted to be free. That's why he had left, hadn't he?

But now, finally, Joanie had been completely replaced. A life she once had was over forever. Richard had B.J. and they were going to have a baby.

"You never told me, Roxanne," Ivy said at dinner. "Why did you and Richard get divorced?"

Joanie froze, her fork halfway to her mouth. All she wanted to do was finish dinner, then sneak a pint of Ben & Jerry's Half Baked in front of the TV, where she could lounge and eat and watch trashy TV and feel sorry for herself. She even had a second pint of ice cream, Häagen-Dazs's Dulce de Leche, in case she was still hungry. Which she probably would be. High-fat ice cream, TV, total self-absorption. She would be home free after this miserable, godforsaken day. She'd fall asleep on the couch in a carbohydrate and sugar stupor. She could hardly wait.

"I told you all about it at the time, Mother," Joanie said. "Richard just wanted out."

"That's not a very satisfying explanation," Ivy said. "What did he mean—he just wanted out?"

"I have no idea why he wanted out, Mother," Joanie said, carefully enunciating every syllable so she wouldn't start screaming dementedly. "Why don't you ask Richard?"

"Well, I never see him," Ivy said.

"I'll give you his phone number," Joanie said. "I'm sure he'd be happy to talk to you and explain all about our failed marriage."

Ivy turned to her salad, carefully sawing away at a big piece of lettuce. "I think I told you that any successful marriage isn't fifty-fifty," she continued. "It's really sixty-forty. The woman has to do most of the work."

"Did you tell me that, Mother? I guess I must have forgotten." Joanie was now incapable of opening her mouth. She was speaking through clenched jaws.

"Oh, yes," Ivy said. She nodded and smiled. As if, Joanie thought, the two of them were having a pleasant, casual conversation of little import. "That's the way it's always been. I know your generation thinks everything is different now. That you can have equality—or whatever it is you call it. But that never works out, you know."

"I didn't realize you were such an expert on my generation, Mother. Most of us have different ideas about relationships."

"Which don't seem to have worked very well, have they?" Ivy said. She looked at Joanie's blotched, flushed face and frowned. "You look angry, Roxanne. What's wrong?"

"*I am not angry!*" Joanie screamed. She stood up and yanked her half-eaten plate off the table. She grasped it so hard her glistening green pile of peas flew off the plate, along with half a chicken leg. The particles of food seemed to hang in the air, like thought bubbles in a cartoon. Then they cascaded onto the floor.

Joanie crouched above the peas and the chicken, her heart pounding. "And don't call me Roxanne, Mother," she said in a low voice that wobbled and shook. "That isn't the name I go by. I've told you that before. I've told you that for years. Everybody calls me Joanie. Except *you*." She slipped a little on the wreckage, her heel squashing a half-dozen peas underneath.

"Whatever you want to be called," Ivy said. She continued to eat her chicken, as if her daughter had just gotten up briefly to stretch or get something out of the refrigerator and wasn't standing in the middle of a compost heap trembling with rage. "I just thought it would be helpful for you to talk. You and the girl seem to be very unhappy and quarrelsome these days. I think you should try to repair your marriage with Richard. He's such a lovely man. Your father and I always thought so."

"We don't have a marriage to repair, Mother!" Joanie screamed. She let the plate drop out of her hand. It smashed on the floor, sending shards in every direction. "And Richard is *not* a lovely man! You know nothing, Mother! Nothing! Richard and his new girlfriend are having a baby!"

Ivy looked up, mildly curious. "So that's what you're so angry about," she said. "A baby. At your age—and after your operation—you can't have another baby, can you?"

"Goddammit, Mother! It isn't that!" Joanie yelled. To hell with the neighbors overhearing this. If they thought this was bad, they'd be very shocked, indeed, when Ivy's lifeless body was found bludgeoned and floating in Lady Bird Lake later on that evening. "It's everything in my life, Mother! My daughter, my ex-husband, my job, my whole filthy, stinking life! And having you here, undermining me every step of the way, day after day, night after night!"

The longer she spoke—or screamed was more like it—the

closer and closer she leaned in to her mother, till their faces were only an inch or two apart. She'd hardly ever seen her mother's face that close-up, she realized, staring into Ivy's faded blue eyes, her wrinkled pink and white complexion, her plump nose with a brown age spot on the right nostril.

Ivy continued to eat, remaining eerily calm. Joanie grabbed Ivy's plate off the table and hurled it to the floor as hard as she could. The food flew and the plate bounced off the floor, shattering.

Joanie lunged out of the dining room into her own bedroom. She slammed the door so vigorously the house shook, then she threw herself on the bed and lay there till she stopped shaking.

Dear David, Ivy wrote, sitting at the computer. I am so sorry to bother you with my problems. I know this must be the busiest time of year for you.

She frowned. She was going to have to be very careful about how she phrased everything. She needed to make David understand how urgent the situation was without getting him too upset. Men were so fragile, in a way. He didn't need to be worrying about her all the time. That wouldn't be fair.

As I'm sure you remember, she continued, your sister was abandoned by her husband and has been going through a terrible divorce. Richard is now very happy with his new wife and they are expecting a baby soon. As you can imagine, this news has greatly upset your sister (who is now calling herself Joanie and insists that I call her that as well). Tonight, I'm afraid to say, she became very violent when I asked her about the matter. She screamed and smashed china. I had to go to my room and lock the door to make sure I was safe.

Ivy had always been a good, fluid writer. She had loved to write long letters and daily entries in journals she kept for herself. Most people hadn't appreciated her letters. She only got back short replies. Sometimes she wished she could get her letters back; if she could read them again, she would be able to remind herself of the hum of daily life when she was younger and busier.

Her journal writing was different. Many nights, while John watched TV or fell asleep on the couch, she pulled out her diary and wrote long reports of what she'd done during the day, what she thought about, what troubled her, what made her happy.

In all their years of marriage, John had never asked her what she was writing. Once, just once, she'd read him something she'd written about an antique china cabinet she'd seen in a store and longed to buy. The cabinet had reminded her of one from her childhood that had sat in her parents' dining room. She could still remember wanting it so badly that it almost hurt to think of it. She'd read the account to John. She didn't know why. Maybe she wanted him to admire her writing. Or that he suggest they buy the cabinet, since it meant so much to her. But he hadn't. He'd just nodded his head when she finished reading, with an odd look on his face, as if he couldn't believe a piece of furniture could be so important to someone. As if she'd been silly to think about it so much, to hope for it. Then he turned back to the TV.

Ivy had never read anything she'd written to John again. The next time she went to the store, months later, the china cabinet was gone. Something else—a rocking chair, she recalled—had been in its place.

She shook her head. She was doing it again—thinking about regrets she still carried with her. Lots of people wrote for no one. Lots of people longed for things they couldn't have. What made her think she was any different, any better, than any of them?

> I just thought you would like to know, David, what is going on here. Please tell me what you think I should do. Love to all, Mom

After she finished, she paused to reread the email to make sure it didn't have any mistakes in it. No, it was clearly written. It didn't ask for anything. It just told the story of what had happened to her today. There wasn't anything wrong with sending it to David. He would want to know about it.

Ivy clicked the SEND key and signed out of her email account. It was late. She needed her rest.

"It gets better," Mary Margaret said over the phone, "when both your parents are dead. You don't have nearly as many arguments with them."

"This is not very helpful, Mary Margaret," Joanie said. She was still seething. She couldn't sleep she was so upset. Her stomach hurt, her back ached, her hands were almost crippled from being clenched into fists. "My mother has the constitution of an ox. She's going to outlive you and me and everybody I know—out of sheer meanness."

"She doesn't seem that mean to me," Mary Margaret said. "She seems kind of sweet."

"Ha," Joanie said bitterly. "She's a snake."

"Send her to your sainted brother, that little New York turd. She's already lived with you—what?—a year?"

"Six months," Joanie said. "Six months of pure hell." She exhaled noisily. "I wanted to kill her tonight. Impale her on a broomstick. Dismember her."

"Yeah? Well, you can borrow my chain saw the next time. It cuts through bones pretty well. Especially old bones."

"God." Joanie sighed. "How did my life become this big, rotten mess?"

"At least your mother doesn't have money," Mary Margaret said. She was always pragmatic about things like this—family relationships, life, bank-account balances. Pragmatic about everything, except for her married boyfriend, Marc. "If they have money—like mine did—then you have to kiss their asses till they buy the farm. They're always threatening to disinherit you. Remember when my mom was going to leave all her goddamn money to the humane society? Jesus."

Fortunately, Mary Margaret's mother had died before she could change her will. Mary Margaret and her sister, Beverly, had thrown a perfectly respectable funeral with a minister who had never met their mother and a lavish wake with heavily spiked pink lemonade, where everyone, even all the Baptists from West Texas, had gotten drunk.

"Your mama was a real pistol," many of them had said, trying to stand upright, wondering why the world was tilting so fast, so violently. "Bless her heart. They don't make women like that anymore."

"I think it's a sad thing to hate your mother," Joanie said now.

"Every woman hates her mother."

"That's not true. Not everybody." Joanie was thinking, in particular, about a girl she'd known at the university who had talked to her mother, long distance, every day. "My mother is really my best friend," she'd once told Joanie. Joanie had almost broken out in a rash, hearing that. She didn't want a best friend. She just wanted a mother who liked her, who didn't pick at her till she bled.

"You know why you're saying that?" Mary Margaret said. "It's because you have a daughter. You don't want to think she'll be hating you."

"I don't care," Joanie said stubbornly. "I don't think it has to be like that. Not always."

"You're messing with the laws of nature, hon. You can't change some things."

"I'm going to bed," Joanie said. "Thanks for listening to me."

"Maybe, if I had a daughter, I'd feel the same way. I just didn't want kids, though. You know that."

"Good night, Mary Margaret," Joanie said. She hung up.

"What grade are you in, Caroline?" B.J. asked.

"She's in high school, B.J. The tenth grade," Richard said. His voice was a little sharp. "I already told you that a couple of times."

The three of them were sitting in Richard and B.J.'s new living room. It had a glass coffee table and a white rug. Richard was drinking red wine, B.J. had a glass of bottled water, and Caroline sipped a Coke. They had already had dinner together at a classic Mexican restaurant, where the noise was so loud they couldn't hear one another. Here, in the condo, it was quiet. That was worse. Caroline missed the noise.

Since he and Joanie had gotten divorced, Richard had had two other girlfriends. There had been Wanda, a long-distance runner, who taught tennis and history at a high school in south Austin, and Leslie, a receptionist at a downtown law firm. Caroline had wanted to die the first few times she'd been around her father with another woman. She knew that, all that time, her mother would be at home, miserable, crying. That scene had played out in her mind as she'd watched her father talk more, laugh louder, act a little too eager to please the new woman. The time he'd patted Leslie on the ass, Caroline had almost had a panic attack. It had been deeply gross.

In fact, Richard looked really different from how he used to look, when he was married to Joanie. He'd lost weight, taken up jogging and yoga, started wearing brighter, tighter, younger-looking clothes. It was strange to see parents change. Weren't they supposed to stay the same while their kids grew up and changed? Yes.

"I guess I forgot," B.J. murmured. She smiled shyly at Caroline. She was very quiet and shy. Blond and pale—but Caroline didn't think she was really an albino, as she'd heard Joanie describe her.

B.J. was trying to be nice to her. Caroline understood that. She was in love with Richard, and being nice to his daughter was part of the package. Caroline was an *object* to her. Caroline hated that. She didn't want to be somebody's object.

"Can I have a little more Coke?" Caroline asked.

Both B.J. and Richard jumped to their feet like they'd been shocked by an electric current.

"I'll get it, sweetie," B.J. said, touching him on the wrist.

Richard sat back down and cracked his knuckles. Caroline had never seen him this restless and strange. She wondered what B.J. saw in him. He was so much older than she was, with graying, wavy hair and a ruddy face. Caroline supposed he was decent-looking, if you liked really old guys. He was twenty years older than B.J. Twenty years! He'd been in college when she was born. When he was twenty, did he go around thinking he'd be dating an infant in a few years? Probably.

"It's so good to have you here," Richard said. His voice was loud and hearty. Too loud. It was the third or fourth time he'd said the exact same thing. Was he losing his mind, maybe? "So great we can spend time together, Caroline. You're growing up so much."

Caroline tried to give him a halfhearted smile, but it froze on her face. She was fifteen. All the kids she went to high school with were probably out with a bunch of friends, having a great time, riding around in cars, going to movies, sneaking into nightclubs, drinking on the sly. Even Sondra had hinted she had plans for the weekend. Sondra! Everybody on earth was out having fun, and here she was, planted in this god-awful living room with her creepy, sex-crazed, child-molester father and his sad, wispy, pregnant girlfriend who was trying to be nice to her because she had to be.

B.J. was probably just buttering her up because she thought she could get Caroline to babysit after she popped the kid out. Yes, that was it. B.J. saw right through Caroline, knew she didn't have any friends, had never been kissed, was a hopeless, flat-chested virgin who spent her whole life thinking, obsessing, dreaming about a good-looking guy who'd barely even noticed her, couldn't have picked her out in a lineup of felons.

"Here you are, Caroline," B.J. said, handing her the glass of Coke. She'd added ice cubes and a lime wedge to it.

Richard cleared his throat and sat up straighter. "I guess your mother has already told you, Caroline, that B.J. and I are expecting a baby."

Oh, no. The happy announcement. Just what Caroline needed. Vomit. Out of the corners of her eyes, she could see B.J.'s pale cheeks pinkening.

Caroline sighed more loudly than she'd intended. She stared at her Coke, at the sweaty glass, at the bright lime wedge. She felt sick to her stomach.

"Instead of the three of us," Richard said, using his hand to indicate Caroline, B.J., and himself, "there are going to be four of us."

His voice dropped off. The room was silent, except for the soft whoosh of the air-conditioning. Caroline stared fixedly at her glass. She examined the ice cubes very carefully, watched the bubbles as they rose to the top of the liquid, then disappeared. There was a whole world there, in that glass of Coke. A whole world of physics, cause and effect, displacement of liquids and solids, changing forms. A small, magical world.

"Caroline—" B.J. began.

Richard waved his hand at B.J. to quiet her. Caroline could see that as she stared at the glass of Coke. She was trying to hypnotize herself, float away, stop caring about anything.

"Don't you have anything to say, Caroline?" Richard asked. His fatherly bravado was over. His voice had an edge to it.

Caroline reached in front of her and placed the tumbler of Coke on the glass coffee table, where it would leave a soggy ring. She was sick, suddenly, of everybody wanting something from her. Of her father wanting her approval, wanting her to pretend she was part of a family that wasn't her family, that wasn't even a family at all. Of her mother being so sad and needy and desperate, and of her going bankrupt. Of a crazy grandmother who wanted her to love Jesus, even though Jesus couldn't get her a car. Of a whole, big outside world that she wanted to belong to—but that didn't seem to want her at all.

"Are you considering an abortion?" she asked. "It's probably not too late."

No more silence or air-conditioning whoosh. She could hear, dimly, her father yelling at her, B.J. bursting into tears, her own thudding heart. But it was better that way. Anything was better than sitting silently, trying to smile and pretend that everything was just swell and perfect. Because it wasn't and it was never going to be.

"Hello?"

"Joanie, what in the hell is going on with you and Mom?"

Joanie stared at her watch. Ten thirty A.M. She'd fallen asleep on the couch, clutching a pillow to her chest, with the phone nearby. Great. She should know better than to answer the phone without checking the caller ID.

But, hey. Even if she had read the caller ID, what difference would it have made? What was it about her that caused the men in her life to telephone her and start abusing her right off the bat? If she were a normal person instead of a perennial victim and toxic-waste dump site, they would at least wait for a minute or two. Right?

"Oh. David. How nice to hear from you. Good morning to you, too."

Silence. Typical. A very hostile, judgmental silence. David used silences to make people talk. He was a trial lawyer. It was Joanie's sick, twisted fate to be surrounded by vicious, aggressive men like Richard and David, who were both lawyers. If she ever ended her ban on sex and got around to advertising on one of those blind date websites, she would include the proviso: *Serial killers, pornography addicts, and mercenaries welcome; lawyers prohibited*.

In the meantime, Joanie wasn't a witness on David's courtroom stand. She was his sister, a little hungover, with a bad headache and a gutful of poisonous, melodramatic family dynamics. He could go fuck himself. She wasn't going to talk first.

A big, dramatic exhale on the other end of the line.

"Joanie," David said, speaking with exaggerated reasonableness, like he was talking to a small and fairly stupid child, "I got a very disturbing email from Mom late last night. She said you were threatening her."

"Really?" Joanie said, wishing she had a mug of hot coffee to wake her up. Somebody evil was playing a bass drum in her head. "And you believed her?"

"She said you were throwing plates at her."

"I was throwing plates at the floor. I only broke two."

"Is that supposed to make me feel better, Joanie?"

"Is that the point, David? To make *you* feel better?"

Joanie flopped back on the couch. Her sleep-clogged mind,

sensitized by months of support-group solidarity, was talking to her. Last night she'd smashed two plates in front of her sweetly malicious mother. She'd never before broken anything in her life, on purpose. And she hadn't backed down, had she? No, she had not.

And look! Now, for the first time in her entire life, she was sort of standing up to her older brother, David, the chosen one, the family genius, the Wall Street lawyer. How you could sort of stand up to someone while you were lying on the couch, she didn't know. But she felt a small jolt of energy and purpose.

Another loud exhale. Did all families communicate by coded breathing, the way hers did? Weren't people supposed to be a little more verbal and articulate than this?

"Joanie," David said, this time with exaggerated patience. The weight of the world, the nobody-knows-the-troubles-I've-seen woes in his breath, "Do you know how hard this is on me? I'm two thousand miles away from Mom and—"

"Try being two inches away from her, David. It's a lot worse. I'll guarantee you, it's a hell of a lot worse."

"I know that, Joanie. And believe me, I appreciate that."

"Do you, David?"

"What are you saying, Joanie? That I don't care about Mom?"

"I'm not sure what I'm saying," Joanie said. "All I know is, I see her every day. I've got a new job and a fifteen-year-old daughter and I'm tired and sometimes, I want to be by myself. But I can't be. Mother's here. Sometimes, it isn't too bad. Other times, she drives me crazy."

The other end of the line was silent. New arguments, fresh methods of attack were being plotted.

"The funny thing is," Joanie added, "you're Mother's favorite, even though you're not here. You didn't want her to live with you, you didn't want her to move to New York. You're still her favorite child."

"That's not my fault—"

"It's nobody's fault. It just *is*. It makes me feel bad. It makes everything harder. She's always been more critical of me. And now she's living with me and she gets to be critical twenty-four hours a day."

"I wish I were closer," David said.

"No, you don't."

"No," he said slowly, "I guess I don't."

There was almost something sad and self-knowing in his voice, a puncture in his usual armor that touched Joanie. For a few seconds, she didn't say anything, wondering about what he might be thinking or feeling. Maybe it would be possible for the two of them to have a real conversation. No brother-and-sister posturing, no guilt, no remorse, no blame. Just a real conversation. They'd never had that, or if they had, she couldn't remember it.

Maybe, for all of Joanie's resentment of Ivy's idolatry of her only son, she'd unconsciously absorbed the same feelings. David was invincible, perfect, couldn't be bothered with the minutiae of others' lives. Maybe Joanie, like her mother, had been wrong about him. Maybe he did care.

"Just a minute," David said. She could hear him in the background, talking to someone with a higher pitched voice—his wife? His daughter?

"I've got to go," he said.

"All right." Joanie lingered on the phone, wondering about

his life, whether he was happy, who it was speaking to him in such urgent tones.

"Just tell me one thing, Joanie," he said.

"What?"

"Is this—is all this trouble with Mom—is it about money?"

Joanie pulled the phone away from her and stared at it for a few seconds. What a creep. What an insensitive lout. If there was a problem, it must be money. Nothing more, nothing less. She placed the phone back at her ear, scowling. "No, David. It's not about money. Not at all."

"Well, I just thought it might be—"

"It's about a lot of things. But not money. That's not even close." She hung up the phone, more disappointed with him than she could ever remember being before.

"I know this is hard on you, Caroline," Richard said. He was driving her back to Joanie's house. "B.J. told me that last night. She said you're afraid the baby is going to take your place."

Caroline rolled her eyes, crossed them, uncrossed them, rolled them again. Why did everybody on earth—including that little lighter-than-air B.J., who barely knew her—"know" how Caroline felt? Nobody knew how she felt. Caroline herself had no idea how she felt—so how could anyone else?

Adults were such big hypocrites. They made so many awful mistakes with their own lives, which they spent all their time justifying and making excuses for, just so they could plow on with the rest of their lives and make the same stupid mistakes all over again. The only difference between them and teenagers was that at least teenagers knew they were a mess.

"We both appreciated your apology this morning," Richard said. "We know you're truly sorry about what you said."

We? *We!* Caroline was so sick of hearing about "we." And that apology? She'd just hung her head and muttered something about being "inappropriate." Inappropriate! She loved that word. Every time you were brutally honest, you could excuse it by saying you'd been inappropriate. Inappropriate was a synonym for honest. Inappropriate and honest were bad; lying was good.

In spite of it all, in spite of the fact that she'd been inappropriate and honest, she'd known she had crossed a line and she hated herself for it. She was just sick of everybody acting happy when they really weren't, and she wanted to ruin it for them, the same way her own life was ruined on a regular basis. But she wasn't that bad, not really. She acted mean, but she wasn't as mean as she acted sometimes. Or was that wrong— just another justification like adults used? Was she growing up to be just like them?

"I'll tell you a little secret," Richard said, reaching over to pat Caroline's knee. "The truth is, I'm not so happy B.J. is pregnant. We didn't plan it. I thought she was taking precautions."

Caroline stared straight ahead, hoping her father was going to run into a parked car and kill them both. Why did he have to tell her something like this? She didn't want to know! And *precautions*? What did he think Caroline was—his best friend? She felt sick to her stomach. Talk about inappropriate. He had no idea.

Richard glanced at her. "Maybe I shouldn't have said that," he said.

Caroline stared at her lap, at her bunched-up knees, like they were the most fascinating thing in the world.

"Caroline?" Richard said. "Are you all right?"

"I'm fine," she said in a low voice.

Richard pulled the car to the curb in front of Joanie's house. He stopped it and grabbed Caroline by the wrist before she could jump out. "Honey," he said, "are you all right?"

"I'm fine," she repeated.

Richard dropped her wrist and placed both his hands on the steering wheel. He looked out the windshield, staring at something or nothing. She didn't know, she didn't care. It was like he was trying to get his balance again.

"I guess grown-ups make mistakes, too," he said—like this should be a shocking revelation to her. "I shouldn't have said that. I'm sorry.

"Can you—can you forget that I said that?"

"Sure," she said, leaving the car, pulling her small overnight case behind her. "Thanks for the weekend."

She ran up the driveway into the house. There were so many things in her life she already wanted to forget. Here was something else.

"How was your weekend, honey?" Joanie asked.

Caroline shrugged. "Okay. I guess."

"You want to talk about it?"

"No."

Caroline felt like a Ping-Pong ball at times like this, getting smashed back and forth between her parents. The minute they'd gotten separated, as a matter of fact, then divorced, she had become something else to the two of them that she couldn't quite understand.

Sometimes, she felt she was a link between her parents. Other times, it was like they both wanted her on their side, were jealous of any affection she had for the other. Still other times, she felt like she was being used as a spy, a microscope into the other's life. Like now. She knew her mother was dying for information about Richard and B.J., but was trying not to push it. Joanie loved Caroline and wanted her to have had a good weekend. But not too good. If she looked happy— which she didn't, God knows—it would have been a problem. It would have made Joanie feel a little worse. Irritating as her mother could be, Caroline didn't want her to feel worse. Joanie already felt bad enough, and Caroline wanted her to be happier.

But she still didn't want to talk to Joanie or have her empty her heart out—the way she had after Richard first left her. Caroline had been exhausted by that, couldn't do it any longer.

Joanie wasn't leaning on Caroline the way she had then. But she still wanted her approval, wanted her to be on Joanie's side. She wanted too much from Caroline. They all did.

"You're just in time for dinner," Joanie said. "I've already got the table set. We're having your favorite meal, Frito chili pie. Good and greasy and fattening. Wash your hands."

Frito chili pie, which required nothing more than dumping canned chili and grated cheese into bowls, then sprinkling corn chips on top, was the one meal Joanie could reliably make without ruining. When Caroline was younger, Joanie hadn't cooked much. But, once Ivy had moved in, she had started cooking more—like she wanted to prove something.

She was getting a lot of practice these days, but she wasn't getting any better.

Caroline, Joanie, and Ivy sat down at the table. Her mother was trying hard, Caroline could see that. It hurt her to notice. Joanie had even plopped some fresh flowers in the middle of the table. And she kept talking, talking, talking, like she had one of those batteries that never died running her mouth.

Wasn't the weather lovely? Had they read about the passenger on a plane who had a heart attack and was revived by the flight attendant? Wasn't that just incredible? What did they think of the latest political debate on global warming?

"Pass the salad, please," Ivy said. She looked directly at Caroline and smiled, even though Joanie was the one closest to the salad.

"Here you are, Mother," Joanie said.

Ivy took the bowl without saying anything. She unloaded a big helping of bright green leaves, glistening with olive oil, onto her plate.

"I've read all about global warming on the Internet," Ivy said, still speaking to Caroline. "It's a complete fraud. There's absolutely no proof of it."

"Every reputable scientist in the world agrees about global warming," Joanie said loudly. She spoke to Ivy. Then, when she realized that Ivy wasn't looking at her, she began speaking to Caroline, too. "You've studied it in biology, haven't you, Caroline?"

"Scientists don't know everything," Ivy told Caroline. "Most of them are atheists, anyway."

"You can see the signs of global warming all around the

world," Joanie said. "Glaciers melting. Polar bears starving. Rising waters."

"I wouldn't believe an atheist about anything," Ivy said. "How can they swear to tell the truth, so help them God, when they don't believe in God?"

"Pretty soon," Joanie predicted, trying to recall what she'd read most recently, "New York and the California coast are going to be underwater."

"I read the Bible," Ivy said. "The Bible tells me everything I need to know. Have you read the book of Revelation, Caroline?"

"The next car I buy is going to be a Prius," Joanie said. "We need to do our part to stop global warming."

"God provided for Noah—and all the animals," Ivy said. "All you need is faith. But some people don't know that."

Caroline tried to bury her face in her Frito chili pie. Her mother and grandmother continued to talk, giving alternate versions of reality, taking turns, but never acknowledging that the other had spoken. An argument—clearly, they'd had a dustup while she'd been with her father and B.J. Caroline had seen the fallout before. Ivy could go for days without acknowledging her mother's existence. It was really kind of amazing when you considered how small the house was.

"I think I'm going to have ice cream for dessert," Joanie announced. "Can I get some for anybody else?"

"I'm not very hungry, Mom," Caroline said, breaking her death-grip stare at her plate and plotting her escape to her room, where she planned to cover her face with a pillow and stop breathing, if possible. "May I be excused?"

"I always wear this necklace, Caroline," Ivy said. "Have I shown it to you? It's a mustard seed. It's based on scripture. Even if you have faith as small as a mustard seed, you can still be saved. You can wear the necklace, if you want. I'm leaving it to you in my will."

"Last chance," Joanie called out from the kitchen. "I'm about to put the ice cream back in the freezer."

Caroline picked up her plate and headed to the kitchen. She couldn't get away fast enough.

chapter 8

"Hello, Lupe," Ivy said. "How are you today?"

"Okay," Lupe said. She placed a glass of water with crushed ice on the place mat in front of Ivy. "Thank you for asking, ma'am. Good to see you again."

Ivy had eaten at the restaurant three times last week and Lupe had been her waitress each time. They were becoming friends, she could tell. Ivy had never had a Hispanic friend before, but a woman in her bridge group in West Texas had had a maid from Monterrey named Elena. Ivy had often nodded at Elena and thanked her for iced tea, but she didn't think this was the same as being friends.

Ivy and John had lived in West Texas for more than forty years. Of course, Ivy had lots of friends there—women she knew through the church, in their neighborhood, in her bridge group. But she'd never had any really close friends, the way other women seemed to. She'd never felt the need to have someone to tell secrets to. She was different, more retiring, than other women.

But she'd missed her circle of friends and acquaintances when she moved here six months ago. There was nobody she knew to nod at in the grocery store or on the sidewalks. Joanie lived in Austin, where the pace was faster and the humidity overwhelming. People here didn't seem to have as much time to talk as they had in West Texas. Or maybe they just didn't want to talk to someone who was almost eighty. Ivy could remember being like that, too. She'd always thought her own grandmother smelled bad—a little soured. She could recall pulling back from her when she was a small child. She regretted that now, all these years later, when she finally understood. Her grandmother couldn't help it if she smelled bad.

Yesterday, Ivy had written her old next-door neighbor, Myra Hawkes. Myra was the friend she'd taken Internet classes with at the library.

She and Ivy had lived side by side for years, trading occasional gossip, political views, talk about religion. They hadn't been particularly close, but Myra had been a part of Ivy's life. They had watched each other—over hedges and fences and through car and kitchen windows—grow from being young women to middle-aged to old. Their children had played together, then, occasionally, their grandchildren.

Suddenly, Ivy missed the company of someone who had known her for years. Who had seen her hair grow gray, then white. Who had watched her middle thicken, and her shoes turn lower and stockier. Someone who knew who she used to be and how she'd come to be what she was. Someone who knew she hadn't started out like this; she had once been someone else, someone vibrant and energetic.

In her letter to Myra, she'd written a brief account of her life in Austin, glossing over the fact that Roxanne was a divorced atheist and Caroline was probably anorexic, and stressing how nice it was to live with your family, to be welcomed. In subsequent letters, once the ice was broken, she'd be more honest. But not in the first letter she sent. A first letter, out of nowhere, needed to be light and general.

"You look busy today, Lupe," Ivy said, as Lupe eased a plate with another tuna fish sandwich—with less mayonnaise this time, after Ivy's careful directions—onto the table.

Lupe smiled. "Too busy. Too many people want things too fast." She smiled at Ivy and patted her on the shoulder. The first time she'd done that, Ivy had drawn back, surprised. But she'd recalled what she'd heard about Hispanics: They were a warm, affectionate people. That was a good thing, the more she thought about it.

"How are things with you, ma'am?" Lupe asked.

Ivy shook her head and sighed. "Well, I'm all right," she said tentatively. "Doing pretty well. You know, I live here with my daughter and granddaughter."

"You do?" Lupe asked. "That's very nice. Very good. Family is always good."

"Yes, it is," Ivy agreed, even though she wasn't so sure.

"What does your daughter do?" Lupe asked.

Ivy tried to remember. She knew that Roxanne—or "Joanie"—worked downtown. She worked for some kind of company. She'd probably told Ivy what the name of the company was several times. But it hadn't meant anything to Ivy at the time. She did something "creative," artistic. That was all Ivy could remember.

"She has a very good job," Ivy said. "She's a—an artist."

"An artist!" Lupe said. Her face brightened. "How wonderful! I always wanted to be an artist, too. What kind of artwork does she do?"

"Oh, all kinds."

"And your granddaughter," Lupe said. "Is she an artist, too?"

"She's a student," Ivy said. "She's in high school."

"You must be very proud of them," Lupe said. "To have a daughter who's an artist!"

"And a son," Ivy added, "who's a big lawyer in New York."

"In New York?" Lupe said, frowning. "That's so far away. He couldn't find a job here?"

"Well, he could have," Ivy said. For some reason, it was making her uncomfortable to speak about her family. How did she explain things? Especially when she didn't really understand them herself. "But he really wanted to work in New York. And then he married a woman from New York and they have two children."

"You have pictures?" Lupe asked.

"Not—not here," Ivy said. David had last sent family photos three or four years ago. The children must have changed so much since then. She wouldn't even recognize them. Did they, she wondered, ever think about her, their grandmother in Texas? Did they ever wonder why they didn't see her?

"Look at this," Lupe said. She reached into her blouse pocket, under her name tag, and pulled out two photos. They had been taken in a photography studio, the subjects formally posed. Lupe smiled out from the center of the photograph, surrounded by three sweet-faced children and a Hispanic man who must have been her husband. "And these are my kids," Lupe added, pointing at the second photo. "My little angels."

She tucked the photos back in her pocket after Ivy had oohed and aahed over them.

"Family is the most important thing in the world," Lupe said, as if this were something she and Ivy both understood and agreed upon.

After Lupe left, Ivy sat and ate her tuna sandwich without much of an appetite. She still had half a sandwich and most of her potato chips left when Lupe returned.

"You need to eat more, hon," Lupe said. She patted Ivy on the back again.

"My daughter," Ivy said, "is divorced."

Lupe shook her head, the corners of her mouth turning down. "That must be very sad for her and for you," she said. "And for her daughter." She picked up Ivy's plate and crumpled napkin.

"It happens a lot these days," Ivy said.

"It's funny, you know," Lupe said. "My parents came to this country for the opportunity. They loved this country."

Ivy nodded.

"But," Lupe said, "they always told me not everything was better here. You can work hard, get rich, buy a big house. But people here don't value friends and family and religion the way they do in Mexico."

Ivy cocked her head, frowning. She'd almost never heard an

immigrant story that didn't sing the praises of the adopted country. Hadn't everybody found a better place when they came here? Otherwise, why did they keep trying?

"People here, I think," Lupe said, "aren't as happy as they are in Mexico." She shrugged. "They're richer. But they're not as happy. Funny thing."

"Funny thing," Ivy echoed.

When Lupe brought her check, Ivy left a bigger tip than usual.

Smoking weed had been Sondra's idea. She'd come back from a weekend in San Antonio visiting cousins with a sly grin on her face. "I've got something to show you," she whispered to Caroline between classes.

After school, they ran to Sondra's jalopy in the parking lot. Inside the car, after craning her neck to make sure no one was looking, Sondra proudly unveiled two joints. She'd hidden them in the car pocket, wrapped in Kleenex.

"Marijuana," Sondra said importantly. "My cousin Blake gave them to me. We spent the entire weekend smoking weed."

Caroline stared at the two ratty-looking cigarettes. She'd heard about marijuana, but had never seen it before. Unlike, probably, everybody else in their sophomore class. What was the big deal? Was this what they'd been talking about? Surely not.

"Getting high," Sondra continued, her round blue eyes widening, "is the most incredible experience. Blake says it's better than sex."

Better than sex. Caroline stared once again at the joints, feeling intrigued. The odds of her getting sex in the next thousand years were about zero. But the odds of her getting high, of experiencing something *just like sex, except better*, had just improved markedly.

They drove to Sondra's small frame house in east Austin, and parked in the driveway. They left their book bags in the car and ran to the front door, giggling already. Running, Caroline already felt happier. She loved the feeling of breaking rules, of being a rebel, of being—what would she call it?—wild and free.

The minute she inhaled the joint, holding her breath, as Sondra told her to, she felt a little crazy. Even though she knew it couldn't be the drug already.

She exhaled a cloud of smoke, trying not to cough, and handed it to Sondra.

"I love this," Caroline said, sinking into the lumpy sofa cushions in Sondra's living room. She threw her head back and cackled like a big, happy bird. "I feel *great*!"

They fell back and forth on the cushions, inhaling and holding their breaths, then exhaling white streams of smoke up into the air. Caroline hoped Sondra's parents didn't have a very good sense of smell. But after a while, she didn't even care. If Sondra's parents had walked through the front door, she would have laughed. They would have laughed, too, she'd bet.

"I'm hungry," Sondra said woozily. Her head was lolling against the couch, making small indentations in the upholstery.

"I am *starving*," Caroline said.

They roused themselves from the sofa, laughing softly, hysterically. Sondra opened all the living room windows and turned on the fan overhead. She wiggled her nose. "I don't think you can smell anything, do you?" she asked.

Caroline sniffed. "I can't smell anything," she reported. "But it does look a little smoky in here." She waved her hands around to clear out the smoke and ended up dancing around the room, her arms flapping, her head gyrating. Sondra joined her. The two of them twirled around the room, waving their arms, giggling, crashing into each other, then finally falling back down on the couch.

"I'm going to die if I don't eat," Sondra said.

She got up, and Caroline followed her into the kitchen. There wasn't anything interesting in the refrigerator, but they found a half-gallon container of chocolate-cherry ice cream in the freezer.

"Oh, my God," Sondra said. "This ice cream is awesome." She put the ice cream in the microwave and pulled out two large spoons for the two of them. After the ice cream softened, they sat at the kitchen table and dipped their spoons into the oozing, creamy lump.

"This is the best ice cream I've ever tasted," Caroline said. She plunged her spoon back in and came up with a fist-sized ball of ice cream. The faster it dripped on the table, the faster she ate it. Sondra's face, she noticed, was smeared with ice cream, her eyes rolling back in ecstasy.

"I have never," Caroline said slowly, deliberately, "felt this different. This . . . this . . . *awesome*."

"See what I mean?" Sondra said. "It's magic." She plunged the spoon back into the ice cream carton and beamed at Caroline.

They began to laugh again. Caroline rubbed her stomach, which was bursting with ice cream and goodwill. She felt happy and full. She felt inspired.

"Sondra," Caroline said, "I just got the most wonderful idea." She leaned forward conspiratorially. "Listen to this."

Jacqueline, pronounced the French way, had kicked Nadine's ex-husband out of her Tuscan-style house. Nadine had found him, first thing that morning, asleep in his pickup truck in her driveway.

"He didn't have anywhere else to go," she told the divorcée group. "So he's staying with me for the time being."

She looked flushed and embarrassed. Joanie understood why. Nadine had always been the first and loudest in the group to accuse the others of total surrender and spinelessness and of waving the white flag when their old mates came sniffing around. "Don't fall for that same old shit!" she'd say. "Remember how it felt when he dumped you? D'you want to go back to that? For *what*? A pity fuck?"

"You're kidding, Nadine," said Lori, who had finally found a new babysitter and was sitting next to Nadine. "Right? Tell me you're kidding." Frowning, her beautiful dark face troubled, she wheeled around to face Nadine. She kicked Nadine gently on the foot. "Kidding. I know you are."

"It's just temporary," Nadine protested halfheartedly.

"But is it good for you, Nadine?" Denise said. She pushed back her hair so she could stare at Nadine intently. "Is it in your best interest?"

"That goddamned little prick is staying with you?" Sharon said, glaring. "Are you nuts, Nadine?"

"Seems like it," Nadine said. She blushed an even deeper shade of red and stared at the ground.

"We're not here to judge you, Nadine," Denise said.

Denise usually said that before she judged somebody, Joanie had noticed, like it inoculated her from blame and them from noticing and criticizing her. After more than a year in the group together, they all knew one another's habits, their weak points, their areas of blindness. It was a lot simpler and less painful than knowing your own.

"This is Nadine's decision," Denise said. "Not ours. But I'm wondering how wise it is."

Nadine shrugged. She sat with her arms crossed in front of her stubbornly. "I'd thought about this happening for a long time," she said, finally, still staring downward. "Imagined it. Thought about Roy coming back, asking me for something. How I'd slam the door in his fucking face."

She paused. Two fat tears slid down her cheeks, then dropped onto her collar. "I guess I just didn't realize how it would feel to see him again. I saw him out in that damn car, asleep . . . and I don't know. Something in me just melted. I didn't want it to. But it did."

Joanie, Lori, Sharon, even Denise were all still, watching her. More tears rolled down Nadine's face, but she didn't do anything to stop them.

Joanie thought briefly about another group member, Hannah, who had eventually taken back a husband who had cheated on her and once blackened her eye. They had argued bitterly with her—all of them. How could she go back to a man who had abused her? How could she give up all the progress she'd made in the group, the grief she'd dealt with, the insights she'd gained, the shaky steps toward independence she'd been making? How could she throw it all away?

"Y'all just don't understand," Hannah had said. She'd been alternately shamefaced and defiant toward them. How could they judge her? Hadn't Denise said, again and again, that their job was to support one another in the paths they chose to go? How did they know this was the wrong path for her? How could they think they understood her and her situation better than she did herself?

That evening, about six months ago, they had ended their meeting angry and fractious. Hannah had finally grabbed her purse and fled the room in tears. The minute the door slammed behind her, they'd all spoken at once. How could Hannah be such a fool? How could they not have tried to save her from what she was doing? Wasn't it their duty to tell her the truth?

Nadine's, of course, had been the loudest, most indignant voice that night. She, Joanie, and Lori had gone out for drinks afterward, heatedly discussing Hannah, furious at her, pleased—Joanie now recognized—with themselves for their own strength.

Hannah had never returned to the group. How could she have? For a few weeks, they'd talked about her, feeling better about their own situations and lives and strong minds. But finally, they'd stopped. There wasn't anything left to say.

Joanie thought about Hannah occasionally, wondering how she was. Maybe her life—miraculously!—had turned out well. Or maybe it hadn't but she'd learned something from it. Joanie didn't know. What haunted her, though, was whether she had been right to join the rest of the group in condemning Hannah. It had been so easy—but that didn't mean it was right.

Don't judge, don't judge, don't judge. It was the mantra of their group, of every support group Joanie had ever known about. Here's what was odd, though: Their judging Hannah had made the group stronger, at least for a while. It had brought them all together in their common outrage. Until it faded and Hannah was forgotten. Until now.

"I know what you're thinking," Nadine said. "I know what every one of you is thinking. Hell"—she gave a mirthless laugh—"I'm thinking it myself. But I did it. And I'm waiting to see how it ends."

Around the circle, eyebrows were raised. Shoulders were shrugged.

"You aren't sleeping with him, are you?" Sharon asked.

Nadine shook her head. Something about the way she shifted her eyes, though, made Joanie think she wasn't quite telling the truth.

Nadine shifted in her chair and stared out the window. She looked alone.

"Any other matters we should talk about?" Denise asked, after a few long seconds of silence. She looked around the group, urging them to speak. What she wanted to hear, Joanie thought, was a story of reasonable progress, occasional but manageable backsliding. A story that reinforced what she wanted them to learn. Nothing messy like real life, like a strong, tough woman named Nadine who'd taken back her husband—temporarily, desperately, whatever you wanted to call it—because she couldn't help herself, she still loved him and wanted him. Nothing like that. Nobody wanted to hear those stories. They were too hard and complicated and real.

Joanie's current dilemma, living with a right-wing Christian mother who believed in Adam and Eve and wouldn't talk to her, and a daughter who alternately hated and loved her, and a shaky job and a fragile boss, just wasn't worth mentioning. Not now. Right now, she felt too tired to even think about it.

"So, good night, everybody," Denise was saying.

Nadine was the first to leave.

Joanie watched her stalk out the door. Nadine might have been running back toward Roy. Or running away from all of them. She couldn't tell. If Nadine could take Roy back, Joanie realized she didn't know anything, didn't understand anyone.

What were they doing in this group? Who were they kidding?

"Which one?" Sondra asked Caroline. She held up two jars of punk hair dye, Flamingo Pink and Violent Violet. They were gorgeous!

Caroline squinted her eyes and tried to focus. It was extremely hard. She'd never really been stoned before. The jars expanded, then shrank right before her eyes. They were both simply beautiful, vibrant, scary, *won-der-ful*.

They had picked them out at the drugstore close to Sondra's house, wandering up and down the aisles, staring at all the fantastic products, their eyes a few inches away from the package photographs of happy, glamorous women with throbbing, bright hair, strobe-like eyes, and dazzling teeth. Who knew there were so many fabulous colors to dye your hair? Caroline couldn't believe she'd spent so many years with ordinary, mousy hair when there was a big, beautiful, pulsating rainbow of color available to her. She must have been blind or stupid. Or sober. That was it. That had been her problem.

"I . . . don't . . . know." Caroline sighed and sat down on the kitchen floor. They were still at Sondra's house and her parents would be at work for another couple of hours. There was time to think. To ponder.

"I know," Caroline said slowly, her voice furling out, swirling, unrolling and flapping like a flag in a breeze. "First, we bleach our hair. *Then* we decide."

"Oh, *yes*," Sondra said. "Yes! That's brilliant."

They had already poured the peroxide into one of the soup bowls in Sondra's kitchen. It smelled strong and chemical and made Caroline's face pucker up.

"I need to put on plastic gloves," Sondra said. She was acting different now that she was stoned—more self-assured, louder, a lot funnier. Everything she said made Caroline laugh. Sondra should probably smoke weed every day before she went to school, Caroline thought. They both should. They'd be happier—like this!—all the time.

Sondra struggled with the gloves, inching them onto her plump hands. Once she finally got them on, she dabbed a small sponge in the peroxide. "Put a towel around your shoulders," she ordered Caroline. Caroline pulled a small dish towel around her shoulders and sat down at the kitchen table.

"Hit me with all you've got," she told Sondra. "Hit me, baby!"

"Dab, dab, dab," Sondra said, poking the sponge on Caroline's scalp and hair. "Ooh, this is pretty."

"Shit, that hurts," Caroline grumbled. Her scalp smarted from the peroxide. It dripped down her face and neck, burning.

"Stop complaining," Sondra said. "I need to concentrate." She stepped back, a couple minutes later, examining Caroline's wet head, which was a little foamy with the peroxide. "I think . . . I've done a perfect job. Now, you do my hair."

Caroline could hardly stand up straight. She felt dizzy, unsteady. She needed to discipline herself, she realized. She picked up the soggy, dripping sponge and attacked Sondra's hair. Sondra had a lot of hair—dark and wavy and coarse. This was going to take a long time.

She worked fast, squeezing peroxide all over Sondra's head. She lurched against the kitchen table, spilling some of the peroxide on the floor. Fortunately, the floor was a light color. It wouldn't matter too much.

Caroline squinted at the directions. Leave in hair for fifty-one minutes, then rinse. Fifty-one? Or was it fifteen?

"Do you have a timer?" she asked Sondra.

"Mother, why aren't you talking to me?" Joanie asked.

She pulled back from the dining table and stared at her mother. She had just gotten back from her divorcée support group, but already, she was tired of getting the silent treatment. After all, this was her house. Joanie wasn't a helpless child any longer. She was a grown-up, a homeowner, a recovering divorcée.

"I don't know what you're talking about," Ivy said. She dabbed her face with the napkin and continued to eat. She was wearing a new scarf that Joanie had never seen before—it was a lovely aquamarine color. "I'm just quiet."

"Yes, you do know what I'm talking about," Joanie said stubbornly. "You haven't spoken to me since I broke those plates."

"Well, you shouldn't have broken the plates," Ivy said.

"They're my plates and this is my house. I can do anything I want, Mother."

"That doesn't make it right," Ivy said. "I get very upset when you're violent like that. I felt threatened." She picked up her napkin again. "It's a very common problem in society. I read about it on the Internet. Senior citizens are often threatened and abused."

"Oh, Jesus," Joanie muttered. She'd thought she'd been hungry, so she'd insisted on starting dinner after Caroline called to say she was eating at Sondra's house. Now, she wasn't so sure. Being around her mother ruined her appetite. She'd already lost ten pounds since Ivy had moved in. She'd be a scarecrow before long. The Move-In Mother Diet. Somebody should write a book, make a commercial, earn a fortune. Better than South Beach, more effective than Atkins!

"Don't talk like that," Ivy said. "It's very offensive to me. If you can't speak without taking the Lord's name in vain, don't say anything."

Joanie stared at the tossed salad. "You are living under my roof, Mother. I want you to be respectful to me, too."

"I brought you up," Ivy said. "Your father and I went through the Great Depression and World War Two. We never had anything. We worked for everything we had. Your generation has no idea what hard times are like."

"What does that have to do with anything?" Joanie asked.

She'd grown up with these stories, heard them night and day her whole life. The Greatest Generation? Good grief! She was sick of hearing how wonderful and self-sacrificing they were and what ingrates their kids were—the baby boomers. Everybody hated baby boomers, blamed them for everything from self-indulgence to the drug culture to the imminent bankruptcy of Social Security.

"It's a matter of respect," Ivy said. "I'm your mother. I don't feel respected."

"Well, welcome to reality," Joanie said. "I don't feel respected, either."

They stared at each other glumly, resentfully.

The phone rang. Joanie broke off her stare and jumped up to answer it. When she could finally understand—through all the noise and crying and swearing on the other end of the line—what she needed to do, she said she'd be there, soon.

"Get up, Mother," Joanie said, wiping her hands on a dish towel. "We've got to go pick up Caroline. There's been some trouble."

"My God," Joanie said. "I need to sit down." She lurched toward the Morrisons' couch.

Ivy still stood in the doorway. "Good evening," she told Sondra's parents. "I am Caroline's grandmother, Ivy Horton."

Her tone was formal and polite, as if she were meeting Sondra's parents at a PTA meeting. As if Sondra's mother—plump and normally jovial—didn't have mascara tear streaks running down her face and as if her father, in a sports shirt and jeans, didn't have his fists extended in front of him like he wanted to pummel somebody. As if their house weren't strewn with newspapers and magazines, as if it didn't reek of peroxide and something else, looking for all the world like a hovel where deranged inmates and other large and bulky animals lived and brawled and threw chairs at one another.

Beyond them, Caroline and Sondra were sprawled on the floor. Caroline's hair was bright pink, sticking out like a dandelion's fuzz. Sondra had a shock of purple hair, just like a clown, unruly and tangled.

"What on earth," Joanie asked, "have you two done to yourselves?"

"That's what I've been asking them," Sondra's mother said. She sniffed loudly. "Sondra always had such beautiful hair. And now—look at it!" She loudly burst into tears. Her husband put his arm around her as she sobbed wildly.

"My hair was boring," Sondra said. She sneaked a glance at Caroline, seeking support.

"I don't know why everybody thinks it's such a big deal," Caroline said. "It's only *hair*. Sondra looks good in purple."

"Hot pink looks good on you, too," Sondra said.

"It's our hair," Caroline said. "Not yours."

Sondra's mother stopped sobbing for a minute. "You can't go to school looking like that, Sondra. You'll get expelled."

"You can't go to church, either," her father said. His voice was a low growl.

"Good." Sondra looked up through her strands of purple hair and smiled. "I hate church."

"I think you're all being melodramatic," Caroline said. "Do you know what some of the kids look like at school these days? They've got tattoos, pierced lips—"

"Pierced nipples," Sondra threw in.

"—shaved heads, Mohawks, spiked hair—"

"All right, all right," Joanie said. "We get the point." She sat back on the sofa and looked at the two girls. They looked absolutely atrocious and completely ridiculous. But they also looked happy and slyly proud of themselves. She hadn't seen Caroline's face look that happy in a long time. If it took pink hair, was that such a big deal? At least she wasn't on drugs or anything. Pick your battles wisely—that's what all the adolescent development books said.

Besides, Joanie kept thinking, trying to control her face, it was all a little funny, when you got down to it. The outlandish hair, the sobbing, the theatrics, the whole bizarre mess.

"Maybe this isn't so bad," she began, tentatively. "We may be getting too upset about—"

"Are you two girls in a gang?" Ivy called out from the doorway.

"A *gang*?" Sondra's mother said, alarmed. "Is that what their hair means?" She whipped her face back around to look at Sondra, her mouth parted into a red *O*. "My God."

"Sometimes it does," Ivy said. "I've got a friend who's Hispanic. She told me all about it. Purple and hot pink might be their gang colors."

"Of *course* we're not in a gang," Caroline said, her voice heavily sarcastic. "We were just being individuals."

"Yeah," Sondra said. "Nonconformists. What's wrong with that?"

"I'll ask which gang it is the next time I see her," Ivy said.

"Didn't you bring us up to think for ourselves?" Caroline asked. "Make our own decisions?"

"Mother, don't get everybody upset," Joanie said. "These girls aren't in a gang."

"Lupe says the parents are always the last to know," Ivy said.

"No," Sondra's father thundered, his face red and furious.

Even his fists turned dark pink, like two hams. "We did not bring you up to think for yourselves! We don't want you to think at all—just obey! You are grounded, young lady."

Sondra's mother began to sob again. "A gang!" she wept. "Our only daughter!"

"Caroline," Joanie hissed. "Get up. We're leaving now."

"Well," Ivy said, "it was nice to get to meet Sondra's parents. They seemed like very nice, Christian people." She straightened her posture and sat up in the front seat, trying to speak to both Joanie and Caroline at the same time. Evidently, she had forgiven Joanie.

"Sondra's father is a psycho," Caroline said from the backseat. "One time, he got fired from a job for punching a customer. He broke the guy's jaw."

"Oh, my," Ivy said. "That doesn't sound very Christian. Which church do they go to?"

"Dunno. He's a cook," Caroline continued. "The customer said his hamburger was burned."

"I never complain about my food in a restaurant," Ivy said. "I don't think it's polite."

"The guy also said he thought the hamburger was made out of dog meat," Caroline reported. "I think he said it tasted like a Chihuahua."

Joanie could see Caroline in the rearview mirror, her hot-pink hair like a blazing neon sign, a big, loopy grin on her face. She remembered bringing Caroline home from the hospital when she was a little baby. Then, you worried about diapers and getting enough sleep and whether you were going to be a decent mother and what your baby would be when she grew up. Somehow, it never occurred to you she'd turn out to be a cranky adolescent with hair the color of psychedelic cotton candy. It also never occurred to you that, all in all, you wouldn't find the hair color that disturbing. What did it have to do with her, anyway? She, Joanie, was trying to find her way. So was her daughter. If pink hair was part of the route, so be it.

"A Chihuahua?" Ivy said. "Those little skinny dogs? The ones with the yappy barks?"

"You've got it," Caroline said.

"I never liked them, anyway," Ivy said.

"I guess I should warn you," Joanie said, speaking quietly into the phone. "Our daughter now has pink hair."

"Pink hair?" Richard said. "What do you mean, pink hair?"

"You know the color, Richard. Pink. It's kind of a light red—but a lot brighter."

"Is this your idea of a joke, Joanie? I've got a lot going on in my life these days. I don't have time to joke around with you."

"I never tell you jokes, Richard," Joanie snapped. "It would be a complete waste of time. You never had much of a sense of humor."

Silence. Good old familiar icy silence—the stock in trade of any of Joanie's hideous, bitter, painful telephone conversations with her ex-husband. Not to mention her brother. She must bring that out in men. Other women got men hot and wild and insatiable. Joanie got them mute and frosty with rage. It was evidently one of her greatest talents when it came to the opposite sex.

Although, Joanie thought to herself, she had to admit her crack about Richard's lack of humor was a bit of a low blow. She had read somewhere that everyone on earth prided himself on having a great sense of humor. If you had a choice between insulting a man about his penis size or his sense of humor, you should always go for the humor and not the penis. So to speak.

"I do have a sense of humor," Richard said huffily.

"That's right," Joanie said. "I forgot. You like puns."

"Which you never respected," Richard said.

"Never did. Is that why you divorced me?"

"We're talking about Caroline, Joanie. Not our divorce. Be serious—for once."

Joanie fiddled with her own hair, wondering how it would look dyed pink. Taunting Richard when he got pompous and uptight was one of the few ways she managed to feel any kind of power around him these days. In fact, there was something almost comforting about taunting him; it made Joanie realize that her behavior had played a role in their evidently unhappy marriage. That was better, she had to admit, than continuing to see herself as a total victim and loser.

But taunting was immature, she supposed. She needed to rise above it.

"She and Sondra got some wild idea about dyeing their hair. That's all. Sondra's mother was throwing a big fit and her father looked like a heart attack waiting to happen."

"Who's Sondra?"

"Caroline's best friend, Richard." Her only friend, Joanie thought. She knew Richard wouldn't want to hear that. He wanted to think Caroline's life was fun, effervescent, happy—

the kind of distorted vision middle-aged people developed about how great it was to be young. Conveniently forgetting how miserable most of them had been in their youths.

Besides, it was easier to keep up those illusions when you weren't around a teenager that much. Richard tried to be a good father to Caroline, she knew. But he was happier to see what he wanted to see, without filling in any uncomfortable blanks with the ugly truth.

"Have I met her?"

"Hundreds of times. She's got long hair—"

"Kind of fat?"

"She has a bit of a weight problem. She'll probably outgrow it."

"Oh, yeah. I remember her."

"Sondra's a sweet girl," Joanie said. "Very creative." She paused to clear her throat. "She dyed her hair purple."

"That's very comforting, Joanie." Richard sighed loudly. "As long as we're on the line, I need to tell you something."

"Yes?" Boy, Joanie didn't like the sound of that. Whenever Richard said *I need to tell you something*, it always preceded something she didn't want to hear.

"B.J. and I are getting married in two weeks."

Joanie grabbed a pen next to her and began to draw on the back of an envelope. She had once taken a drawing class when she was in college, and she could draw a shotgun pretty well. It was hard, getting the barrel just right.

"Joanie? Are you there?"

Joanie gripped the pen more tightly. She ground the ballpoint into the paper, trying to get the image perfect. Then she drew ammunition blowing out of the end of the barrel.

"Joanie?"

Joanie dropped the pen. She tried to breathe normally, slowly and deeply. Her heart was racing and something was rising up into her chest. "I don't know what to say," she said, finally. Her voice sounded odd, shaky, high.

"You could try congratulations."

"Yes, I could." Joanie gouged the pen into the paper tablet, making vicious inky marks. Too bad Richard wasn't there. She could plunge it into his so-called heart. Creep, fucker, liar, jerk, Neanderthal, asshole, swine, vermin, prick.

"I said, you could try—"

"I heard you, Richard. I'm not deaf." Joanie drew in a cleansing breath, then let it out slowly. She made a hideous face. She bared her teeth. She clenched her fists.

"Congratulations, Richard," she said finally. Her voice, she was pleased to note, sounded almost normal as she slammed down the phone.

chapter 9

Caroline scooted from her mother's car into the high school as easily and anonymously as anyone with psychedelic hot-pink hair could. She'd taken particular care with her outfit this morning, wearing a blue T-shirt Sondra had once assured her was flattering and denim shorts that fit like a wet coat of paint. She'd lingered in front of the full-length mirror in Joanie's bedroom, watching herself from all angles, in a variety of poses.

The color of her clothes seemed to complement her pink hair. They were a harbinger of her new life, with crazy hair, extracurricular weed-smoking, her recently found rebellious change of personality. Of course, rebels, wild women, and free spirits weren't named Caroline. She needed a new name, too. Something with a single syllable that started with an *X* or a *V*. Vann, maybe? Vex?

Walking through the clusters of gathered students, she tried to throw her head back and act like she didn't care. The way fashion models she'd seen on TV walked, sauntered, looking self-assured, devil-may-care. How did they get that kind of look?

"Hey, Pinkie!" a male voice called out from behind her.

Caroline turned around to look and tripped over a planter. She fell in slow motion, her arms flying out in front of her like a tilting windmill, and crashed down on the pavement. A few inches behind, her backpack slammed down on her spine.

She lay there for a few seconds, her eyes closed. Above her, there was nothing but silence. Then, slowly, she could hear laughter and catcalls spreading, getting louder. "Did you see that?" a male voice—maybe the same one—called out. More laughter, giggles, snorting.

What if she stayed there, her eyes closed, pretending to be unconscious or, better yet, dead? Her back hurt, her stomach hurt, she ached all over. She could feel tears filling her eyes and that made her want to die. She couldn't cry at school. If she did, she could never come back again. She would have to kill herself or escape to a foreign country, where she would shave her head and meditate twenty-four hours a day and live by herself in a tiny hut close to the Indian Ocean.

She breathed in fiercely, scraped her palms against her cheeks and wiped away the damp tears. The bell rang and she could hear people moving toward the door, losing interest in the spectacle she had made. "Well, that's a great way to start out the day," she heard a girl say. Then laughter, more laughter, but it was receding into the distance. Doors were banging open and shut, cutting off snatches of conversation and noise and screeches of hilarity. The concrete was cold and hard, but it was growing a little warmer the longer she lay there. Maybe, hopefully, Caroline had a concussion. Even better, maybe she would develop amnesia. Soon, very soon, it would set in. She couldn't wait to forget.

"Are you all right?"

It was another male voice, somehow familiar. Caroline kept her eyes pasted shut and pretended to be unconscious. Maybe he, whoever he was, would leave. Only a very cruel and depraved person would bend over a girl who had just crashed on the concrete floor and ruined her whole shitty life. Either that or some kind of predatory religious nut wanted to save her for Jesus. If the meek inherited the earth, the clumsy and unpopular would probably get the moon or an asteroid. Great.

"Hello? Are you all right?"

Uh-oh. Caroline knew that voice. Jesus fucking Christ. It was *Henry*. That did it. She now officially wanted to die and be reincarnated as a caterpillar or a praying mantis.

Now what? Caroline tried to formulate a plan of action. She could, of course, continue to pretend to be dead. But that required acting skills. Ha. Fat chance. She'd tried to act confident one single morning in her life and look where it had gotten her—flat on the ground, possibly crippled for life, the morning's entertainment for the whole high school. She'd gone from being the biggest nonentity in high school to being the biggest joke.

Still, though. Shut up, she told herself. She needed to do something. Fast. In the meantime, she couldn't help herself—she needed to look at Henry, just to make sure it was him. She fluttered her eyes.

"Oooohhhh," she moaned. Caroline had never moaned before. She thought that sounded just about right, though. "Ooooohhh." She squinted through her stubby eyelashes (which even that extra-volume, vibrating power mascara she'd bought last week for $10.99 couldn't help) and saw a blurred masculine image. Dark hair, tanned face, yellow shirt. Holy shit, *yellow*!? She'd never seen Henry wear yellow before. He must look divine in it.

Lust ratcheted her eyelids open like shades snapping up a window. It *was* him and he looked incredible in yellow. He was bending over her, just the way heroes do on the covers of romance novels.

For just a nanosecond, Caroline almost sighed blissfully. Then she realized how the women on the covers of romance novels always had jutting, enormous breasts that were about to pop out of their dresses. The romance-novel women also had long, floating cascades of blond or dark hair and they were always fainting, which required a strong arm to support them, and they looked ravishing, always ravishing, against the voluptuous backdrop of green grass or a roaring hearth.

In short, they weren't flat-chested, pink-haired klutzes who tripped and collapsed face-first in front of crowds of vicious adolescent thugs straight out of *Lord of the Flies*. Caroline was on the cover of some novel, all right, but it wasn't a novel she wanted to be in.

Henry frowned. "I know you," he said. "Don't I?" He looked puzzled.

"Excuse me," someone else said to Henry. "You need to get to class. The bell rang five minutes ago."

Henry stood up. Caroline looked up at him briefly—tall, tan, gorgeous, heartbreaking. He still looked a little confused. The great love of her life, the man she thought about all day, every day, every night, the guy she lusted over, pined for, and day-dreamed about constantly, moved toward the classroom door. He didn't even know who she was. How could that be? Wasn't that impossible—with all the mental, psychic, and sexual energy Caroline was emitting into the universe? Oh, hell, yes, it was possible. The universe sucked.

"Let's get you up." It was the woman who'd told Henry to go. She was crouching next to Caroline and she helped pull her to her feet. She frowned at Henry's retreating back. "There's always someone," she said, to no one in particular, "who wants to get out of class. Typical."

"Urghh," Caroline said. Standing up suddenly, she wavered.

"Sit down here," the woman said, pointing to the planter Caroline had tripped over.

Caroline sat. She felt dizzy and exhausted and dirty. Both her knees were skinned and bloody and so was her left elbow. Her T-shirt had been ripped a little and she had black marks on her shorts. She looked like somebody had beaten her up.

"Are you all right?" the woman asked.

Caroline shrugged. "I'm okay."

"Hello," the woman said. She stuck out her hand for Caroline to shake. "I'm Karen Abrams." She pulled a Kleenex out of her purse and set the purse next to Caroline's feet. She swabbed the scrapes and scratches on Caroline's knees and elbow, dabbing at the blood. Caroline watched her, feeling limp and passive.

"I'm Caroline Pilcher," she said.

"You're a student here," the woman said. She had steady blue eyes that looked up, settling on Caroline's face.

"Well, yeah, at the moment. But I'm probably going to be dropping out."

"Why? Because you fell?"

"I was already unhappy," Caroline said. "I hate high school. I don't have any friends, except one." This came out in a rush. Of course she was unhappy, miserable, desperate. But you didn't go around saying that to people, especially strangers, especially strangers who were grown-ups. That proved she probably had a concussion.

The woman sat down on the planter next to her. She shifted her legs out in front of her. She was wearing expensive-looking sandals.

"Who are you?" Caroline asked.

"I work in the guidance office," the woman said.

"Doing what?"

"I'm an intern. Working on a master's in social work."

"So," Caroline said, "you help people. Students."

"Yeah. Sometimes."

They sat for a few seconds, staring in front of them. It was getting hot already, but a small breeze stirred.

"You probably think I need help," Caroline said.

Karen Abrams smiled. "I go around looking for people who are sprawled out on the pavement. It beats waiting in my office."

"Now," Caroline said, "you're going to tell me that everybody in high school is unhappy."

"No, I usually wait a few minutes to say that."

Caroline nodded. "Then you'll say that you were unhappy in high school, too. And, if I just wait a few years, everything will turn out okay."

"Who'd you hear that from?" Karen asked. "It's pretty good."

"My mother. She tells me that all the time."

"I guess you don't listen to her. Since she's your mother."

"No," Caroline said. "Why should I? Her life is pretty fucked-up, too." She'd never used the word "fuck" around an adult before. But it seemed permissible, under the circumstances.

"Most people's are," Karen said. It was a very odd thing for a social worker to say. She stood up and extended her hand to Caroline again. "C'mon. We need to get you to the school nurse. She'll want to dump antiseptics all over your cuts."

"How's the report coming?" Zoe asked Joanie.

As usual, she had sneaked up on Joanie and was peering at her computer screen, reading it. Fortunately, Joanie had just switched her screen away from the mental health page website on divorce, depression, despair, and rejuvenation.

The website was currently running a contest called "How Bad Is Your Ex?" Frankly, Joanie felt that the woman who'd written in about a husband who wanted her to have sex with their German shepherd should win. *He even wanted me to wear a dog coller and rabies tag while Rommel and I did it!* the woman had written. Joanie was pretty sure that if Richard had wanted her to have sex with a dog, she might have misspelled "collar," too. Fortunately, they hadn't had a dog. Richard was allergic to all animals.

"Fine." Joanie sat back in her chair and gave Zoe what she hoped was a reassuring, I'm-in-control grin. "I've got all the stats on numbers of employees, sales figures, advertising budget. I've analyzed their print ads, direct mail, follow-ups after purchases, TV and radio commercials.

"Right now, I'm working on suggestions for a new ad campaign and branding."

"Terrific!" Zoe said. "I've been thinking about this campaign night and day." She flopped into the chair next to Joanie's desk and began to talk more loudly, her hands flying. "We have the opportunity to take Frontier Motors into the twenty-first century—and attract a whole new client base for them!"

She flashed a big, hysterical grin at Joanie. "This account could make our agency!"

Zoe jumped up out of the chair. "We've got a big, creative meeting Thursday. We'll use some of the methods from my MBA training—techniques that encourage innovative thinking.

"Two o'clock!" she said, patting Joanie's shoulder.

"I've got it on my calendar," Joanie said, watching Zoe sail out of her office. Then she turned back to her computer screen.

Joanie, someone hissed. It was Tanya, the office brown-noser, leaning into Joanie's office. She came in and shut the door. Tanya was a desk squatter. She sat on the edge of Joanie's desk and leaned over to whisper.

"Have you noticed," Tanya said, "that Zoe's acting a little strange?"

"She's always been a little high-strung," Joanie said cautiously. Could she trust Tanya? She had no idea. Tanya might be bearing a grudge since Joanie had never taken her up on her offer to help Joanie learn to message more effectively.

On the other hand, hadn't Bruce told her that Tanya was gunning for Zoe's job?

"I think she's drinking again," Tanya said.

"*Again?* What do you mean?"

Tanya shrugged. "Zoe was in rehab for three months before she came here. Everybody knows that. Did you smell anything on her breath?"

Joanie frowned, searching her memory. "Not really."

"Well, maybe I'm wrong," Tanya said in a voice that indicated she knew she was right. She stood up and smoothed her skirt. "Don't tell anybody I said that."

"My God," Sondra said. "What happened to you?"

"Nothing," Caroline said sulkily. "Just my vile, vomity, sucky life. It keeps on happening."

She settled onto the grass, next to Sondra. They usually sat outside at lunch, eating their sandwiches, then feeding the leftovers to the swarming ants and black grackles that honked from the trees. The grackles, fed junk food by generations of high school students, had dull-colored, sparse feathers and hearty appetites. It wasn't pretty outside, communing with stinging insects and malnourished birds, but anything was better than sitting in the school cafeteria.

"Your knees are all bandaged," Sondra pointed out, sounding puzzled.

She was probably the only person in the high school who hadn't heard about Caroline's nosedive on the school patio. Sometimes it was good, Caroline reflected, to have a friend no one else spoke to.

"I fell," Caroline said vaguely. She pulled a smoked turkey sandwich made with whole wheat bread out of the plastic wrapper. As usual, the school cafeteria was trying to get the students to eat healthier. White bread had been banned last year. Oh, please. Like it was really going to make a difference.

"Your hair looks great," Sondra said. She flipped her head around and her purple hair cascaded down her back. "Very sophisticated."

"What happened after I left your house?"

"Oh, you know. Lots of drama. My mom kept asking me about the gang we're in."

"You should tell her you can't say anything or you'll get killed," Caroline suggested. "Execution-style."

"Jeez, I can't, Caroline. That's not funny. You don't know my parents. They take everything super seriously. They're already talking about transferring me to a parochial school. They don't want me turning out like Sean—working as a parking-lot attendant."

"Also, tell them about the gang initiation ritual where we had to drink a vial of bat vomit mixed with dog blood."

"Caroline! Stop!"

Caroline almost smiled. She was feeling a tiny bit better. Sondra was so easy to rile. It made Caroline remember her own new and wild persona. Maybe it couldn't be derailed by humiliating herself in front of the whole school and learning that the love of her life didn't know who she was. Maybe, instead, that would just feed into her legend as a crazy, out-of-control pink-haired girl who Did Not Care.

"Did your parents smell the weed?"

"Oh, God, no. I'd already be in a convent or something if

they had. I told them we'd been burning incense." Sondra pulled out a few ragged pieces of lettuce and tossed them to the grackles. "You're lucky," she added. "Your mom is a lot cooler than my parents. At least she didn't totally freak out."

"My mom?" Caroline said. She frowned, thinking. In the midst of all the screaming and hysteria at Sondra's house, Joanie *had* been surprisingly laid back. Also, she seemed to like Caroline's hair, kind of. "I guess," she said cautiously. "But at least your parents aren't divorced."

"They're Catholics," Sondra said. "My mom told me that they have to stay together even if they hate each other."

"Did she tell you that after your dad punched out that customer and got fired?"

"No, it was after he gave her herpes." Sondra sighed and tossed the rest of her sandwich to the grackle cotillion. "I'm never going to get married."

"Me, neither," Caroline said.

"I've got the other joint in the car," Sondra said.

"Let's save it," Caroline said. "For now, anyway. When are you going to San Antonio again?"

Ivy was now a regular at the restaurant. She always sat at the same, two-person table in the corner, close to a window. Lupe knew to bring her iced tea the minute she sat down and she always smiled at Ivy and asked if she wanted "the usual." Ivy always did. She loved being a regular, someone who was recognized right away when she came in.

"I think my granddaughter is in a gang," she told Lupe today.

"Oh, no!" Lupe looked horrified.

Ivy nodded. "I'm afraid so. She and another gang member dyed their hair very strange colors. Purple and pink."

"Really?" Lupe frowned. "I've never heard of that."

"I understand it, though," Ivy said. "It's because her mother didn't bring her up in a church. Also—you know—she's the product of a broken home." She shook her head from side to side. "I can't say I'm surprised."

She'd spent the morning reading about youth gangs on the Internet. It had been very eye-opening. More girls were getting involved in gangs. They got initiated by being beaten up or being forced to do certain sexual acts Ivy had never heard of before and certainly didn't want to mention to Lupe. She was planning to inspect Caroline the minute she got home from school to see if she'd been beaten up recently. The dyed hair was probably just the first step. She wondered whether Caroline and Sondra were already carrying knives to protect themselves. Or guns?

"I'm so tired today," Lupe said, when she returned with Ivy's sandwich. She had dark circles under her eyes.

"Is something wrong?" Ivy asked.

"My husband, Jesus. He got rounded up at work. He has, he's got—immigration problems."

Ivy put down her sandwich and frowned. "I thought you were a citizen."

Lupe shook her head. "I am. The kids are. But Jesus—he's from Mexico."

"He's illegal?"

As a matter of principle, Ivy didn't approve of illegal aliens. They were breaking the law and taking away jobs from good, hardworking American citizens. But this was different. She'd seen a photo of Jesus. He was married to her friend, Lupe. They had children together.

"He's lived here for fourteen years," Lupe said. "He works hard. We pay taxes. We're good citizens, good Americans. So how can he be illegal?"

"I don't—really know what the law is," Ivy said. "Where is he now?"

"Detained," Lupe said. "In a concrete cell." Her eyes filled with tears.

Ivy reached out and touched her hand, squeezing it. Lupe squeezed back, hard. "I'm sorry," Ivy said. "I don't know what to say. My son-in-law, my daughter's ex-husband, is a lawyer. Maybe he can help."

"I don't know," Lupe said. "I don't think we can afford a lawyer. I'm scared." She leaned down and picked up a napkin from the table and wiped her eyes. Someone from another table called her—"Oh, waitress! Can you get our order? We're in a hurry"—and she walked slowly away.

Ivy looked down at her sandwich—the same sandwich she tore into day after day, leaving a plate completely clear, except for tiny crumbs. Today, the sandwich looked as appealing as ever, carefully browned, with feathery leaves of lettuce poking out of the sides and bright tomato slices. But her normally healthy appetite had vanished.

"Tanya says Zoe's drinking again," Joanie told Bruce at lunch.

Bruce looked up from his half-eaten lasagna. "If I had to manage Tanya, I'd be drinking, too."

"Did Zoe really just get out of rehab?"

"Joanie, half the agency's just out of rehab. Including Tanya."

"Seriously?"

"Yeah, if you listen to gossip around the office. Which I don't advise." Bruce dipped his bread in the olive oil. "These kids have been watching *Entertainment Tonight* for too many years. They think rehab's a good thing. A sign of creativity. Sensitivity."

"I can never tell when you're kidding," Joanie pointed out. Which was entirely different from her interactions with Richard, she suddenly realized. Richard had never, *ever* been kidding.

After a few lunches and coffee breaks together, Joanie knew much of Bruce's professional background. He was in his late fifties and had spent his whole post-college life in advertising. In the 1970s, he created a series of brilliant ads for a start-up airline in San Antonio. The ads, still regarded as classics in the industry, had helped the airline become one of the top carriers in the country.

"Sold my stock in it of course," Bruce had told Joanie, grinning wryly. "Could have been a multimillionaire if I'd kept it." He'd shaken his head. "That's a pattern in my life. Bad decisions."

Bruce had been married twice and had two grown daughters he was close to. Both his marriages had collapsed because of his obsessive work habits when he was younger. But maybe, he'd told Joanie ruefully, they would have collapsed anyway. His pattern of bad decisions, you know.

"I liked the ad agency business a lot better when it didn't

take itself so seriously," Bruce said now. "Back when creative people were ashamed to be in the business. It was a lot more fun then—when we all knew we were hacks."

He grinned at Joanie, half-serious, half not. She was getting used to that.

Bruce was a sweet guy, Joanie had decided. It was nice to have a friend close to her own age at work. She'd often read about the idea of having men as friends—and nothing more—but she'd never really believed in it till she started working with Bruce. There was something easy and comforting about their friendship. They talked, they laughed, they gossiped, they gave each other unsolicited advice. It was nice.

Every time Bruce mentioned his lifelong pattern of bad decisions, though, it made Joanie uneasy. He was so cheerful about it, so resigned. Joanie couldn't understand it. She was turning fifty and she'd already made enough bad decisions for a lifetime. She didn't have time left for more mistakes in her life.

"Your turn to pick up the check," Joanie said to Bruce.

Beethoven. Plus, a very odd photo of Richard with a big grin and a cowboy hat (a *cowboy hat*?) now appeared on Caroline's phone whenever he called. He'd put the new photo on it the last time she'd spent the weekend with him and B.J. Caroline had wanted to suggest he put on Beethoven's picture, instead. She was saving that particular remark for the next time he really irritated her.

"Yeah?" Caroline said.

"Caroline? It's your dad."

"I know."

A short pause. Then, "Hey! I hear you have pink hair!"

"Yeah." Oh, great. Terrific. Joanie must have ratted her out. Caroline had looked forward to the shock on her father's face. Now it was ruined.

"Hey, work with me, honey. Can I get a little more enthusiasm out of you?"

"Dad, I've got homework."

"I know. But I need to talk to you about something important."

"What?" Caroline pulled a piece of her hair in front of her face and examined it for split ends. She wasn't in the mood to talk to her father. That was the trouble with cell phones. People thought you should be available night and day. Also—and this was the part that really sucked—almost nobody called her but Sondra and her father, anyway. If she didn't start getting a few calls, she was going to have to write her number in the boys' restroom stalls.

"Well, I wanted you to be the first to know. B.J. and I are getting married."

"Really?"

Richard started talking faster, the way he always did when he was trying to convince himself of something. How he and B.J. were "so happy" he couldn't believe it. And so thrilled about the baby (like he'd forgotten everything he'd told Caroline about it). They were going to have a small wedding and they wanted her to be in it. Of course they did. They couldn't get married without her there! Both he and B.J. were adamant about it.

Caroline put her hand to her forehead. She couldn't stand

this. He didn't love B.J. If he did, he wouldn't treat her the way he did—almost like he treated Caroline, except a little worse. He didn't want the baby, hadn't planned on it. (Probably he hadn't wanted Caroline, either, now that she thought about it.)

"We'll just have to find you a dress that goes with your new pink hair," Richard said.

"When's the wedding?" she asked.

"Two weeks from Saturday. The twenty-fourth," he said. "Mark your calendar, Caroline."

"How's it going?" Joanie asked.

Nadine squirmed a little bit. Her face pinkened, then blossomed into a sweet smile. "It's going just fine."

Oh, lord. Joanie knew what that happy, blushing face meant. Nadine and Roy were sleeping together and they were having great sex and Nadine was happier than she'd been in years. Which was all fine, great, perfect.

But Joanie had finally reached a point in her life that she distrusted that sweet flush of joy. It didn't last. She knew that. Everyone over the age of thirty knew it. It would end, eventually. But how it ended was of utmost importance.

Did it gradually ebb into something comforting and familiar and warm, even though it had lost its white-hot intensity?

Or did it just snap off abruptly, plummeting someone like Nadine into a free fall, into more despair than any human being could stand?

Joanie knew which alternative was far likelier. The funny thing was, she knew Nadine knew that, too. But she couldn't stop herself. What kind of masochistic nut could say no to this kind of blinding joy? Weren't they always supposed to *go for it* no matter what age they were, whether they knew better or not?

Look at her friend Mary Margaret, obsessed with a man who only showed up to criticize her, then fuck her, then criticize her again, before he went back to his wife, whom he would never leave. Joanie had given up trying to talk any sense into Mary Margaret. Joanie just listened to her. She'd been listening for years. Hell, she'd go into a nursing home or the graveyard still listening, nodding her head, never saying what she really thought.

"I don't feel like I can go back to our group," Nadine said.

"Why not?" Joanie said. The minute she said that, she realized how idiotic it was. Of course Nadine couldn't go back. "We'll miss you," she said. "It won't be the same without you."

"Yeah." Nadine bent over and sipped some of her beer. They were at their usual bar, where the lights were low and the music was quiet and adults got drunk politely and quietly, eventually oozing onto the floor.

Technically, Joanie was cheating on the divorcée group by being here. Was she going to tell them she'd seen Nadine? Was it any of their business? She didn't know. She'd think about it later, when she wasn't drinking. The truth was, she'd gotten a little tired of the group herself. For a while, she'd found camaraderie and compassion there. These days, though, it almost seemed formulaic. Was it her imagination—or did they keep having the same conversations over and over?

In the meantime, leaning over drinks and relaxing, Joanie thought how much she still liked Nadine, valued her friendship. There was something honest and unpretentious about her that Joanie loved and respected. If Nadine was making a tremendous mistake, there was nothing Joanie could do about it, was there?

"You ever think about dating?" Nadine asked abruptly.

It wasn't the first time Joanie had heard that question. The whole world asked her that. Told her to get back on the horse that bucked her and start living again. She was tired of it. People had no idea what she needed. They just thought they did. They thought they should repeat themselves over and over till she discovered the error of her ways and desperately propositioned every man within a fifty-mile radius. No way. She was finished with sex, was deeply distrustful of romance. It lasted too briefly and hurt too much. She couldn't afford it in her life.

Joanie smiled. "I think about dating," she said. "And then I think *no*."

"Why not? You're pretty. You must meet guys at work. It wouldn't be hard for you."

Joanie shook her head. It was hard to explain something she didn't quite understand herself. It was just something she *knew*. "I just feel like I need to spend time by myself. I've never had that before. I need to think about my life, bring up my kid, do my job, try not to let my mother drive me crazy.

"With a man—I don't know. I think I wouldn't be able to do the rest. I think I'd just forget again and start drifting. Letting things happen to me. You know what I mean?"

"Kind of," Nadine said. "You're smarter than I am. You think more about stuff like that."

"I'm not smarter," Joanie said. "That's bullshit, Nadine.

College doesn't make you any smarter. It just gives you bigger words—"

"Makes you think more," Nadine said.

"You think as much as I do. You need to get over the idea that you're not as smart as people who went to college."

It was hard, sitting there with Nadine, trying to explain her life. For the most part, Joanie felt that getting involved with someone would be for the wrong reasons. If she had a new romance, she wouldn't be able to face her life, somehow. She needed to look at herself, understand her life better than she did. Love didn't help you do that. Love helped you *not* to do that. She didn't need that kind of distraction now. Maybe she'd never need it.

Sex and love and romance and idealism had been part of Joanie's youth. Since then, she'd begun to grow up, slowly and painfully. She'd put away childish things. She didn't want to go back.

"I guess," Joanie said, "I've spent too much of my life drifting along, not thinking. I need to change that. A man wouldn't help.

"By the way," she added, "Richard and B.J. are getting married."

"Oh, Jesus God." Nadine narrowed her eyes. "When?"

"Don't know. Next month, maybe. He couldn't tell me. I kind of hung up on him."

"Prick," Nadine said.

"And I'm about to turn fifty," Joanie said, turning the number over in her mouth. Fifty. Half a century, five decades, the gateway to old age. Oh, yeah, she wasn't supposed to look at it that way. She was supposed to think of herself as a fox, a cougar, on the prowl. Fifty was the new thirty. What utter bullshit. She'd already been thirty and that was twenty years ago.

"Fifty. That's not so bad. What are you going to do?"

"I don't know. I haven't been thinking about it."

"We could have a party," Nadine suggested.

"Yeah. Maybe. I don't know."

"Seems like you should do something. Especially with Richard and B.J. getting married."

Oh, right. Fly off to Paris. Visit the Pyramids. Go on an African safari. Except she didn't have the money to do any of that. Maybe she should just get blotto, morosely drunk, at her house and pass out. Joanie didn't know. But she had a week to figure it out. She'd think of something.

"Is Roy different now?" she asked Nadine.

There was something about that question that was wrong, that spoiled the mood.

"Roy's the same," Nadine said. For a second, her smile faltered.

So, there it was. Joanie didn't need to say anything, deliver any sermons, offer her ancient, tarnished trove of wisdom. Nadine, who was far smarter than she knew or gave herself credit for, knew what she was doing, knew how it would turn out. She was just buying a little time, that was all. Right now, that was enough for her.

chapter 10

"Great hair," Henry said. He grinned at Caroline—a dazzling, sexy, overwhelming sight.

She could feel her cheeks grow hot. If she hadn't been sitting down, she would have probably fainted.

"Thanks." She tried to breathe calmly. How did other girls do it? They managed to talk to good-looking guys and walk without tripping and actually say semi-intelligent words. Where did they come from? How did they get to be the way they were? Sometimes she watched them, trying not to stare—just trying to understand how all their little gestures and expressions and postures came together to make them desirable and confident.

"Hey," he said. He looked at her directly, for once, with the same puzzled expression she'd seen yesterday. "You're the girl who fell on the patio yesterday. Right?"

"Right," Caroline said miserably. She tried to think of something, anything that would make her loserdom a little more bearable. "I guess I was a little wasted."

Henry nodded. "You gotta watch that. On a school night."

"Yeah. But that's hard to do."

For just a second, Caroline felt dazzled by her own wit and bravado. She and Henry were having an actual conversation, even if it was based on a big lie. But being a teenage alcoholic sounded a lot better than the alternatives. Like being a freaking giraffe who tripped over her own feet.

"Did you do the homework today?" Henry asked. He grinned again, his mouth parting into a showstopping display of white.

A tiny part of her realized he knew how good-looking he was, what a perfect smile he had, his effect on her. But, so what? She didn't care. Sure, she was smart, the way Joanie always insisted she was. But that had absolutely no effect on her stupid heart, which was about to burst out of her chest, or on that weak feeling she got deep in the pit of her stomach every time she saw Henry or even glimpsed him in the hallway. She knew things, but it didn't matter. Who cared?

So Caroline knew, as she whispered a couple of the answers to Henry, that he wouldn't be paying attention to her at all if she weren't useful to him. She knew, but she didn't care. Henry looked happy as he filled in a few blanks and he touched her wrist when he thanked her and she stared at that part of her arm even after he removed his hand. She could still feel the warm glow and knew she would think about it late at night when she lay in bed and stretched her head back and dreamed about things that made her whole body light and arching and rapturous, as if she could almost fly.

"Hello?"

"Richard? This is Ivy."

"Oh." He cleared his throat. "Ivy! Well, this is a pleasant surprise. Good to hear from you."

Ivy had always liked Richard. She didn't know why Roxanne hadn't stayed married to him. People gave up on marriage too easily these days. They didn't understand how important stability was. Who said you had to be in love with the other person? Roxanne could have learned a lot from the Hispanic culture. Ivy wondered whether Roxanne had any Hispanic friends. She liked to think she was a big liberal. But it was Ivy who was really open to new experiences, different people.

"How are you?" Richard asked.

"Oh, I'm fine. And you?"

He said he was doing well, just fine. "You've probably heard I'm getting married again."

No, she hadn't. Roxanne never told her anything. Neither did Caroline. "Well, congratulations, then," Ivy said.

Richard started talking about his wedding plans with someone whose name sounded like a couple of initials. He'd always been talkative, unlike Ivy's husband, who went for a week without saying more than a few words. That was one of the many things Ivy had liked about Richard. At least you knew he was awake. Sometimes, with John, Ivy hadn't been certain.

"It all sounds lovely," she said. She supposed she and Rox-anne wouldn't be invited. Too bad. She would have been in-terested to see this young woman with the initials, the one who was taking her daughter's place.

He agreed.

"I guess you're wondering why I called," Ivy said. "I need to ask you for advice—for a friend."

She explained about Lupe, how hard she worked, what a good person she was, how devoted she was to her family. How she and Ivy had become friends.

"But her husband, Jesus, has problems," Ivy said. "He's been detained by immigration."

"Is he illegal?" Richard said. It was the same question Ivy had asked Lupe. But somehow, coming from him, it sounded more abrupt and impatient.

"Yes." For the first time, she was struck by what odd terms these were—*legal* and *illegal*. How could a human being be illegal? It didn't seem right to her. Did the government know what it was doing? She supposed so. There were so many things you never questioned. She'd just always assumed they were handled well. Why wouldn't they be? If you couldn't trust your own government, whom could you trust?

"You know, Ivy, this isn't my area of specialty," Richard said. "I work with estates and trusts. That's all."

"Does anyone at your firm—" Ivy began.

"We don't handle any immigration cases," Richard said.

For a few seconds, they were both silent. Richard cleared his throat again.

"I'm sorry, Ivy," he said. "There's nothing I can do. This just isn't—what I do."

Ivy thought about Lupe and the photos of her and her family. It was funny how you could dismiss people so easily—especially people associated with someone who was illegal—when you didn't know them.

"It was good to hear from you, though," Richard said. "I'm glad you're doing well."

Ivy wished him well in his new marriage. She meant it. People should try to be happy. Maybe Roxanne hadn't made him happy and the girl with the initials would.

She hung up, then stared at the phone. She wondered what on earth she could do for Lupe and her family. Weren't friends supposed to be able to help each other?

"I talked to Richard today," Ivy told Joanie.

Joanie, who was sautéing salmon on the stove, stopped. "You did? Why? Did he call here?"

"No," Ivy said. "I called him. At work. I had something I needed to discuss with him."

The salmon crackled in the pan. Joanie turned it over, with a loud, greasy slap, frowning and furious.

"You didn't tell me," Ivy said pointedly, "that he was getting married again." She paused and adjusted her new scarf. It was a bright floral pattern. She'd just acquired it that morning.

"Well, I hardly knew it myself," Joanie said. She turned off the burner and stared at her mother. "He just told me about it yesterday."

"He said he's quite happy," Ivy said.

"Then I imagine he is." Joanie stabbed the salmon with a fork. It was undercooked. She turned the burner back on.

"I suppose he always wanted more children," Ivy continued. "Maybe he wanted a son."

"Why are you telling me this, Mother?" Joanie asked. She looked up at her mother, who stood primly next to her, lips pursed, eyes calm.

Ivy ignored the question. "I've always thought," she said, "that your generation wanted too much."

"What do you mean?"

"You expected some kind of love we never did."

"I don't know what you're talking about, Mother," Joanie said, fuming. A small flame appeared at the edge of the pan. She was going to burn the house down. Good.

"You expected to be happy, to be loved," Ivy said. "You wanted something out of life that wasn't there. As if it were owed to you."

"And that's wrong? To expect so much out of life?" Joanie jerked the pan away from the fire. She stared at her mother, whose face had turned more severe, harder. This was a face she'd seen before, disapproving and angry. The face of a generation that had brought her and all her friends up to want so much—then became furious with them for their expectations.

"I believe you're misunderstanding my point," Ivy said. "You never learned to be grateful for what you had. You always wanted more. You should see some of the people I know—Hispanics. They'd be happy just to be citizens of this country."

Joanie pulled out a platter and shoved the salmon on it. The fish was coming apart where she'd poked the fork in it.

"What do Hispanics have to do with it?"

"I'm just using them as an example."

"So—we expected too much," Joanie said, her voice rising

with each new syllable. "Permanent love, happiness, every-thing. Yes, I guess we did. But you know what? We didn't get it. We didn't even come close. Does that make you happy, Mother?"

By the end, she was almost screaming. But at least she'd kept her wits about her. Even though her mother had pro-voked her, she hadn't thrown any plates this time.

The salmon was charred and ratty-looking. Caroline tried to pick out a few edible pieces without looking too obvious.

She could tell Joanie and Ivy had been fighting again. Frost lingered in the air, right above the charred salmon. Ivy's face was puckered like she'd just chomped on a lemon and Joanie's mouth was twisted to the right—the way it always got when she was upset about something.

Caroline sighed and poked at the salmon some more. When Ivy first moved in with them six months ago, Joanie had claimed she wouldn't be staying long. "She'll probably be mov-ing into a retirement home soon," her mother had said. "She's just staying with us for a few weeks."

Nobody had asked Caroline about it, whether she cared. Of course not. People never asked kids for their opinions. Or, if they did, it was just a sham. They'd ask your opinion and go right ahead and do whatever it was they were planning to do originally. It just made them feel better to ask, so they could pretend they were living in a democracy.

As far as she knew, Caroline was the only kid in high school who was stuck with a grandparent in her home, sharing her bathroom, forgetting to replace the toilet paper, leaving the whole room so smelly Caroline almost got asphyxiated. And her snoring! Night after night, Ivy sounded like an airplane coming in for a landing, with all the engines honking and roaring and thundering. No wonder Caroline felt so tired all the time. She was sharing her house with a 747.

That was bad enough. But her mother and Ivy's relationship! It was like living in a war zone on nights like this. Caroline should be getting combat pay.

"I've been reading about immigration law on the Internet," Ivy announced. "Do you know that if you're in the country illegally, the authorities can put you in jail and deport you?"

No one answered. Joanie was staring bleakly at her salmon, which she'd cut up into little black pieces. But Ivy didn't notice. At times like this, she was like a TV set somebody had just pushed the remote control on—she'd talk for hours if she felt like it. Caroline and Joanie could probably leave the table and she'd go on talking forever. She was lonely, Joanie had told Caroline. That's why she talked so much sometimes. They needed to try to listen to her.

"That doesn't seem right to me," Ivy said. "Hispanics are very good people. They work hard. They're religious. They're devoted to their families. You'd think we would welcome them into our country."

"I thought you wanted to build a wall at the border, Grandma," Caroline reminded her. She was still smarting from her grandmother's accusation that she and Sondra were in a gang. "A wall to keep them out."

"Well, I've changed my mind," Ivy said. "I have a good friend who's Hispanic. She and her family are having immigration problems. I'm trying to help. I've consulted a lawyer for them."

"Is that why you called Richard?" Joanie asked suspiciously.

"I thought you said intermingling the races was bad, Grandma," Caroline said.

"I have lots of new ideas now," Ivy said.

"What did Richard say when you asked him to help, Mother?"

"People think that just because you're old, you can't have any new ideas," Ivy said. "That's not true. I go out every day and get exposed to new people and their experiences. I Goggle on the Internet."

"That's *Google*, Mother. Do I have to spell it out for you again?"

"I read about lots of things—like immigration and teenage gangs." Ivy frowned at Caroline, suddenly aware of the bandages on her granddaughter's arms. "Why do you have those Band-Aids on your arms, Caroline?" She slid her head around and looked under the table. "And on your knees, too?"

"I fell at school," Caroline said. "I'm all right. I don't want to talk about it." She'd already gotten the third degree from Joanie, who had received a call from the school nurse. Joanie was sure that the shoes Caroline had been wearing, with their three-inch heels, had put her "at risk," as she called it. You couldn't have any privacy at all when you were living with a couple of busybodies like her mother and grandmother. How could she develop her new, exciting persona when she was living in this House of Constant Surveillance?

"Caroline and I have already discussed her injuries,

Mother," Joanie said. "You don't have to concern yourself. So, what did Richard tell you about immigration?"

"They look like gang initiation injuries to me," Ivy said triumphantly. "What's the name of your gang, Caroline? Did they torture you for very long?" She was so excited, she belched loudly.

"Oh, God," Caroline said.

"She's not in a gang, Mother," Joanie said. "Richard didn't tell you anything, right? He wouldn't."

"I hope you still have your virginity, Caroline," Ivy said. "It's a young girl's most precious asset. Don't let your gang members tell you otherwise."

Caroline stood up. The Band-Aids on her arms and legs stood out—stark white—because her skin was so flushed. "I am so sick of living in an insane asylum!" she announced. "Sick of it!" She picked up her plate and stalked into the kitchen. "Of course I still have my virginity, Grandma! I couldn't get anybody to take it from me if I begged!" She loudly stomped down the hall.

Joanie looked down at her salmon. It was still burned, dammit.

"Mother," she said after Caroline had loudly banged her door shut and locked it. "You need to stop picking fights with Caroline. She has enough problems." She paused to catch her breath. "And she's not in a gang, for God's sake. She just fell at school. It might have happened to anyone."

"It could have happened to any gang member," Ivy insisted. "That girl is covered with wounds—and God knows what else all over her body. Her hair was the first sign something was wrong. Do you know what they do to girls when they initiate them into gangs? They—"

"Please stop it, Mother," Joanie said wearily. "Caroline's a little confused. She's a teenager. She fell at school. But she's not in a gang."

Ivy rose from her chair, straining for dignity. She ostentatiously wiped her eyes with a napkin. "I can see my advice is not welcome," she said.

Joanie considered that. "You're right, Mother. It's not. I think there's only room for one mother at a time here. It's a small house."

"I'd think you'd want to take advantage of my long years of experience as a mother. But I guess you don't." Ivy let her napkin drift down onto the plate.

"I guess I don't." *Only one practicing mother per household,* Joanie thought. Beyond that, it was chaotic and hopeless. Her mother was right: Joanie didn't want to take advantage of what Ivy knew. This wasn't a democracy and it wasn't a competition. It was her house and her mother was a guest. Joanie just wanted Ivy's support, ached sometimes for her mother to tell her she was doing a good job. Or even a not-bad job. But she could never say that.

"And the salmon was badly burned," Ivy added as she left the room. "That's why I didn't finish it. No wonder your daughter is so painfully thin."

After Ivy left the room, Joanie stuffed a stringy piece of salmon into her mouth. Sure enough, it tasted as burned and bitter as it looked.

chapter 11

Four days later, after Caroline's constant prodding, Sondra finally convinced her parents to let her spend the night on Friday.

"I had to promise them we wouldn't dye our hair any different colors," Sondra reported. "I have to call them the minute we get to your house."

Caroline examined her own hair. It wasn't quite as blindingly bright as it had been the first day. Or maybe she was just getting used to it. "Did you bring the weed?" she asked. She loved saying that word, *weed*, casually and carelessly.

Sondra leaned over the steering wheel and patted the car pocket. "Right here."

"Cool." It was clear to Caroline that spending time at her house was better than hanging around Sondra's house with its presiding nutso parents. At least Caroline only had one parent to worry about. Joanie was so preoccupied with work these days and Ivy had spent three days straight crying ever since she heard about some old neighbor dying a few months ago. Nobody would notice what they were up to. "I've got the brownie mix already," she said.

Sondra guided her car under a tree in front of Caroline's house. It lurched to the curb, then died loudly, like one of those aging animals on a nature show.

It was the season when live oaks molted yellow leaves and pollen saturated the air. People went around sniffling and sneezing and griping about the mess. Sondra's car would be covered with dead leaves by the next morning. But, given how lousy her car already looked, that might improve its appearance.

Caroline eased the plastic package of marijuana into her backpack. Sondra's cousin had mailed it to her a couple of days ago, with a burnt orange University of Texas T-shirt wrapped around it. It had been marked DELICATE! HANDLE WITH CARE! "Blake's got such a great sense of humor," Sondra had said. "He's even funnier when he's stoned. Just hilarious. You've got to meet him."

"Grandma! You there?" Caroline screamed out as they entered the house. If they were lucky, Ivy would be hanging out at that diner she was always yakking about. They could start baking the brownies right away.

"Is that you, Caroline?"

Caroline's heart sank. There was Ivy, standing at the end of the hall. Light flooded around her, and she looked smaller and more rounded than usual. Caroline felt fairly certain that Ivy had shrunk two or three inches since she'd moved in with them. Pretty soon, she was going to be a midget. It was bad enough to have a grandmother around—but a midget grandmother? The indignities never stopped.

"Hi, Grandma." Caroline tried to smile. Ivy's gray hair was plastered down with hairspray. It smelled like old, dead flowers, heavy with moldy perfume. Ivy smiled back, delighted.

"Hello, Cassandra," Ivy said, holding her hand out to Sondra.

"Sondra. Not Cassandra," Caroline hissed.

Her grandmother ignored her, beaming up at Sondra. "At least you're not too thin, like Caroline. Eating disorders are very common among teenage girls these days. I've read a lot about it."

Sondra blushed the color of a ripe watermelon. She was a good thirty or forty pounds overweight, which she never, ever talked about. Other girls spoke constantly about needing to go on a diet, but Sondra never did. Even when Caroline was feeling cross and mean—at least forty times a day—she would never mention Sondra's weight.

"You look like a very strong girl, Cassandra," Ivy continued approvingly. "I think you look good, no matter what anyone else says. Don't get brainwashed by the fashion magazines. They're up to no good."

"I won't," Sondra said faintly. She looked dazed, uncomfortable.

"What are you two girls doing this afternoon?" Ivy asked.

Caroline and Sondra exchanged glances.

"Nothing," Caroline said quickly. "Just studying."

Ivy nodded. "I'm going for a walk," she said, pointing to her white athletic shoes. "Will you two be all right?"

"Fine. Don't worry about us, Grandma."

By the time they were in Caroline's room, the front door slammed. "She's usually gone for an hour," Caroline whispered to Sondra. "She's on some kind of weird exercise kick. How long do the brownies take?"

"Forty-five minutes," Sondra whispered back.

"We've got time," Caroline said, "if we hurry."

According to the Internet, physical exercise was the most important thing an elderly person could do to maintain her health. That's why Ivy had bought a pair of white walking shoes two days ago.

People think they need to run or jog to get a good cardiovascular workout, the AARP magazine said. *Well, this just isn't true! Scientists have found that a regular walking regimen is just as beneficial as running—plus, it results in far fewer injuries.*

This week, Ivy had gone walking at the same time every day, in the late afternoon, when she could stay in the shade. It helped to have something to do in the long afternoons after she got back from the diner. She always felt kind of lost and sad when Caroline came back from school and Roxanne from work. They usually asked her, very politely, what she had done during the day. But she could tell they didn't find her Internet reading or her visits with Lupe to be terribly interesting. It helped to have somewhere to go, so she might be getting back just as Roxanne and Caroline did. That way, it looked like they all had busy, productive lives. Ivy didn't want them to think she sat around the house every day, even if she did.

She couldn't stop thinking about her old neighbor, Myra Hawkes, who had died suddenly of an aneurysm four months ago. Ivy wondered whether Myra simply hadn't taken good care of herself, hadn't exercised every day. She recalled that Myra had been several years younger than she was. So she would have been in her late sixties—a very young age, even if Caroline and Roxanne wouldn't have thought so.

Ivy paused and sat down at a bench under a tree in the small park that was nestled at the end of a street several blocks from Roxanne's house. It was hot today, with puffy white clouds floating overhead and a faint breeze that was moist and listless. Ivy pulled out a carefully creased handkerchief and patted her face.

After receiving her returned letter to Myra, it had taken her two weeks to find out what had happened to her friend. She had tried to call another old neighbor, Francie Davis, whose line had been disconnected. Ivy had never liked Francie that much; Francie had a shrill, unpleasant voice and was far too nosy about other people's lives. Once she had asked Ivy why David never came home to see her and John. She had watched Ivy's face closely, looking for the precise sadness and unease Ivy was trying to conceal. Francie's eyes were a nasty yellow green that gleamed like a cat's.

But that was exactly why she'd tried to call Francie. If any disaster had befallen Myra, Francie would know about it, would relish telling the gory details. Why had Francie's phone been disconnected? Ivy hadn't been looking forward to hearing Francie's shrill voice, but she felt oddly disappointed not to make contact. Even an old neighbor she hadn't liked was still part of her past. She didn't want Francie to disappear without some kind of notice, as Myra had. It showed that life was far too uncertain and dangerous. Ivy already knew that, but she didn't want to be reminded of it.

Finally, she called the Second Baptist Church, where Myra and her husband had worshipped for years. The woman who answered paused a long time when Ivy asked what had happened to Myra, then Ivy could hear a muffled conversation going on at the other end of the line.

"Mrs. Hawkes—we think she died of an aneurysm," the woman said. Her voice was soft but firm, the kind of voice that could gently call you to Jesus, then remind you that you were going to hell if you weren't a Southern Baptist who'd been fully dunked in a baptismal pool. Ivy, a lifelong Methodist, had always found Baptists to be a bit gung ho. Methodists sprinkled instead of dunking when it came to baptisms, which she found far more dignified.

"Oh, dear," Ivy said. "So, it was sudden?"

"She dropped dead in her front yard," the woman said. "Just like that. I remember it now. It was in the newspaper. She lay there for hours before anybody found her. *Hours.*"

Ivy blinked at the phone, thinking of Myra's front yard. She'd always had flower beds full of impatiens this time of year. Maybe she'd died taking care of them. That would be a happy way to go. Wouldn't it?

"People don't watch out for each other anymore," Ivy said. "They're not caring, the way they used to be."

"People have forgotten God," the woman said. She cleared her throat loudly. "Were you a friend of Mrs. Hawkes?"

"We were neighbors for many years. I was trying to get back in touch with her."

"Would you like to make a donation to the church on her behalf? It would be a lovely way to honor her memory."

"No. Thank you. I don't think so." Ivy frowned, trying to think. "Wasn't Francie Davis also a member of your church?"

"Francie? Francie Davis? Oh, yes. Yes, she was. She moved to Houston to live with her daughter. She had been ailing for quite a long time." The woman sighed. "She has Parkinson's. She couldn't live by herself any longer."

Ivy wondered about Myra's and Francie's husbands. Probably they had died, too. Or were infirm. But she couldn't bring herself to ask. She had heard enough for one day.

"You could make a donation in both their names," the woman suggested. "One would be *in memory of* and the other would be *in honor of*."

She paused, waiting for Ivy to speak. Then she went on. "Or you could donate a beautiful display of flowers for this Sunday's service. We could list you and your friends in the program. What kind of flowers did they like?"

Ivy thought about Myra and her impatiens, saw her sprawled out in her front lawn for hours. She thought about Francie and about how elderly people simply disappeared, from one town to another, leaving no memories or forwarding addresses behind—as Ivy herself had done. They simply vanished, unmourned.

"They didn't like flowers," Ivy said abruptly. "Either of them."

"*What?*" the church receptionist asked, her voice catching with surprise. "But everybody likes flowers."

"Not Myra and Francie. They absolutely hated flowers. Myra started sneezing every time she got around them. One time, she wound up in a hospital because of some carnations. Asthma attack, I think. It was almost fatal."

"We wouldn't have to have carnations. We could have roses or—"

"Francie once got stuck by a rose thorn," Ivy said. "Her whole hand got swollen and infected. Gangrene. It was terrible. Gory. They had to cut off her hand, eventually. She wore a prosthesis for the rest of her life."

"A prosthesis?"

"It was very lifelike. It had red nails. She used to get a manicure on her other hand to match. The nail salon gave her half price."

"That's—that's very odd," the woman said. She sounded aghast and deeply shaken. "I never heard that. Those are awful stories. Awful. I never knew anybody who hated flowers—"

"Well, I guess you didn't know them very well," Ivy said.

She hung up the phone, feeling strange. What was she doing? She wasn't a liar. She'd never even told polite white lies like other people. The truth, plain and harsh and unlovely, was always better for everybody. She knew that.

But here she was, making up a whole string of crazy, outlandish lies, going on and on. It was terrible of her. Sinful. She should feel deeply ashamed of herself. She should call the Second Baptist Church back and apologize and give them money. "We Try Harder!" the Second Baptist Church often proclaimed on its gaudy little marquee. Ivy should help them try harder, after upsetting their snooty little receptionist and spreading a pack of lies.

But she didn't feel at all bad. Instead, she felt good, almost triumphant. Everybody had forgotten about her and Myra and Francie. No one cared about them. Myra had lain in her front yard for hours and no one had noticed. Francie and Ivy had both disappeared, leaving no trace of themselves behind in the small, windswept city, where they had lived the core decades of their adult lives.

Now, they would remember. Myra and Francie would be known as the women who hated flowers. Carnations had almost killed Myra. Roses had amputated Francie's hand. If the truth came out eventually, Ivy would be remembered as a serial liar and lunatic who had lived among them for years, quietly spinning falsehoods and spreading tiny seeds of malice wherever she went. Well, good. Let them think that. Let them be a little fearful of the barely visible, hardworking women who lived among them—tending houses and yards and children and silent husbands who watched TV and died—growing older, fading away. Let them beware.

Now, sitting on the park bench in the hot afternoon, Ivy still felt defiant and flushed with silly pride about her late-blooming career as a fabulist. She wished she had someone to tell the story to—a friend who would laugh and shriek, "Oh, my Lord, I can't believe you did that, Ivy! Did you really say *that*?" Ivy had never had a friend like that, even when she was young. She had always been too serious, and her few friends—serious, too—had usually pulled their lips into halfhearted smiles when they talked about their children and husbands, but never themselves. Life was hard. You didn't laugh about it.

Roxanne—"Joanie"—wouldn't understand the story. She would probably insist on taking Ivy to a medical professional so she could be institutionalized immediately—the same way she would if she ever figured out how Ivy had collected so many attractive scarves. And Caroline? No. Ivy could read the look on Caroline's face as clearly as any highway billboard— the exaggerated patience, the irritation, the boredom. Nothing Ivy said could possibly interest or amuse Caroline. Lupe? No, she had too many troubles of her own. Ivy hadn't seen her smile in days, her ordinarily cheerful face was drawn and tight. David? Ivy felt her ribs tighten with pain. She hadn't emailed David in days, maybe even weeks. She wondered if he'd noticed. Maybe he had simply been relieved.

The sun had moved, casting the tree's shadows away from Ivy. Sunlight settled on her, clutching at her exposed arms and face. It felt indifferent and pitiless, burning the grass, the leaves, the solitary elderly woman on the bench.

Ivy rose, heavily, to her feet and returned home. She'd traveled far enough today.

The house smelled heavenly as Ivy walked in. Something sweet and warm and fragrant was baking in the oven. It had been so long since she'd stepped into a home and smelled something so good and welcoming. Roxanne, the ambitious, overheated career woman, never baked anything.

"What are you girls making?" she asked, pleased. Maybe Caroline and her friend—what was her name, anyway? Cassandra?—had been disillusioned by their gang and had turned to wholesome, domestic pursuits. If Caroline were interested, Ivy could teach her to cook. Ivy had failed—miserably—to teach her own daughter, who had always felt she was too creative and intellectual to cook. But a grand-daughter might be more willing and open-minded. Along with her friend of course.

"Brownies," the girl with the purple hair said. She smiled nervously at Ivy.

"We got tired of studying, Grandma," Caroline said. "We were hungry."

"Well, I think it's very industrious of the two of you to bake something," Ivy said, with an approving smile. "Too many young people don't even know how to cook for themselves these days."

"No, ma'am," Caroline's friend agreed. *Ma'am!* That was good. That showed she had been brought up well. Ivy was sick of a younger generation that wanted everybody to be on a first-name basis, so they could be equal. Well, they weren't equal. Ivy was old, almost eighty. She deserved respect, not equality.

Ivy sat down at the kitchen table, across from the two girls. "Did you use my recipe?" she asked.

"Oh—no. Just a mix," Caroline said vaguely, glancing at Sondra.

"That's fine," Ivy said agreeably. "I often used mixes, too. But you know what I did? I always added something special to the mix—to make it my own. Did you add anything special to the mix today?"

"No," Caroline and her friend answered very quickly, almost in unison.

"Next time," Ivy said, "use half a cup of whipping cream." She placed her elbows on the table and propped up her chin. "That was always my secret ingredient. People loved my brownies. They couldn't get over how rich they were."

Behind the girls, the oven timer went off. Both girls jumped. Caroline pushed her chair back, grabbed a pot holder, and opened the oven an inch or two, moving like a tall, startled stork.

"Are they done?" Ivy asked. "Sometimes they take more time than the package says."

Caroline turned on the oven light and peered in. "I can't tell," she said. Her voice was hoarse and jittery.

"I'll help." Ivy picked up another pot holder and bent over the open oven door. She pulled out the rectangular glass container and placed it on top of the stove. The brownies were a lovely, golden brown. Ivy stuck her forefinger into the surface and watched the indentation slowly fill in. "They're done. They look wonderful." She smiled at the girls. "They're especially good when they're like this—still hot and soft. We can put some vanilla ice cream on them, if you'd like."

"But, Grandma," Caroline said. "We can't—"

"Don't worry," Ivy said. "I won't let your mother know you've spoiled your dinner. She doesn't have to know everything that goes on here. Your grandmother can keep a secret if you girls can."

"Yes, ma'am." The purple-haired girl's voice was faint. She and Caroline sat down at the table while Ivy bustled around.

"I didn't know how hungry I was," Ivy said, "till I smelled those brownies. In fact, I was in a sad mood before I came home.

This is making me feel much better." She cut the brownies, then ran a spatula under them. They oozed onto plates, where she added a fat ball of ice cream on top of each one. The ice cream began to melt, covering the brownies with a creamy glaze.

"Grandma, those are awfully big helpings," Caroline said. Her spoon hovered over the plate.

"Stop worrying about eating too much, Caroline," Ivy said. She nodded in Sondra's direction. "Look at Cassandra and me. We both have healthy appetites." She plunged her spoon into the thick, gooey chocolate, dipping it into the melting ice cream, and put it into her mouth. "It's wonderful," she said, taking another hearty spoonful, with a big, happy grin on her face.

Finally, at long last, Zoe's insane frenzy about the car-dealership account had infected all of them. It was like a virulent disease, like the Andromeda strain.

All around Joanie, everybody at the agency was pumped up with take-out lattes and other high-energy drinks that were probably poisonous. They had spent the entire day pitching ideas back and forth, screeching with laughter at unfunny jokes, raking their fingers through their hair, taking off their glasses to clean them repeatedly. It had been a madhouse, an insane asylum. About six thirty that evening, Joanie had officially stopped caring.

They talked about movies she'd never heard of. Musical groups that were "cool, dude, cool." Video games—at least she'd thought they were video games. Maybe they weren't.

Maybe they were another medium she'd never heard of. No matter. Joanie would never have asked, didn't want to call attention to her own status as the ancient coworker, the over-the-hill divorcée, the colleague who wore panty hose because she couldn't bear the sight of her puffy knees and the faint purple of her varicose veins. As the day had worn on, she'd noticed only she and Bruce had grown quieter. Everyone else had become hysterical and raucous.

They didn't intend to be unkind. It wasn't like that. Joanie knew they liked her, kind of, appreciated her work and breadth of knowledge. They just forgot about her, spinning around in their own quicksilver orbits of youth and energy and a common culture she'd never been a part of. Didn't want to be a part of, even if she could have been. Didn't care for.

"Man, can you believe it?" one of the youngest designers said to the others. "I'm turning twenty-nine next week!"

Catcalls, laughter ensued.

"You're old, dude! It's all downhill from here." That was from one of the secretaries, Rachel, who was just out of college. Joanie saw her emails sometimes. Unlike many of the others, who eschewed capitalizations, Rachel often capitalized random words. Joanie couldn't figure out the logic of her approach. Maybe her native language was German.

A short silence. Someone must have nodded a head toward Joanie, quietly warning the others. Joanie stared at her hands under the merciless fluorescent lights, tried to sit very still, but look comfortable, like she was enjoying herself the way everybody else was, even though she hadn't said anything in hours and always laughed a couple of beats after the others. She knew she had that pained half-grin on her face. It had stayed there, like a thick coat of makeup, almost the entire day. She'd never felt so old and useless in her life.

Sometimes, she was okay, she was fine with this group. She didn't pretend to be their age. Didn't, really, want to be as young as they were. They would never have believed that, but it was true. She had been their age. She knew how uncomfortable they were, how unfocused and searching. What did they want to do for their adult lives? Whom would they marry? Did they want children? What could they do to avoid making the horrible mistakes their own parents had made, pursuing boring, money-grubbing work, married to people they had long grown tired of?

I understand you, she wanted to tell them. I understand your bravado and your fears that you won't amount to much. I understand why you laugh so hard when it isn't even funny. I understand you so well. But you don't have a clue about me—or about your parents, either. You won't for years, until it's too late. You have no idea what it's like to be our age until you get there.

Zoe flipped her hair back and fanned her face with a writing tablet. She smiled suddenly, brilliantly at Joanie, noticing her for the first time in hours.

"Don't you have a birthday coming up, too, Joanie?" she asked cheerfully. Her voice was deafening, like a foghorn.

Joanie felt her face redden in a way she'd thought she'd outgrown. So much for her desperate assumptions about the grace and poise of middle age. She might as well be thirteen, with pimple medicine on her cheeks and a deadweight on her tongue.

"Oh . . . yeah," she said, shrugging. She pulled a soft-drink can up to her mouth, trying to look unconcerned. The liquid was warm and flat and she almost spilled it all over herself.

"You're how old? Forty-nine?" Zoe persisted.

"Wow," one of the young men muttered under his breath. Somebody must have elbowed him in the side, because he jerked a little.

"You look so young!" Rachel trilled helpfully. "My mom isn't nearly as old as you are and she—"

"No, you're going to be *fifty*!" Zoe said, undeterred by any discomfort in the room. "I remember your birth date from your resume."

"My mom doesn't look nearly as good as you," Rachel continued, uncertainly.

Joanie placed the can, now empty, on the table. Fifty! She could feel it, this chill spilling out over the room, spotlighting her wrinkled face, her feeble attempts at being with-it, one of the gang, a valued member of the company.

"We'll have to give you both a party!" Zoe said. "A big party! After all of this"—she spread her arms out over the mess on the table—"is over. After we've won the account!"

Joanie smiled as gamely as she could. When she finally looked up, nobody met her gaze. Except for Bruce. His tired face was cocked to the side. For just a second, he shook his head and smiled at her with a sympathy that was deep and decades old.

"Ohmygod," Caroline shrieked. "Is she dead?"

Sondra moved to Ivy's side, laying her head on Ivy's back.

Ivy had just sprawled down, face-first, onto the table. Her head, landing on the table with a loud thump, had narrowly missed her second heaping bowl of brownies and ice cream.

"She's still breathing, I think," Sondra reported.

Caroline grabbed Ivy's right hand, turning it over. Frantically, she tried to remember from her long-ago Girl Scout training where to find a person's pulse. There it was. She could feel it, thank God, a steady, rhythmic beating. Girl Scout training had never prepared her for a grandmother who had overdosed on marijuana brownies.

"Turn her head over so she can breathe," Sondra directed Caroline. She sounded very authoritative, bossy. But that was good. Caroline was a mess, hyperventilating and choking. A semi-stoned mess who may have killed her grandmother or put her into a coma. Would she and Sondra get the death penalty?

They hoisted Ivy's head up, then gently laid her on her right ear. "Should we get a pillow?" Caroline asked.

Sondra nodded. Caroline raced to the living room and came back with a small cushion. They lifted Ivy's head again and put the cushion under her.

Ivy's eyes fluttered open. "I feel so happy. I just had the most wonderful dream! It was about . . . it was about—" She lifted her head and frowned. "What *was* it about?"

"Be careful, Grandma," Caroline said. "You kind of passed out." She reached over and held Ivy's hand. "Are you feeling all right?"

Ivy straightened her posture to its usual erectness. "I'm perfectly all right. I feel excellent."

Her head swooped alarmingly in one direction as she stared up at the light above the kitchen table. "What a perfectly gorgeous light. I really never noticed it before. Look at the way it—it—*glistens*. Have you ever seen anything quite so beautiful?"

"Would—would you like some water, Mrs. Horton?" Sondra asked.

"Why, yes, dear. I'd love some water." Ivy's voice, normally precise and crisp, had taken on a languid, loopy quality. So had her neck, which was usually rigid and upright.

Ivy ran her nose along the surface of the wooden table, then spread her fingers across its surface. "Look at this workmanship. The surface is so very smoooooth." She ran her hands back and forth over the wood, smiling like a happy toddler.

Caroline's eyes bulged out. She grabbed Sondra's arm as her friend deposited a tall glass of ice water in front of Ivy and pulled her back into the kitchen. "What are we going to do?" she hissed.

Sondra lifted her eyebrows and shrugged. "She seems sort of okay. I mean, I wouldn't take her out in public or any-thing—"

"That's not funny, Sondra," Caroline snapped, aware that she was ordinarily the more outrageous of the two of them. "It's not your grandmother who's dying from a marijuana overdose."

"She's not dying. Look at her. She's really, really happy."

Sondra nodded in Ivy's direction. Ivy had moved on from exclaiming about the smoothness of the wooden table to mi-nutely examining the tiles on the dining room ceiling, her neck slithering around like a snake's. She was humming a spirited tune Caroline couldn't recognize, with whispered lyrics and accompanying hand motions.

Caroline listened more closely. The tune was familiar,

somehow. It came from that ancient record album Ivy had insisted on bringing to their house. One day, she'd played it on their stereo, carefully placing the needle on the record. The album, Caroline now recalled, was from an old musical Ivy liked. *South Pacific*.

She watched Ivy's pink fingers scratching her firmly sprayed hair, and she finally understood the lyrics her grandmother was singing. She was gonna wash that man right outta her hair and send him on his way.

The TV was on, loud and blaring. Joanie crept into the darkened living room, past the two girls sleeping on the couches, and turned it off. She sighed loudly. Was she the only person in the household who worried about bills, about saving energy, salvaging the environment? Evidently so.

Thinking about it now—while she turned off the lights— Joanie was glad no one else was awake. She couldn't have borne talking to anyone else that night. She was sick to death of pretending that everything was all right, that she was having a good time, when she wasn't.

She left the two girls stretched out in the living room, and went into the kitchen, which smelled faintly of something warm and sweet. It was completely clean, almost sterile. Ivy must have done it. Caroline always left a mess. Joanie poured herself a nice, full glass of wine, then drank the first couple of inches so she could walk without spilling it.

Carefully balancing her wine, she headed down the darkened hallway, past Ivy's closed door. She could hear her mother's snores, regular and loud as factory machinery. Inside her own room, Joanie threw herself on the bed and spilled most of her wine on the bedspread.

Wonderful. It was the perfect ending to her whole misbegotten day. By now, she was too tired to care.

Thank God it was a weekend. Joanie pulled the covers over her head and sank into sleep.

chapter 12

Caroline's phone rang. She picked it up from the coffee table and checked it in the blinding morning light. No photo, just a regular ring. Who was it? Probably a wrong number. That was all she ever got. Other people got obscene phone calls, at least.

"Hello?"

"Hello, Caroline?"

She recognized the small, tentative voice. It was B.J.

"Oh, hi."

"It's B.J."

"I know."

"Well . . . how are you?"

"Okay."

"Uh—I guess this is kind of strange," B.J. said. "But I need to go shopping for my wedding dress."

Caroline sat up and rubbed her eyes, looking around. She couldn't even remember falling asleep, but there she was, on the couch. She felt a lot better than she should, after the brownies and Ivy's overdose. She hoped her grandmother was still alive. She and Sondra had half-led, half-carried Ivy to her bedroom. Then they had come back to the living room, too scared and stoned to talk. They must have passed out after that. Sondra was still asleep on the other couch, her arm cradling her purple hair.

"And I was wondering," B.J. went on, so softly that Caroline could barely hear her, "if you'd like to go shopping with me."

She sounded so hesitant, like she was asking Caroline for a big favor. *Hey, Caroline! Can you lend me, like, a million dollars?*

"We could shop," B.J. said. "Then we could go out for lunch. If you'd like."

Caroline groaned silently. She couldn't imagine anything worse than going shopping for a wedding dress with her father's pregnant girlfriend. On a Saturday, too! She had lots of better things to do.

Like—let's see, what? Well, *nothing*. She and Sondra had already used all the weed in the brownies. And Sondra's parents were expecting her home before noon. So it would just be Caroline, as usual, hanging around the house with her mother and her drug-addled grandmother, trying to avoid her mother's questions about what they'd done the night before. It sounded awful. Like every other weekend in her life.

"Sure," Caroline said tentatively. "It sounds like fun."

"Really? That's great! Then, then maybe—you could come

over here to spend the night. Your father's out of town. On business. I'm just here . . . by myself." All of B.J.'s sentences ended up sounding like questions. She sounded sad and lonely to Caroline. It was almost like listening to her own voice.

"Oh. Yeah. I guess so."

Caroline hung up the phone, wondering what she'd promised. Joanie was going to have a fit. Caroline knew that. This was "her" weekend with Caroline. Her daughter's making plans with Richard's girlfriend—worse, his pregnant, bridal-dress-hunting fiancée—would infuriate her. Maybe Caroline should call B.J. back and cancel the plans. But no. She couldn't do that. B.J. had sounded so desperately happy when Caroline said she could come. Caroline didn't want to disappoint her. How did she get into binds like this? She was the victim of excessively bad karma.

Caroline eased herself onto her feet, then stuck her head into the kitchen. It was empty. That was odd. Joanie was one of these morning people who were always up and cheerful at the crack of dawn. It made Caroline want to scream. She didn't like talking to other people—especially her mother—till at least noon. But Joanie's not being up, humming loudly, forcing some kind of inedible "nutritious" breakfast on Caroline—well, that was even stranger.

Her mother's bedroom door was closed. It was almost eleven, too. Caroline knocked quietly. A noise inside. She opened the door. The room was dark.

"Mom?"

Joanie sat up in bed. She pushed her hair back from her face. "God," she moaned. "What time is it?"

"Almost eleven."

Joanie plummeted backward, like someone in an iced tea commercial, hitting the pillow. "I'm still exhausted." She turned over, pulling the covers back over her face. "I'm going to sleep some more, Caroline. I'll see you later."

"Well—that's what I want to talk about, Mom."

"What?" Joanie asked sulkily. She lowered the covers a few inches so she could look at Caroline.

"I—I'm going shopping today. With B.J."

"That's fine." Joanie still sounded groggy.

"And then—well, I told her I'd spend the night. At her—at *their*—place."

Silence. Joanie was snoring softly.

"Is that all right, Mom?" Caroline used a louder voice this time.

Joanie opened her eyes. "It's fine," she said crossly. "I may sleep all day." She pulled the pillow over her head.

"Well . . . okay."

Caroline stood uncertainly by the door. She'd been dreading a big, guilt-inducing blowup with her mother about spending precious weekend time with her father's girlfriend when it was time Joanie and Caroline should be spending together. It was going to be terrible, with her mother reduced to teary stoicism, a tinge of bitterness in her voice, emitting whispered, offhand remarks about Richard and B.J. Yes, it was going to be painful, awful, unbearable.

But now—*this*. Her mother was hardly even reacting to Caroline's news. In fact, she seemed bored by it, preoccupied with getting back to sleep. *Leaving Caroline alone to make her own decisions.*

It was exactly what Caroline wanted from her mother—to

be left alone, to be treated like an adult. But, this was so sudden. She'd been geared for an argument, a screaming match. And then, nothing happened. It was like bending over, heading into a stiff wind, pushing ahead, then all of a sudden, the wind dies down and you lose your balance. You almost fall on your face.

Yes, it was exactly what she wanted. But now she felt curiously off center and uncertain. She hated to admit it, but she was a little disappointed. Didn't Joanie care about her?

It was only a little fire. Ivy couldn't figure out why Joanie made such a big fuss about it. During her years as a housewife and cook, Ivy had started several small fires on the stove top. All you had to do was smother it with a pan or something. But she hadn't been able to find a pan quickly enough, and there was Joanie, getting all hysterical about how she was burning down the house and screaming bloody murder till she found a fire extinguisher and shot out a bunch of white foamy stuff that put out the fire but made a big mess everywhere.

"Mother, are you sure you should still be cooking?" Joanie asked.

"What a question," Ivy said. "Of course I'm sure. I was just heating up a little soup. Maybe there's something wrong with your stove."

"You're the only person who starts fires with it," Joanie said. She sat down at the kitchen table and pushed her hair back. "What time is it?"

"Noon. That's why I was so hungry."

"God," Joanie groaned. "How did I sleep that late?" She

thought about her long, hideous day yesterday. Oh, that's right. She'd wanted to go to bed forever and never get up. Well, at least she'd gotten a start on it. She'd never slept till noon before in her life. Maybe it was a new habit that came along with her upcoming fiftieth birthday. Old age was bearing down on her, a vulture that would pick at her weary carcass.

"Where's the girl? And Cassandra?" Ivy asked.

"Who? Oh—Caroline went shopping with somebody. And Sondra, well, I guess she slept in our living room last night. Is she gone, too?"

"The girls made brownies last night," Ivy said. "We put vanilla ice cream on them. They were delicious."

"I've never known Caroline to cook," Joanie said doubtfully.

"Well, she and her friend are quite accomplished at brownies." Ivy moved around the kitchen slowly, trying to clean up all the white foam. "You would have been proud of them."

Joanie ran her fingers through her hair, realizing she was way overdue for a haircut. She was probably starting to resemble one of the more unattractive breeds of dogs that herd sheep. Another item for her weekend to-do list. Another expense. Maybe she should go to a punk hairdresser and get a completely new identity. Maybe she should just let Caroline and Sondra color her hair. Anything. But, no. What she needed was a new, young brain and a body to match.

Ivy sat down at the table, across from her. "We don't have to eat here, do we? Maybe I could take you out to the place where I go to lunch."

"Sure," Joanie said. "Let's go now." That was why she went around looking like a homeless person, a middle-aged fashion degenerate most of the time. She'd always rather eat than get her hair cut.

"How does this look?" B.J. asked.

She was standing in front of a three-way mirror at Nordstrom, trying on an ice blue silk dress. With her long, blond hair and wispy body, B.J. looked like Alice in Wonderland. The dress was slim and smooth, and Caroline could see just the slightest hint of B.J.'s pregnancy below her rib cage.

"It's pretty," Caroline said.

B.J. turned to the left, looking at the new angle in the mirror. "Do you think it looks tasteful?" she asked.

"Yeah. I guess." Caroline sat back on the waiting room couch and tried not to look bored. It was hard. B.J. had already tried on six or seven other dresses. They all looked alike—pale and a little shimmery. Kind of traditional-looking. She didn't know why B.J. needed her help.

"Really?" B.J. craned her neck to look at Caroline in the mirror. "Are you sure?"

"Really." B.J. needed to be reassured about twenty times an hour. Maybe that's why she wanted Caroline around. A parrot would have been about as useful.

"It looks lovely on you." It was Monica, the saleswoman they hadn't seen in about an hour. She was red-haired and about six feet tall, careening on heels that looked like stilts. Caroline could never wear heels like that. She was already clumsy enough.

"Do you really think so?" B.J. asked.

"It's dreamy," Monica said definitively. "Just divine." She cocked her head to the side. "Perfect for any number of occasions. Where are you planning to wear it?"

"Well," B.J. said, "to my own wedding." She smiled shyly and her face grew pink.

"How *perfect*," Monica said, clasping her manicured hands together. "Congratulations. You'll make a beautiful bride. Just lovely." She moved back a step or two and stared at B.J.'s reflection, smiling blindingly. "Do you have a planner for your wedding—or is your mother doing it herself?"

B.J. looked down, examining the dress's hem. "No. It's just me."

"A small wedding," Monica said approvingly. "I particularly adore small weddings."

"Me, too," B.J. said.

"This dress," Monica said, "will be perfect for a fall wedding. Is that what you're planning?"

B.J. shook her head. "No. We're getting married sooner than that."

"Oh." Monica frowned. "When?"

"In two weeks."

"Two weeks!" Monica clapped her hands together so loudly that Caroline jumped. She hated people who went around clapping their hands. Monica acted like she had a nervous disorder or something.

"Two weeks! And you're just shopping for a dress now?"

B.J. nodded. She looked almost panicked, like she had done something terribly wrong.

Monica's red-tipped fingers flew up in the air. "That is so ro*man*tic!" she exclaimed. "Almost like you're eloping!"

B.J. smiled timidly. "Do you think so?"

"Absolutely!" Monica said. She leaned over and adjusted the straps on B.J.'s dress. "Have you known him long?"

"Well—three months."

"Three months!" That seemed to please Monica even more—like B.J. had been on some kind of reality TV show and had waltzed off with the bachelor while all the other brazen little hussies plotted and fumed and vomited in the bathroom so they wouldn't get fat. Losers! "Was it love at first sight?"

"Kind of." B.J. glanced at Caroline. Monica was now messing with B.J.'s hair, pulling it back from her face, where it always hung.

"You should wear your hair up—like this." Monica pulled it up and twisted it around. "See how great it looks this way?"

"Yeah." B.J. nodded, then turned her head to admire her hair. It looked pretty shitty, in Caroline's opinion.

"What does he do? Your fiancé, I mean."

"He's a lawyer."

"A lawyer!" Monica said. "You really hit the jackpot, honey!" She leaned over and gave B.J. a little hug.

"I know." B.J. looked at her image in the mirror, with Monica crowding in like a sorority sister. She avoided Caroline's eyes and smiled at Monica's reflection in the mirror. "I'm really, really lucky."

"Is Lupe here today?" Ivy asked the waitress. "She always waits on me."

The waitress was plump and middle-aged, with a gray

coiffure so tight it looked clenched, like a statue's hair. Her glasses magnified her pale eyes. According to her name tag, her name was Barbara.

"Who?" Barbara shifted her weight from one leg to the other and rattled her notebook. She looked cross. She was there to take their orders, not to make idle chitchat.

"Lupe. Lupe Ramirez."

Barbara took out a wadded Kleenex and loudly blew her nose. "Oh, yeah," she said, wiping a nostril. "Her. She's gone back to Mexico."

"Mexico?" Ivy said. "What for? A vacation?" The instant she said it, she knew it wasn't true. She felt sick to her stomach.

Barbara stuffed the used Kleenex back into her pocket. She shook her head. "Nah. She's gone for good. Took the family, everything. Moved back. She's from there."

"No, she's not," Ivy said. "She was born in Dallas. Dallas, *Texas*. Not Mexico."

Barbara ignored her. "You want drinks?" she said.

"Diet Coke," Joanie said. "Please."

"Lupe's Hispanic," Ivy said. "Not Mexican. Some people don't know the difference."

"Anything to drink?" Barbara asked Ivy.

"Just water," Ivy said.

Barbara shuffled off.

"It must be hard to be a waitress at her age," Joanie said. She could already tell her mother had taken an instant dislike to the new waitress. Maybe Joanie's remark would help her be more charitable. Ivy needed to try to look at the world through other people's eyes, for a change. "Staying on your feet the whole day, I mean."

Silence. Joanie looked across the table at Ivy, whose face was stony. Just a few minutes ago, she'd been talking and relatively cheerful. Ivy was becoming very moody the older she got.

"Is something wrong, Mother?" Joanie asked. "You seem out of sorts."

"I don't know what you're talking about," Ivy said.

"Here's your Coke." Barbara set it down in front of Joanie, spilling a little, then placed a glass of water in front of Ivy. "That Lupe you're talking about," she said to Ivy, "she didn't even give notice or nothin'. They were lucky I could go to work so fast.

"Used to be different," Barbara continued, suddenly chatty. "Used to be, you could trust people that worked for you. These days . . ." Her voice trailed off and she made a small, sour face. They would understand, she seemed to say, what she'd left unsaid. Times had changed for the worse. Life was going down the toilet. Brown-skinned infidels were blowing up buildings and swarming over the border.

"She ordered a Diet Coke," Ivy said. Her normally bland face had gotten stern and angry. Joanie had seen that face before—just a few times in her life, like the time she'd run over her mother's flowers when she was learning to drive. But she still remembered it. It was a danger sign.

"What?" Barbara said.

"My daughter ordered a Diet Coke. Not a Coke."

"It's all right, Mother," Joanie said. "It doesn't really matter to me—"

"If you're going to be a waitress, Barbara," Ivy said, "you need to get people's orders right."

"Mother, it's fine. Really. I'll just go ahead and drink this."

Joanie picked up the Coke. Barbara reached for it, too, but Joanie yanked it away. "It's fine," Joanie said. "I don't know why I ordered a Diet Coke. Cokes taste better, anyway, and—"

"Give her the Coke, Joanie," Ivy said. "She needs to make things right." She reached across the table and pulled the glass out of Joanie's hand. "Will you please get the order correct this time?" she asked Barbara.

Joanie watched as Barbara's large frame stalked behind the counter. "What is this about?" she hissed to her mother. "I've never seen you act like this before, Mother."

"I don't like bad service," Ivy said.

"It isn't bad. It's just—"

Barbara slammed the Diet Coke down in front of Joanie. "Here," she said. She grabbed her notebook and pulled a pencil from behind her ear. "You ready to order?" It sounded more like a threat than a request.

"I'll have a cheeseburger, please," Joanie said.

"You need to work on your attitude, Barbara," Ivy said. "You're not supposed to throw drinks on the table."

Barbara's eyes were pale and furious. "You wanta speak with the manager? He's my cousin, Fred." She glared at Ivy. "My *first* cousin."

"Send him over," Ivy said. "I need to have a talk with him."

Barbara slapped her notebook back into her pocket without writing down Joanie's order. "Yes, *ma'am*," she snapped.

"Wasn't she wonderful?" B.J. said, sipping her decaf cappuccino. She and Caroline were back at Richard's condo with drinks they'd picked up on the way home.

"Who?" Caroline had already dumped three packages of sugar into her latte. It wasn't enough. She added a fourth. When was she ever going to get used to the taste of coffee?

"Monica. The saleswoman." B.J. leaned across the coffee table and swept up all the little sugar packages Caroline had left. She grabbed a napkin and tried to clean up all the sugar crystals. "I mean, she was so helpful. And supportive. I really liked her."

"She was okay." Caroline sipped the latte. It was almost drinkable, but she could still taste the espresso too much. "That's what she gets paid to do. She wants to sell you stuff."

B.J. frowned. "I guess." She stirred her drink with a little silver spoon. "I'm not used to going to such nice stores," she said after a long pause. "Like you are."

"I don't go to nice stores," Caroline said. "I don't even like to shop. Anywhere."

"I don't mean that. I mean, you're used to nicer things than I am." B.J.'s voice didn't have its usual sweet, singsong quality. It had a sharper edge to it. Caroline must have pissed her off, but she didn't know what she'd done. That was the story of her whole life. Everybody hated her.

"No, I'm not," Caroline said stubbornly.

B.J. was still staring at her cappuccino like she was going to talk to it. "I'm just saying you're lucky."

"Lucky? Are you kidding? My life sucks."

Caroline watched B.J.'s face, the way it had screwed into a little pout. Definitely pissed off about something. That's all Caroline knew. God Almighty. If B.J. thought Caroline had such a wonderful life, then why was she out shopping with her father's pregnant girlfriend on a Saturday? She should be out giving her boyfriend a blow job. Except she didn't have a boy-friend. And she'd need a training manual to give a blow job. *Lucky?* Did B.J. live in an alternate universe?

"You're so spoiled," B.J. said, "you don't even know how lucky you are." She picked up her cappuccino and spilled a little around her lips, but she didn't notice. Her face was getting red again. She wasn't as pale when she was angry about something. "You don't know what it's like to want something. Things other people have—but they don't appreciate. Like you." She stared at Caroline angrily.

"It's a free country," Caroline said sulkily. "You can do any-thing you want. Nobody's stopping you." She felt like she was reciting something from a civics class about how great the country was. But she believed it. Didn't she?

"Your parents love you. You're smart. You can do anything you want." B.J. set her cup down on the coffee table and it spilled brown drops everywhere. But she didn't even notice that, either. "You don't know what it's like to want something so much you can hardly stand it," she added, her voice rising. "Do you?"

Was B.J. insane? Caroline spent her whole life wanting things she couldn't have. Didn't B.J. notice what went on in other people's lives—how they spent their days and nights yearning to be different, yearning for something better, some-thing exciting, anything but living in the sad reality of their own lives?

"I don't know what you're talking about," Caroline said. "What do you want so badly?"

B.J. stared at Caroline like she was an idiot. How, her face seemed to say, could Caroline not understand?

B.J.'s hands opened slowly, moving along the small mound of pregnancy, then extending out to indicate the furniture, the room, the kitchen beyond, the whole manicured, stainless-steel, stained concrete world that was secure and luxurious and stylish and whole. Her face softened, as she stared at Caroline, almost pleading with her to understand. How could Caroline fail to see or appreciate this perfect world that surrounded the two of them right now? Couldn't she see how important it was, how much it meant?

"You don't know," B.J. said softly, "the kind of place I came from. The kind of family. You have no idea."

Tears slid down her face. She dropped her hands into her lap, then moved them protectively over the small hump of her baby-to-be.

Caroline sighed. She felt bad, she felt confused, she felt irritated, she felt inadequate. Everywhere she went, she was surrounded by people like her mother and father and grandmother and now B.J., who wanted something from her. She was tired of it. Why should she want to grow up when every adult she knew was so crazy and needy and demanding?

Was it Caroline's fault that B.J. had some kind of awful family or something? No. She hoped B.J. didn't start talking about it—about the abused mother, the alcoholic father, the drug-addicted brother, the sister who was the town tramp. Caroline watched *Oprah* sometimes. She knew about all those stories. She didn't want to hear more.

Maybe B.J. was getting hysterical because she was pregnant, though. People got totally crazy when they were pregnant. Caroline had read about them, too. They became lunatics and went around eating dirt and swinging machetes at people who irritated them. B.J. might be temporarily insane right now. Caroline would have to lock her door tonight.

She watched B.J. cry, then gradually grow quiet. She seemed all right, finally.

"I'm sorry," Caroline said, even if she didn't know what she was apologizing for. "I'm tired. Do you want to watch TV or something?"

B.J. nodded. But she stayed in her chair while Caroline walked into the living room.

Good grief. Joanie had never—in her life—gotten thrown out of a restaurant. Not even late at night, when she was drunk. Not even when she was young, for God's sake, and one of her friends had vomited into a potted plant, then fallen asleep underneath the table, hugging the legs of a chair.

But here she was now, at the advanced age of almost fifty, standing on the sidewalk after being firmly escorted out of the Gladiola Café with her ancient mother. Good Lord. She hoped nobody she knew was in the café, after the ruckus Ivy had raised.

"We're going to be filing a lawsuit," Ivy told Fred, the restaurant manager who had suggested they leave. "My son and my daughter's ex-husband are both lawyers."

"That's your privilege, ma'am," Fred said wearily. He was a tall, round man who was very polite. But Ivy's deliberately pushing over a nearby chair had been too much for his sense of decorum. Now, standing in the hot sun, he mopped his forehead with a dish towel. "It's a free country." He closed the door firmly behind them.

"Not so free!" Ivy screamed at the closed door. "You discriminate against Hispanics! And elderly women!"

Joanie wrapped her hands around Ivy's elbow and pulled. "Come on, Mother. You're making a scene."

Ivy yanked her elbow away. "Stop pulling on me, Roxanne." She crossed her arms in front of her chest. She was breathing heavily. "I am not a child." She turned and walked to a nearby bench, where she sat down unsteadily. "I need to rest now."

Joanie sat down beside her. Sunlight had warmed the bench and it felt almost cozy. She could fall asleep sitting here. If she wasn't so hungry. She wondered what had happened to her cheeseburger.

She heard a noise—suspiciously like a sniff—coming from Ivy. Ivy's face was still, but tears coursed down her plump cheeks. Joanie realized, suddenly, that she'd never seen her mother cry before. Not even when her father died.

"Mother? Are you all right?" Joanie reached for Ivy's hand. "What's wrong?"

"Everything," Ivy said. She stared straight ahead. Tears fell on her blouse, on her and Joanie's intertwined hands.

Joanie scooted over the bench, next to her mother. She pulled Ivy's head onto her shoulder and patted her hair. She leaned her head against her mother's and stroked Ivy's hair as she would a child's.

Funny that she'd never done that before in her life. They had never been a warm or "touchy" family. Over the years, they'd watched one another warily. Not especially affectionately, but closely. They were a family, a collection of people who lived under the same roof. They had obligations to one another. Meals were served, bills were paid, manners were minded. That was enough. You didn't expect anything more.

That was all true—the distance, the wariness, the lack of warmth—except for Ivy's slavish devotion to her son. Often, growing up, Joanie watched her mother's face soften as she looked at David. Everything about her seemed to change when she was around her son. Even Ivy's pale cheeks took on a rosy glow when David was there.

How long ago had it been that Joanie had noticed that connection? Forty-five years, thirty years, just last month? She had always been aware of the indelible current that ran from her mother to her brother. Why dwell on it? It was a simple fact, a part of her life. It shouldn't matter—she might have told herself that, consciously or unconsciously, many times. No one could help it or change it or enlarge it to include her. It just *was*.

But wasn't it strange how it still pierced her with a sliver of sharp pain—even after all this time? Life was just hopeless sometimes. Even when you thought you had grown up, had put those childish things away. Progress, adulthood, maturity— what a crock. You didn't improve, you didn't get better. You just got older.

"Lupe was my friend," Ivy said. "She listened to me."

Joanie peered into her mother's face and dabbed it with a napkin she'd carried from the restaurant. All the anger had drained from Ivy's face, leaving it sagging and more tired than Joanie had ever seen it before.

Ivy looked, Joanie realized suddenly, like she was weary of

living, ready for it all to be over. Joanie crumpled the damp napkin in her hand and placed it on the bench. She pulled Ivy's head back on her shoulder so they could sit together for as long as they needed to.

The clock said three twenty-four when Caroline woke up. She felt that familiar sticky feeling between her legs. She pushed her hand inside her panties and pulled out her bloody fingers. Oh, God. Not that. She yanked the covers back and looked at the new white sheets. She'd left a big pool of blood on them.

She should have known—as cranky and irritated as she'd been the whole day—that she had PMS. She could have put in a tampon, just to be safe. But, no. As usual, she'd been stupid and forgetful. She probably didn't even have a tampon with her. Of course she didn't. They were at home, in the bathroom she shared with Ivy.

What could she do? She slipped out of bed and opened the door. The bathroom was several feet away. She was probably going to be dripping all the way, all over the fluffy white carpeting in the hallway. She grasped her crotch to try to catch any blood before it hit the floor.

Inside the bathroom, she used her elbow to turn on the light. She sat down on the toilet and stared at her panties with the bright red stain. Now what?

She hated having periods. When she'd read Anne Frank's diary last year, she'd been amazed that Anne thought having periods was so great. Like having some kind of wonderful secret, Anne had written. Caroline was really sorry Anne had died in a concentration camp, but she still thought Anne was weird about periods. Maybe, she'd thought, it was because Anne was European and Europeans liked blood more than Americans did.

Besides, having a period wasn't exactly a big secret when you went around drenching other people's beds and sheets with blood and you didn't even have a tampon with you. Caroline pulled a big clump of toilet paper off the roller and tried to clean herself up.

By the time she rinsed out her panties, cleaned up the sink and toilet, and sneaked back into the guest room to put on a new pair of underwear, she was exhausted. She hung the wet panties on a rod in the shower and sighed. Now, what on earth was she going to do about the bed?

"Caroline? Are you all right?"

Caroline opened the bathroom door. B.J. blinked and rubbed her eyes in the light. "I thought you might be sick," she said.

"I—my period started. I forgot to bring a tampon."

B.J. stepped inside the bathroom. "I've got plenty here," she said. "Haven't used them in four months." She opened a box and handed one to Caroline. "Here. You need some extras?"

Caroline took the tampon. "I kind of—well, I messed up the bed, too."

B.J. frowned. "The bed? You got blood on it?" She sat down suddenly, on the side of the tub. She looked alarmed. "I can't be around blood. It makes me sick to my stomach. Scared . . ." Her voice trailed off. She covered her face.

"Just tell me where the sheets are," Caroline said.

"Over there." B.J. pointed toward the cabinet, her other hand still covering her eyes. "Get the beige ones. They're on top."

Caroline pulled the beige sheets out of the cabinet and carried them into the bedroom. Well, even if Joanie couldn't cook, she had at least taught Caroline how to strip and make a bed. Caroline pulled the bloody bottom sheet off the bed. Fortunately, the blood hadn't stained the mattress. B.J. would have probably had a breakdown if that had happened.

"Can you start the washing machine?" B.J. called out from the bathroom. "The detergent is already out in the laundry room."

Caroline wadded up the sheets and carried them to the washing machine. Everything was perfectly in order, with a plastic lavender bottle of detergent sitting on top of the machine. How much detergent should she put in? She didn't want to ask B.J. about it, didn't want to bring up the awful word *blood* again. She poured in a fistful of the white soap and started the machine.

Outside the laundry room, in the kitchen, B.J. was brewing tea. She still looked pale.

"Everything's all right," Caroline said. "It's not going to stain. The mattress was okay, too."

B.J. nodded, as she poured steaming water into a cup, still not looking at Caroline. "I just love those sheets. Did you notice how soft they are?"

"They're nice," Caroline said. They had felt like regular sheets to her.

"It's a four hundred thread count," B.J. said. "My favorite kind. Would you like some tea?"

Caroline nodded and B.J. poured a cup for her, with the tea bag floating around on top.

"I'm sorry," B.J. said finally, still looking down at her hands.

"I'm just scared to death of blood. It makes me panicky, I guess."

"It's all right," Caroline said.

"I know it seems silly—"

"No, it doesn't."

They sat quietly, drinking their tea companionably, with the washing machine sloshing in the background.

"Do you want to feel the baby?" B.J. asked. She raised her eyes and searched Caroline's face.

Caroline definitely didn't want to feel the baby. She thought babies and pregnant women were kind of gross. But she couldn't think of any way to say no without hurting B.J.'s feelings—after she'd already messed up B.J.'s sheets and upset her about all the blood. So she stuck out a tentative hand.

"Here it is." B.J. guided Caroline's hand to her abdomen and pressed it down. It was surprisingly firm. Caroline had always thought pregnant women looked fat, but this bump didn't feel like fat. She left her hand there for several polite seconds, then quickly pulled it back.

"Isn't that just incredible?" B.J. asked. "Sometimes, when I'm really still, I think I can feel the baby move. It feels like the wings of a little bird." She smiled at Caroline. "I love being pregnant. I haven't had morning sickness once."

She poured more tea for herself and Caroline, then settled back into her chair and wrapped her pink quilted robe tighter around her middle.

"But weren't you—like—shocked when you found out you were pregnant?" Caroline asked. "It must have been hard."

B.J. brought the teacup to her lips. She smiled kind of indulgently, like Caroline was some kind of really young kid who didn't understand anything. She lifted her eyebrows and smiled a little more, this time to herself. "Not really that shocked."

She set the teacup down and reached across the table to grasp Caroline's hand. "Can you keep a secret?"

"Sure." What else could Caroline say? She could keep a secret, but she wasn't sure she wanted to hear it, though. But B.J. hadn't asked that.

"Well," B.J. looked down at their intertwined hands and squeezed, "the truth is . . . I wasn't really surprised at all."

"You weren't? But I thought—I mean, my dad said—it was an accident." Having her hand clasped so hard by B.J. was starting to feel funny. Caroline didn't quite understand why. But it was like she was being held on to too tightly. Like something was passing from B.J. to her that she didn't really want. But it was too late to say no. Some kind of strange weight had already been transferred to her and she couldn't give it back.

"That's what he thought," B.J. said. She squeezed Caroline's hand again, then let it go. Her hands returned, once again, to cradle the small bump of her abdomen. "I guess I just . . . let it happen."

Caroline tried to breathe normally. She felt sick. She thought of her father's face when he told her about the pregnancy. How it was an accident he regretted. Like B.J., he'd told her something she didn't want to know. They'd both dumped their lives into her lap, then leaned back to watch her. They'd felt better, she guessed, after telling her their secrets, letting her into their adult worlds. Maybe they'd both thought she'd be pleased to know more about them.

The truth was, they hadn't thought about Caroline. Not at

all. They'd just thought about themselves and how good it would make them feel to tell someone else.

"Maybe I shouldn't have told you that," B.J. said. Her voice was a whisper. "You look upset. I didn't mean to upset you."

Caroline sighed. She closed her eyes. She didn't want to look at B.J. any longer. Didn't want to see her eager face or her pregnancy bump. "I'm just tired," she said. "I need to go back to bed."

B.J. nodded understandingly. She gave Caroline a little hug and told her to sleep well.

Back in the guest bedroom, Caroline lay on the fresh sheets and watched the ceiling fan spin above her. She couldn't sleep. She just stared at the fan, hearing voices and seeing faces. She thought of how Joanie had told her the facts of life when she was eleven. Her mother's face had been serious and cautious. She had talked about men and women and penises and vaginas, carefully using the clinical terms. Caroline—who had heard rumors and read widely on the Internet—already knew a lot of information and misinformation. She felt sorry for her mother as she struggled through her little presentation about sex and reproduction and responsibility. But Caroline hadn't interrupted her. She'd just pretended to listen.

The facts of life. What a stupid term. Talking about vaginas and penises didn't tell you much of anything. It just gave you shapes of body parts and how they fit together. It didn't tell you one thing about how complicated and ugly and bogus it could be, how people sweated and panted together and talked about love when they didn't mean it, how they lied to each other before they had sex, while they had sex, after they had sex. Then lied to their kids once they were born.

"Sex can be beautiful," Joanie had said. "But it can also be dangerous. You have to make the right decisions and protect yourself."

Sex can be beautiful. That was the biggest lie of all. Caroline knew that now, even though she had never had sex and probably would never have it because she was ugly and awkward and everybody hated her.

It was horrible enough that people lied to the people they were having sex with. But it was even worse that they went around telling other people—like Caroline—how they had lied. Caroline wasn't supposed to tell anyone what she knew. She was supposed to be their secret keeper.

B.J. was carrying a baby that had begun as a lie. Whose father didn't want it. So that was how people came into the world, every second of every day. Unwanted and unloved and lied to.

Joanie always accused Caroline of being pessimistic and seeing the worst in things. She told her she would probably grow out of it when she got over her "adolescent angst." Another lie. The older Caroline got, the more she knew, the more painful it was. At times like this, it was unbearable.

Caroline rolled over in bed and pulled her knees up to her chest. It was only four thirty-four, according to the bedside clock. She knew she wouldn't be sleeping anymore tonight.

"Caroline! What's wrong with you?" Joanie asked the next day.

Her daughter's eyes were scrunched into her face like a stuffed animal that had lost his button eyes and all you could see were the indentations where the eyes should be. She looked terrible.

Caroline shrugged. "Nothing." She gripped a cup of hot milk with a little bit of coffee mixed in. "I didn't sleep much last night," she said finally, grudgingly, like it was none of Joanie's business, but she was trying to be polite.

Joanie felt her forehead to see if she had a fever and Caroline wrenched her head away. "I'm not sick," she said. "Just tired."

"Did you have a good time?"

Another one of those fuck-you-for-asking shrugs, Joanie noted, accompanied by some kind of preliterate grunt that could have meant anything in cave-people society.

Good Lord. Joanie spent half her life trying to keep up a totally one-sided conversation with a morose, crabby fifteen-year-old daughter, to keep the lines of communication open the way all those talk-to-your-teen books told her to. Why did she bother? Why didn't anyone ever ask how *she* was doing, anyway? ("You look kind of depressed, Mom. Are they treating you like the petrified remains of the dinosaur age at work? Are you worried about money? The future? Do you have days when you want to throw yourself off the top of the parking garage? Tell me about it." "Thanks for asking, Caroline. I just want to shoot myself some days. Can you give me one good reason why I shouldn't?")

Ah, yes. A conversation!

But, no. Forget it, perish the thought. Mothers didn't talk like that. Not good mothers, anyway. If Caroline thought Joanie was such a bad mother, she should know how hard Joanie tried to be a better parent. But good mothers didn't talk about that, either.

"Well," Joanie said, "your grandmother and I had an interesting day yesterday."

She waited for some kind of affirmation from Caroline. A
nod. A little eye contact. Audible breathing.

Nothing. Well, tough. If Joanie waited around for encouragement from her daughter before she spoke, she might as
well sign up for classes on how to become a mime. To hell with
it. She was going to go ahead and talk.

"We got thrown out of a restaurant."

Caroline's pouched eyes opened just a little wider. So,
Joanie, taking this as encouragement (which she now defined
as a state of mind that didn't indicate obvious and total con-
tempt and loathing), went on. She talked about Ivy's getting
into a fight with the waitress, about her pushing a chair over,
about being escorted out of the Gladiola Café and told never
to return. Her voice rose and fell and she exaggerated a few
details, just to make it a little more dramatic. It was a good
story, if she did say so.

"Why did Grandma do that?" Caroline asked. "She doesn't
usually act that weird."

"I don't know." Joanie had been wondering about that herself. "She lost a friend. She was so upset about it, she cried. I'd
never seen her cry before." Joanie shook her head. "I think
she's depressed."

Caroline considered that. She nodded, companionably
enough.

"I'm making an appointment for her at the doctor," Joanie
said. Caroline nodded again, which was practically as good as
having a long, intimate conversation these days. Maybe they

were making progress. Maybe she was coming out of her adolescent funk and didn't hate Joanie as much as she had seemed to recently. Like yesterday.

"So, you went shopping with B.J.," Joanie said. Her voice was deliberately light and nonchalant. She even turned toward the kitchen and took some lettuce out of the refrigerator so she could begin to tear it up for a salad and look preoccupied and completely casual. "How was that?"

None of it escaped Caroline—the studied nonchalance, the lettuce-tearing, the refrigerator. *How could her mother do that?* Did she think Caroline was a simpleton? Everywhere Caroline looked, she saw articles and books about how parents took their kids too seriously, catered to them too much, made them the center of their existences. What a stinking crock. Parents treated their kids like accessories, they pumped them for details. They didn't love them. They used them. They emptied them out.

"I'm going to take a nap," Caroline said. She pushed her chair up to the table so hard it made a satisfying bang.

"I didn't mean to—" Joanie began, but Caroline was already gone.

chapter 13

"Good weekend?" Bruce asked.

Joanie shrugged. "Fair."

He sat down in the chair next to her desk. "Then why don't you look happier to be here on a Monday morning?"

"Because I don't like it here," Joanie snapped.

"How many times have you said that? Why don't you quit?"

"Because I've got a kid and a mother and a mortgage," Joanie said. "I've got to think about it before I do anything rash."

Bruce clasped his hands behind his head and grinned at her. "Want some advice?"

"No. I'm sick of people giving me advice."

"I don't care. I'll give it to you, anyway. Stop talking and start working on it."

"Why don't *you* quit? You're not happy, either."

"It's too late for me," Bruce said. "I'm stuck in this whole world. The money's too good. I'm too old."

"I feel like I spend half my life," Joanie said, "listening to melodramatic bullshit like that."

"I create bullshit for a living," Bruce said. "But it's innovative, state-of-the-art bullshit. I'm proud of it—no matter how much I complain."

He chuckled and looked pleased with himself, for some reason. He was almost cute when he grinned like that, in a fuzzy, older kind of way. If Joanie ever stopped being celibate, she might think about him. Ten years from now, say.

"Bye," Joanie said briskly. "It's time for me to get to work."

"Have you ever heard of multiple personality disorder?" Caroline asked. "That's what I have."

Karen Abrams, the student counselor who had picked up Caroline when she took her nosedive on the school patio, nodded her head. "Why do you think that?"

Caroline heaved a sigh. She was getting out of algebra class to come to Karen's office and talk about her problems. "Are you in crisis?" the receptionist had asked her. My whole life is a crisis, Caroline had thought. "Kind of," she'd said.

"Well," Caroline said, "I'm extremely moody. I get depressed a lot."

Karen nodded. Unlike Joanie, she didn't immediately become hysterical when Caroline said she had problems. She seemed calm. It was nice for Caroline to have someone calm in her life. A big change.

"Do you ever notice when it is you get depressed?" Karen asked.

"It comes and goes," Caroline said vaguely. She wished Karen wouldn't ask her so many nosy, prying questions. "That's the way it is with multiple personality disorder."

Karen nodded again. "You know, Caroline," she said slowly, "multiple personality disorder is very rare."

"You mean I don't have it," Caroline said.

"Probably not," Karen said.

Caroline shifted in her chair, feeling miffed. "Then, what's wrong with me?" she snapped. She should have known better than to come here. Karen was like every other adult she knew: manipulative and sneaky and selfish. "Don't tell me I'm a normal teenager—and everybody goes through this."

"Okay, I won't," Karen said. She sat back in her chair and folded her hands. Her face was placid and alert. She watched Caroline squirm and sulk.

"Do you want to know what I think?" Karen asked after a long, uncomfortable silence. At least it was uncomfortable for Caroline; Karen herself seemed perfectly composed. What a bitch.

Caroline shrugged. "Go ahead," she muttered resentfully.

"All right. I think you're a very sensitive, intelligent young woman. Based on what you've already told me, I think high school is difficult for you—well, socially, anyway. And you're trying to navigate between your parents the best way you can."

"Yeah. So what?"

"So—what you're doing is tough. You get down about it. That's a normal reaction—and not a clinical illness."

"Isn't there a pill I can take?" Caroline asked. "I'm tired of feeling shitty all the time."

Karen shrugged, her hands extended in front of her, flat. "You know, I'm sure there are lots of pills you could take—and lots of doctors out there who'd give them to you. But I don't think that's what you need."

"You're not a doctor," Caroline pointed out. She was getting a little tired of all the airs Karen was putting on. Like she knew everything. Like she knew all about Caroline—that particularly rankled. Caroline was an extremely complicated person, a very special and unusual person, whether Karen knew it or not. But Karen probably had no idea. Nobody did. Even Caroline herself occasionally suspected she might be ordinary. Ordinary! Like everybody else! It was a horrifying thought. Nobody had ever told Sylvia Plath she was ordinary, Caroline felt sure.

"No, I'm not," Karen said. "But I'm a pretty damned good observer."

"I smoke weed," Caroline said, even though she'd had no intention of bringing it up here. "I love to smoke weed—"

"You know it's illegal," Karen said mildly.

"I also smoke cigarettes. I think I may be addicted."

"Cigarettes are very addictive," Karen agreed.

"I hate myself."

"I know you do," Karen said.

That was when Caroline started crying like a two-year-old, which was mortifying. Karen handed her a Kleenex and she swabbed her cheeks and blew her nose, and tears and snot still slithered down her face. Finally, she stopped crying and just sniffed occasionally.

"Why don't you come back and see me next week?" Karen asked. "I think that talking about all of this can help."

"I'll think about it," Caroline said. "But I'm really busy. I don't know if I have enough time."

"I can understand that. Just let me know."

Caroline nodded and stood up. She looked at Karen briefly before she left the room. She had the feeling Karen *did* understand; that Caroline wasn't busy at all. That she was lonely and would love to talk to someone. That she was bitterly disappointed she didn't have a serious addiction or multiple personality disorder, didn't need to be hospitalized or committed immediately. That she hated herself and her life—but it wasn't particularly alarming.

There was something sobering about being listened to and treated with respect by an adult. But it reminded Caroline of something she didn't really want to know: She was a small actor in a big world of many people. Her own worldview—dominated by herself and her misery and her inadequacies and her crazy family—wasn't the way other people viewed life. She might be smaller and less significant than she ever wanted to know.

"Thank you," Caroline said. She felt emptied out and lighter and borderline gloomy, all at the same time. Just like someone with multiple personality disorder, whether Karen thought so or not.

"Is this Roxanne Pilcher?" the voice asked.

"It's Joanie Pilcher," Joanie said, irritated. "Roxanne is my first name, but I never use it."

"But you're the daughter of a Mrs. Ivy Horton?"

Joanie's hands froze on the computer. "Yes. She's my mother. Is she all right?"

A brief silence, during which Joanie's stomach churned and she wanted to vomit. Then, finally, "Yeah, she's fine. But I'm calling from the downtown police office. We have her in custody now. She's been arrested for shoplifting."

"When's your dad getting married?" Sondra eased her way onto the grass. She was carrying a salad plate today—iceberg lettuce that was brown and wrinkled around the edges, with an enormous globule of blue cheese dressing on the top. It was the kind of meal they served to death-row prisoners in the movies.

"Yech," Caroline said. "That looks horrendous." She frowned, taking in Sondra's round face and wide eyes. Something about her friend looked different. Makeup. That was it. Sondra was wearing makeup on her eyes and blush on her cheeks. If she hadn't been sweating, she would have looked all right. But Sondra tended to sweat a lot. "Are you really going to eat that?"

"Yeah." Sondra plunged a plastic fork into the salad. "My mom's taking me to Weight Watchers. She even got me a food diary. I'm supposed to fill it out every day so I can lose weight."

"That's weird." Caroline was still feeling deflated after learning she didn't have multiple personality disorder and that she was probably a completely ordinary, insignificant person. She tried to contemplate what Sondra would look like if she lost weight. Joanie always said she had a pretty face. If Sondra lost a lot of weight, she might look entirely different. A lot better. She might not want to be Caroline's friend anymore. She'd probably make a bunch of new and better friends. Then Caroline wouldn't have any friends at all. Sondra would pass her in the hall, like everybody else did, not really looking at her, surrounded by a big circle of her popular friends.

Caroline stared at her own half-eaten cheeseburger. Sondra always said she was lucky not to have a weight problem. Maybe she was. But at least Sondra knew what she needed to do to look better—eat barfy-looking salads. Caroline had no idea what to do. She couldn't think of anything she could do to look better, except grow big breasts. Mothers couldn't take you to support groups for that.

"When's your dad getting married?" Sondra asked again. "Are you going to be in the wedding?"

"Soon." Caroline put her cheeseburger down and wiped off her hands with a napkin. "Thanks for reminding me."

She felt bitter and resentful, all of a sudden. Sondra was starting a new, skinnier life without her. What did Caroline have to look forward to? An awful wedding with her father trying to look younger and happier than he really was and B.J. holding in her stomach the whole time so it wouldn't look like the shotgun wedding it really was. Also, Joanie would be stomping around the house, crying and probably getting suicidal again. Why did everything in Caroline's life have to be so awful?

"*Sor*-ry."

Sondra's voice sounded partly sarcastic, partly hurt. She was changing already. Getting as tired of Caroline as Caroline was of herself.

Caroline suddenly felt like crying. She spent most of her life saying things that were mean and ugly and seemed to come out of a place inside her she couldn't control. Sometimes she felt as though life hurt her so much, she had to strike back. But that was stupid. She always ended up snapping at people like Sondra or Joanie, who meant well. Never at the people who really hurt her. The people who didn't even know she existed. Her priorities were totally screwed up.

"I went shopping with B.J. Saturday," Caroline said. "For her wedding dress."

"Weird." Sondra shook her head, toying with the salad and plastic fork. "What was that like?"

"OK. Fine. Not too bad." Caroline told Sondra about the shopping and the saleswoman and spending the night at Richard and B.J.'s condo. She didn't mention the blood-soaked bedsheets, though, or how B.J. accused her of being spoiled. Or how the baby hadn't been the accident everybody thought it was.

As she talked—with Sondra looking kind of interested, even if she was already on her way to dumping Caroline as a best friend—Caroline realized something strange. She wasn't sure how much she liked B.J. But she felt oddly protective of her. She thought of the look B.J. got on her face, as she touched the sheets in the guest room, the granite counter in the kitchen, the leather seats in the car she drove. There was something on her face that Caroline recognized—the desperate longing for things she wanted, but couldn't have. Caroline knew that look, understood it with everything in her body. She felt it from the inside every day of her life.

"I have everything in my life I ever wanted," B.J. had told Caroline that morning before she left. "*Every*thing."

It had been the kind of remark B.J. was prone to making: A comment that required a follow-up question.

Finally, Caroline had complied. "Like what?" she asked.

B.J. extended her fingers, touching them one by one. "Well," she said, "I'm getting married. I'm having a baby. And I have my own house."

She'd smiled so blissfully after she said that that it made something inside Caroline ache for her. She recognized that same sense of despair in B.J. that she had herself—that feeling of wanting something so badly that you felt your soul would shatter if you didn't get it. That you would do anything, however insane or dishonorable, to get that object of desire.

It made Caroline feel that she knew B.J. better than she really did, understood something about her she couldn't have explained to anyone. She didn't like her, but for some reason, she cared about her. How weird was that?

"So, do you like B.J. now?" Sondra asked. She pushed her paper plate away, with the browning salad mostly uneaten. "I know you didn't used to."

"I don't know," Caroline said. "I guess. Kind of."

She watched Sondra pull a candy bar out of her purse and begin to peel the wrapping paper off it. It was a 3 Musketeers, Sondra's favorite kind.

"Are you going to record that in your food diary?" Caroline asked.

Sondra wiped a little chocolate smear off her upper lip with her finger, then popped the finger in her mouth. She grinned slyly. "What food diary?"

Caroline felt guilty about how good that made her feel—that Sondra wasn't already newly thin and beautiful and lost to her. She watched Sondra swiftly finish the candy bar. Then the two of them picked up their trash and threw their crumbs to the birds before they walked back inside the school together.

"Tell me, Roxanne," Ivy said. "Did you ever—"

"It's *Joanie*, Mother. Do we have to go through that again?"

Joanie jerked the steering wheel sharply. Wasn't it enough that she was taking off from work so she could bail her seventy-six-year-old mother out of jail, then schlep her to the doctor, where she'd already bullied the medical receptionist into giving them the first available appointment since Ivy was in a "state of crisis"? Oh, no. Evidently not. Ivy still had to torment her.

"I'm so sorry," Ivy said. "I won't do it again."

"It's okay," Joanie said grimly.

She tried to put the look on Zoe's face out of her mind—the panic, the betrayal, the veiled fury that Joanie, good old rock-solid, almost-fifty-year-old Joanie, had to take the morning off to escort her elderly mother to the doctor at a time when the office was in crisis and deep turmoil and Zoe herself had gone without sleep for days, bingeing on Red Bull and Nicorette and looking for all the world like a rodent that had been shocked repeatedly for feeding from the wrong container. Joanie could see it now. Zoe had assumed that Joanie, at her advanced age with zero social life, would be a steady hand, a ballast, a life preserver on their sinking ship. And now what? At their darkest hour, she was deserting them.

"Well, if you *have* to go," Zoe had said, her eyes bulging with ad-agency drama.

"I have to go," Joanie had answered. She had carefully omitted the fact that, before she could take her mother to the doctor, she had to spring her from jail. No need for the entire office to know that Joanie was the daughter of an elderly criminal.

"What I was going to ask, *Joanie*," Ivy said now, "is whether you ever wished Richard had died, instead of divorcing you."

"Mother!" Joanie front-loaded her voice with as much horror as she could muster. Had she ever wished Richard had dropped dead? Only every hour of every day for every month since he'd walked out the door. She had dreamed, again and again, of being a widow. So much better than being a divorcée! She looked good in black, and she could have been so attractively, photogenically tragic, with an air of mystery about her. She would have carried an embroidered handkerchief with her at all times, clutched in her hand, which she would have used to dab at her eyes, without smearing her carefully applied mascara, as she hinted at what a perfect relationship she and her recently deceased husband had had. Just perfect! She couldn't even think of remarrying. "Mother!" she repeated. "Of course not!"

"Well, at least you would have had his life insurance," Ivy pointed out.

Joanie pulled into a parking place. Her mother was the only person she knew who could turn emotional tables so abruptly that the two of them were talking about Joanie as a potential murderer, instead of Ivy as a known kleptomaniac.

Where had that come from? How long had Ivy been shoplifting—and why? And why had Joanie failed to wonder about Ivy's growing collection of high-fashion scarves? Joanie knew why. She was too busy trying to earn a living in a job she was growing to hate, too busy trying to keep her own sanity welded together, watching over a teenage daughter, whose emotions simmered like a volcano about to blow. It had never occurred to her that her mother—a self-righteous, upstanding, lifelong Christian, member of the Greatest Generation—might be a common thief.

"You can't tell me you haven't ever thought about it," Ivy continued. "I know *I* would have."

"Mother, why don't we talk about your problems, instead?" Joanie asked.

Ivy stared straight ahead. "I don't have any problems," she said.

"You're looking hot today," Henry said. He flashed his gorgeous white grin at Caroline.

She could feel herself blush—that hot, prickly feeling that crept over her cheeks and down her neck. Caroline hated to blush. It told the world everything about you—turned all your hidden insecurities and desires into a billboard people could point at and laugh. Caroline was so unnerved that she stared down at her book and avoided Henry's eyes.

"Very pretty," Henry said.

Oh, please. Even though Caroline wanted to believe it, she knew she looked bad right now. She hadn't been sleeping much since she'd stayed at B.J. and Richard's condo. When she'd examined herself from every possible angle in the mirror for about thirty minutes this morning (after her daily and disappointing breast check), she'd seen the dark hollows under her eyes, the way her skin was pulled tight over her face. She looked like one of those refugees from a war-torn country, even though she didn't dress quite as badly.

Still—Henry was paying attention to her. Complimenting her. Even though he was glancing over her shoulder to wave at other people, too. Maybe he liked her, just a little. She blushed even more, thinking that, and her heart thudded loudly, like a car with a flat tire. She needed antianxiety drugs. *Prescription: Xanax. Take as directed every time you go to Spanish class and sit behind the love of your life and want to touch him so badly—just to stroke his hair, his neck, his arm, that's all—that your stomach rotates and your cheeks blaze and you feel like you want to vomit. Refill as needed.*

"Thanks," she managed finally, still staring down at her book. They were studying the subjunctive tense this week. She tried to look interested, peering at the small print.

"Buenas tardes," Senora Schmidt said loudly.

Caroline looked up and found Henry staring into her eyes, then smiling again, before he turned around to face the front of the room. Those gorgeous chocolate-colored eyes, warm and liquid! She could have drowned in them, happily, perfectly content forever, surrendering to everything that was sweet and dense. Transported.

After that, Caroline didn't notice much of anything. The class went on. Senora Schmidt stood in front of the class, pacing and sometimes clapping her hands to get their attention. Other students spoke. Senora Schmidt frowned because they didn't understand the subjunctive. She looked around the class, searching for a right answer, for someone who understood and could explain. Normally, that would have been Caroline. But not today.

Caroline sat with her chin in her hands, staring at the back of Henry's neck, watching the rise and fall of his breath. He reached his hand back to rub his neck, his strong fingers pinching his smooth skin. She was so close, she could have reached out and touched his hand, linking their fingers together, squeezing them to say everything she wanted to say aloud, but couldn't.

If she were brave, if she were beautiful and desirable and everything else she wanted to be, she would have done it.

Wait. That was it. The subjunctive tense. There it was. Her whole, dismal life was in the subjunctive tense—something she dreamed of, but that wasn't real. Like Henry. Like her idea of Henry. Like her dreams that something somehow someday would change and she would be happy.

Caroline snapped her head back and sat with her arms crossed, staring at Senora Schmidt pacing in front of the classroom. Her mouth, with its deep red lipstick, moved rapidly, but Caroline couldn't hear anything.

"Ivy!" the woman behind the desk announced. "Are you ready? The nurse is here."

The woman had a voice very much like a hog caller Ivy had once heard at the Texas state fair. She was clearly another one of those dreadful people who thought everybody on earth should be immediately familiar and chummy. Ivy loathed chummy. If she hadn't felt so heavy inside, so burdened by everything in the whole fast, indifferent world, so insulted at being branded a common criminal, she would have said something. As it was, it was hard enough to drag herself to her feet. Even with Joanie helping her.

"Come on, Mother," Joanie whispered.

The nurse, who introduced herself as Dolores with a frosty, antiseptic smile, led them down the hall. "We'll stop here," she said, pointing to the scales. She adjusted the arrow as Ivy stood there, edging it slowly upward. One hundred and thirty. That wasn't bad. Ivy had weighed that amount for years. At least she hadn't gotten fat, like a lot of old people.

Then Dolores snapped out a long metal rod and eased it onto the top of Ivy's head. "Five-two," she said, writing it down in Ivy's record.

"I'm afraid that's incorrect," Ivy said, politely. "I'm five-four. I've always been five-four—ever since I was sixteen and concluded my growth."

"Well, you're not five-four anymore." Dolores pushed the rod back in with a loud snap. "People shrink as they get older, Ivy. You've already shrunk two inches. You'll probably shrink more."

"I've always been five-four," Ivy insisted. "Your measuring device must be wrong."

"Is she always this feisty?" Dolores asked Joanie, rolling her eyes.

"I wish you wouldn't call me by my first name," Ivy said. (At least they had politely referred to her as "Mrs. Horton" when she was being booked at the jail.) "And I object to the word *feisty*. It's demeaning."

"Most of our patients prefer for us to call them by their first names," Dolores said. "We run an informal office."

"Have you asked any of your patients what they prefer? Or are you just assuming what they want?" Ivy's voice sounded shaky and querulous. Like an old woman's voice, she noticed. Like her neck, wobbly and mottled.

"So, what would you like to be called, dear?" Dolores asked. She cocked her head to the side and gave Ivy a big, goopy smile, like she was a misbehaving toddler. "I'll write it in your record."

"Mrs. Horton will be fine."

Ivy watched as Dolores wrote *Do not call patient by her first name. She objects. Also, do not call her fiesty. She objects to that, too.*

"It's *feisty*," Ivy said. "You misspelled it."

Dolores snapped the record shut. "What?"

"It's all right." Joanie grabbed Ivy's elbow and squeezed. "You don't have to correct everything, Mother."

"Follow me, please," Dolores said.

They walked behind her, Joanie yanking at Ivy's elbow, Ivy pulling back huffily, following Dolores's squishy white shoes down the polished hall.

"Hey," Henry said. For a moment, he looked confused.

"Caroline," she said.

"Caroline." He shook his head. "My memory's shot."

"Yeah. Mine, too." She giggled too loudly.

They were walking out of the Spanish classroom door, pushing against other people. Caroline thought Henry might have touched her arm, but she wasn't sure. Maybe it was somebody else brushing up against her. Still, since it might have been him, it was like an electric current. Her arm was on fire.

"What's your next class?" Henry asked.

"Algebra Two."

"You must be smart. I'm still in geometry. For the second year in a row." He smiled ruefully. If failing a class bothered him, it didn't show. No big deal. When you looked as hot as he did, who cared about math?

"I just study a lot. My mother makes me." That was such a big lie. But it sounded better than admitting she was smart. Who wanted to be smart? Nobody—not even a loser like Caroline.

"Maybe we could get together sometime. After school. You started on that Spanish paper yet?"

Caroline concentrated on putting one foot in front of the other. Her breath was caught high up in her chest and it wasn't moving. It was stuck. She might become asphyxiated any moment now.

"Yeah. Sure." She tried to say it very casually. It was hard to be casual when you couldn't breathe, though.

"What's your number?"

Caroline stopped short, like somebody had jerked her from behind. If she'd been an amputee, she could have still counted the number of times she'd been asked that question on the fingers of her remaining hand. She tossed her pink hair back and mumbled the number. Jeez, she hoped it was the right one.

"See ya later." He definitely touched her left elbow this time. Caroline kept on walking, even though the most important interaction of her life had just occurred in this school hallway, which she had always dismissed as dark and depressing and banal. Now, all of a sudden, it was filled with glorious golden light and birds that sang sweetly and riotously, and she could feel every part of her soaring and joyful.

"You look, like—really happy." Sondra cocked her head and stared at Caroline.

Caroline shoved her Spanish book in her locker, pausing just a moment to touch it for good luck. She had been carrying that book when Henry suggested they get together. She would always remember that book, that first real conversation, that invitation.

"I've been talking to *him*."

"Oh, my God. Really?" Sondra slammed her locker door shut and faced Caroline. Her eyes were huge. "What did he say?"

"He wants us to get together." Caroline was trying to get back into casual, sophisticated, no-big-deal, I'm-cool mode, but it wasn't working. Not at all. Her voice sounded squeaky. "He asked for my number."

"A—well, a date? You're kidding!" Sondra reached out and jiggled Caroline's arm, which caused Caroline to drop her algebra book and sent her notebooks flying.

They bent down to pick up the scattered papers as students walked past, some of them stepping on Caroline's notes. At one time, earlier in her life—like yesterday or two hours ago, say—that would have bothered Caroline. But not today. They could stomp all over everything and she wouldn't care.

"This is so exciting," Sondra whispered. Her face was flushed with happiness. She looked as happy for Caroline as

Caroline was for herself. For the first time in ages, Caroline realized that her best friend was a better person than she was, a better friend to Caroline than Caroline was to her.

"I'll tell you about it after school," Caroline said, standing up. She smiled at Sondra and told herself sternly that she needed to be a better friend, too. Just because her social life had just taken off didn't mean she was better than Sondra. Not really. Just luckier, for once. That was all.

"Hello, Ivy," the doctor said. He extended his hand. "I'm Dr. Bednar."

"Mrs. Horton," Dolores said. She pointed to her note in Ivy's records. "The patient doesn't want to be called by her first name."

"Mrs. Horton. Oh, yes. Of course," the doctor said smoothly. He grasped Ivy's hand and shook it. "Why don't we all sit down?" He motioned toward the chairs and sat down himself. He smiled at Ivy and Joanie. "Now, what can I do for you today?"

Ivy sighed. It was a loud sigh that came out of nowhere, as far as she was concerned. She wasn't the kind of person who sighed. Then she sighed again. She couldn't think of anything to say. She felt like she had a basketball buried in her chest, pushing against her. It almost hurt to breathe.

Dr. Bednar continued to smile encouragingly, his smooth pink face expectant. When Ivy didn't say anything, he looked down at the file in his hands. "Good weight," he said, nodding. Then he frowned and looked closer. "What's this? *Fiesty*?"

Ivy stopped midsigh. "Feisty," she said. "It's misspelled."

"I'm a nurse," Dolores said. She was standing by the door, like a hall monitor. "Not an English teacher." She stood up straighter and smiled. "I never could spell very well."

"I'll just correct that," Dr. Bednar said, pulling out his pen. He looked up at Ivy. "I don't like misspellings, either."

The door banged shut. Dolores had disappeared. They could hear her squishy nurse's shoes heading down the hallway.

"Now, what's wrong, Mrs. Horton?" Dr. Bednar asked.

Something strange was happening to Ivy. Just the sound of his voice—soft and courteous and low and *male*—triggered something almost violent in her. Her eyes flooded, then overflowed with tears, soaking her blouse, spotting her skirt. Something about that voice broke her heart, she thought helplessly, leaning over, almost blinded by the tears. When, she wondered, had a man ever spoken to her that tenderly? Even John, solid and dependable and regular as a wound clock, had never really used that tone with her or stared at her quite so intently and sympathetically. "But he's always there, isn't he?" Ivy's mother had once told her when she complained about her husband's silences and lack of interest in her life. Yes, he had always been there. You didn't complain about a man who was always there. A woman couldn't afford to be that kind of fool.

Ivy felt, rather than saw, Joanie leave the office, easing the door shut behind her. She wept till she was empty and exhausted. Dr. Bednar pulled Kleenexes from a nearby box and handed them to her. Finally, she sat there, quietly. It was like peering out of a storm shelter after a tornado had passed through. What had happened? She had no idea. Outside, the world had tilted and made itself into something new.

~~~~~~

"Do you think he wants to have sex with you?" Sondra asked. "Like, soon?"

Caroline, who was carefully inhaling a cigarette, almost choked.

"I don't know," she finally said, between coughs. She searched her already well-trod memory of her romantic hallway encounter with Henry, which had probably lasted a good thirty seconds. Had he been hitting on her—and she just hadn't realized it? She was so naïve. Nobody had ever hit on her before. How would she know it if it happened?

"I think he really likes you," Sondra said. "He wouldn't talk to you all the time if he didn't."

Caroline shook her head. Then she shrugged helplessly. If there was anyone on earth who knew even less about guys than she did, it was Sondra. If Sondra hadn't looked so eager and happy for her, Caroline would have said something mean. Had Karen been wrong about her multiple personality disorder?

They sat in Sondra's car, puffing halfheartedly on their cigarettes. Outside, other students moved past them in the parking lot, yelling and revving their cars and laughing loudly. Why was it that other people always seemed to be having more fun than they were?

"If you have sex with Henry," Sondra said solemnly, "you've got to remember to use protection." She stubbed her cigarette out in the ashtray. Above it, she'd hung one of those car deodorants you could get at local car washes. It was scented like a pine forest, so, with the lingering smoke, her car now smelled like a burning forest.

You must be smart. Maybe we could get together sometime. After school. Caroline let the words float, once again, through her mind, drinking them in and feeling giddy from the romance and the smoke and the smell of the pine forest. She knew there had been something more to the conversation, something about a Spanish paper. It bothered her, just a little. But, still. Was it really such a big deal? Henry could have asked for help from anybody else in the class. But he hadn't. He'd asked her. It meant—well, it had to mean *something*.

"You might also want to get a push-up bra." Sondra was waving her hands around in the car, trying to get rid of the smoke and the smell. "They're really sexy. My cousin says guys love them."

Oh, please. Was there anything Sondra didn't talk about with her cousin? Caroline wished Blake would keep his opinions about women's lingerie to himself and start sending them more weed on a regular basis. Caroline missed the loose and loopy way marijuana made her feel—like it opened up her real self, freeing her from being the skinny, nervous, uptight loser everybody thought she was.

She could really, *really* use some weed right now. Joanie had been flapping around the house like a deranged bird lately, moaning about how Grandma seemed strange and depressed. Clinically depressed, Joanie had said, like that made a difference.

"Don't you have anything to say?" Joanie had asked Caroline. "I'm worried Grandma may be suicidal."

"I'd be suicidal, too, if I were her," Caroline said.

"Caroline, that is a horrible thing to say!" Joanie had reared back and stared at her like she was a demon seed.

"Well, it's honest," Caroline said. "Don't you want me to be honest?"

No, of course Joanie did not want Caroline to be honest. She wanted her to pretend her life was unbearable because her grandmother was depressed. She had no idea that Caroline's whole life was already unbearable and it had nothing to do with her depressed grandmother.

"I'm going to be old someday soon, too," Joanie had said, her reading glasses falling down on her nose, glaring at Caroline. "I hope you'll treat me with greater consideration than you're showing toward your poor grandmother." Her *poor* grandmother. Like Joanie just loved having Grandma in the house and like she hadn't totally ruined their lives by moving in.

"I don't have anything to push up in a bra," she reminded Sondra. "You do." Sondra's boobs were big, but big fat deal, so was the rest of her—kind of like one of those big balloons in the Macy's Thanksgiving Day Parade. She was very insensitive about how much Caroline suffered from being flat-chested.

"I'd rather be skinny like you." Sondra reached for the ignition key and the car started with its usual asthmatic wheeze. "My mom's going to be on my butt about what I ate today. She's forcing me to get weighed every week at Weight Watchers." She glanced over her shoulder and eased the car into reverse. "It is so totally humiliating to get weighed in front of all these old fat people. What happens if I gain weight?"

"Why does your mom even care?" Caroline tried to imagine Joanie trying to run her life the way Sondra's mother did. Joanie was a pretty big busybody, but at least she didn't hound Caroline about what she ate.

"She says I'd be happier if I was thinner." Sondra ran a stop sign and a car honked at her. "She wants me to be popular. Like that's going to happen."

The driver honked again. Then he loudly passed the two girls and turned around in the seat and shot Sondra the bird. Sometimes, it was hard not to take it all personally.

Ivy hadn't talked this much in years. Now that she'd dried her eyes, the words flooded out of her the way her tears had. She'd always been a quiet, reserved person. What had happened to her? Had she been saving up these words, these long, rambling sentences for her whole life?

"I miss my home," she said. "I loved having my own place. Everything was where I wanted it to be. I didn't have to infringe on anybody else."

She didn't even look up at Dr. Bednar to see whether she was boring him. She didn't care, for once. She just talked on and on.

She spoke about the view from her old kitchen window of the tree she and John had planted forty years earlier. About the furniture they'd bought at garage sales when they were first married. About the comfort of looking around and knowing she was at home and safe. She knew it didn't mean anything to anyone but her—the collection of decades of life in one place—but she missed it terribly. It had anchored her in the world, told a comforting story. And now, it was sold or packed away, gone. Yes, she had a place to live. But she felt homeless, in a way.

"I used to feel useful in my own house," Ivy said. "Now, I don't. I'm an intruder. I try not to intrude much—but I can't help it. I'm where I don't belong."

She paused, finally, and looked at Dr. Bednar. He was nodding gravely, watching her, taking occasional notes on his pad. When he bent over to write, she could see a faint bald spot on top of his head. He'd combed his hair carefully to cover it. How old was he? Late forties? Early fifties? She couldn't tell any longer. They all looked young to her, indistinguishable from one another. How could he ever understand her? He was still in the very thick of life. Somebody needed him. He had work, a home, a family, no doubt. He still recognized himself when he looked in a mirror, even if he was probably concerned about his bald spot. He didn't flinch when he saw his reflection, as Ivy often did, wondering who that old woman was. He didn't look at hands mottled by age and wonder who they belonged to.

He also didn't resort to occasional shoplifting just because— well, just because *why*? Why, why, why? Ivy had no idea. Just because she had saved her money and sacrificed and done everything right—but had still gone broke. Just because she ached for beautiful things sometimes and she couldn't afford them. Because they made her feel good, for at least a little while, added some excitement to her dreary life. Because life seemed so unfair and mean, and she was tired of it and bored and sad. Why ask why? Maybe she should have been asking, Why not?

Dr. Bednar looked up at her. He had light gray eyes behind his bifocals. "You seem very upset, Mrs. Horton."

"I'm not usually like this," Ivy said.

She hoped he wouldn't launch into some tirade about how lucky she was to be living with her daughter. People always told you how lucky you were when you were old—lucky you weren't living in a filthy nursing home, begging on the streets, living in a ditch, getting assaulted by a motorcycle gang. He'd probably tell her about all the horror stories he knew from the older people he saw in his practice who were bruised and abused and malnourished and dazed by dementia. Ivy, in contrast, was lucky. She should count her blessings and stop shoplifting.

Ivy knew that. She didn't have to hear him say it. She knew her life wasn't as bad as other people's. Yes, it could be so much worse. She understood that. But that made her feel worse, instead of better. She was fortunate, yes. So, what was wrong with her for being so unhappy?

"After listening to you," he said, "I believe you're depressed."

"I am not depressed," Ivy said quickly. "We don't have mental illness in my family."

Dr. Bednar shook his head. A lock of his comb-over came loose and he smoothed it back in a practiced movement. "You're sad and you feel useless," he said. "That's textbook depression." He reached his hand over to hers and touched her gently. "It's all right. It happens to everybody sometimes."

He pulled out a prescription notepad and began to jot down some words. "I'm prescribing an antidepressant for you that should help. I want to see you again in a month to see if it's working."

He continued writing, in some kind of terrible doctor scrawl they called handwriting these days, which Ivy couldn't even read upside down.

"But I don't believe in drugs," Ivy said. "They're habit-forming. And I think you're completely wrong about my being mentally ill."

After all her emoting, her complaining, her whining, her voice sounded faint and unconvincing, even to her.

"Can you please trust me on this, Mrs. Horton?" Dr. Bednar said. "I think it will help. You know, seeing a counselor—someone who specializes in geriatric issues—would also be good for you."

"I don't like to talk about my problems," Ivy said. "It's self-indulgent."

"Well, then," Dr. Bednar said. "Let's try this."

He handed her the piece of paper. She clutched it, staring at the chicken scratch on it, still unable to decipher it.

Depression. Maybe it wasn't a mental illness anymore. It was what they now called old age.

chapter 14

"David?"

"Yeah?"

"This is your sister, Joanie Pilcher."

There was a long, ominous silence, punctuated by the sound of papers being rattled in the background, like David was trying to swat a fly or a fellow human being with them.

"Joanie," David said finally, huffing with exasperation, "it's a Tuesday morning. I'm in the middle of a big bailout that's worth billions of dollars. *Billions.* The last thing I need this morning is your sarcasm." He cleared his throat loudly. "Now, do you have something to tell me?"

Pompous creep. Self-important toad. Like Joanie wasn't involved in lots of extremely significant things, too, like an ad campaign for a crappy, near-bankrupt car company that might be worth tens of thousands of dollars. If they got the account. If Zoe stayed on her meds and didn't have a nervous breakdown. If Joanie didn't get fired.

Yes, indeed! David wasn't the only one who had a life.

"I thought you might be interested to know," Joanie said, slowly drawling her words out to further irritate her brother, the billion-dollar hotshot lawyer who now affected a brash, hurried, New York accent even though he had been born in Midland, Texas, "that Mother has been diagnosed with depression."

"Mom?"

"Yes." Joanie stared hard at her clenched fist and fell silent after that one brief syllable. Let it sink in, she thought. Wallow in guilt. Wrestle with your conscience, if you've got one.

"Well," David said, "are you sure she's been properly diagnosed? And cared for?"

"Yes, David," Joanie snapped. "We have hospitals out here in the sticks. And many people with M.D. after their names."

"Or—no! Wait a minute. I guess I could put Mother on the plane so you could take her to a proper New York doctor for a better diagnosis. She'd be a lot happier living with you, I think. It might even clear up her depression."

"I don't know how you can joke about something this serious, Joanie."

"That's because I *live* with something this serious, David. It makes you say inappropriate things after a while. Sorry."

Joanie thought fleetingly of Ivy's heaviness, her slow-moving body, her sad, lined face. She had still been asleep when Joanie left for work that morning. Ivy, who always rose at dawn to bustle around the kitchen and poke around on the

Internet. For months, she and her mother had battled about living together, calling occasional truces, easing themselves into a routine—even if it was an uncomfortable routine. It surprised Joanie to realize that no matter how much her mother had irritated and upset her, she had still depended on Ivy to remain as she was—opinionated, energetic, even judgmental. Her mother oriented her somehow. Anchored her. Now Joanie was flailing in midair. How strange.

"Oh—and before I forget," Joanie added, "Mother also got arrested for shoplifting." David, as an officer of the court, might find that interesting. Jerk.

"Shoplifting?" David sounded completely aghast.

"The doctor thinks it's related to her depression," Joanie said.

"Shoplifting?" The line fell silent, then a little staticky. David must be contemplating the fact that he was the son of a hardened criminal. "Good God. What did she steal?"

"We're not sure," Joanie said. "Mostly scarves. They're very stylish these days. Everyone's wearing them."

"Is she going to jail?" David still sounded like he was in the middle of a nightmare that would play out in the New York tabloids: Sticky-Fingered Mom of Wall Street Lawyer Tasered! Neighbors Said Gray-Haired Widow Was a "Loner."

"No, she wasn't even charged," Joanie said. "She's going to be doing some community work." She cleared her throat. "Actually, the depression is a bigger deal than the shoplifting. The shoplifting was just a symptom, the doctor said. It's common in the elderly."

Silence.

"Don't you have anything to say?" Joanie asked.

"What can I say?" David snapped. "You call me up, out of nowhere, to tell me our mother is a mentally ill criminal—"

"She's depressed. Not mentally ill—"

"—running around town, stealing things—"

"Only a few things. Calm down, David. You sound hysterical."

More silence. Men hated to be called hysterical.

"So—what do you want from me, Joanie?"

The words and tone were flat. What did Joanie want from him? She had no idea. She'd just called him—well, why? To be comforted. To have someone else know and care. To feel less isolated and alone. She should have known that wouldn't work. Speaking to her brother almost always made her feel more alone.

"I thought you'd want to know," she said.

"Of course I want to know," David said quickly. The paper-rattling in the background resumed, then stopped. "I just— well, you call me and dump it all in my lap. What am I supposed to do?"

"I want you to care."

"I *do* care." He paused for several seconds. "I just don't know what to do."

"You could come and see her, you know." Joanie omitted another line of potential sarcasm about how they had airports in Texas, too. David's voice had dropped some of its fast-paced arrogance, becoming a little plaintive and uncertain.

"I could," he said. "I *should*."

"Yes, you should." Joanie relaxed her balled-up hand and wiggled her fingers. They were always sore and achy these days. Arthritis? Probably. She sighed. "You think about it. And call me."

For once, neither of them hung up on the other. In fact, there was a brief silence of several seconds before they both disconnected the call at exactly the same time.

Ivy sat and stared at the prescription bottle for about fifteen minutes before she opened it. Inside, the pills were a lustrous light blue. They were Prozac, also known as fluoxetine. She had read all about it on the Internet. They were used to treat depression, bulimia, and anxiety. Sometimes, they made you break out in a rash or get restless. They also interfered with sexual pleasure.

The last, Ivy thought, would not be a problem. Not now, anyway. She had greatly enjoyed sex during the years she and John had been married, had felt a rush of happiness whenever he turned to her in bed. Sometimes, she had almost felt she enjoyed sex a little too much. Other women her age usually complained about it. "You know how men are," Myra had once complained to Ivy, raising her eyebrows heavenward. "They're always after you. I got sick and tired of that years ago." Myra had scrunched up her face in distaste and Ivy had nodded companionably enough. She hadn't said anything, though.

But then Joanie and her whole loudmouthed generation had come along and all they could do was talk about sex and prance around almost naked and discuss orgasms on TV programs with sympathetic hostesses who frowned and lectured about being "satisfied sexually." For a while, all they could talk about were G-spots. Ivy had no idea whether she had a G-spot or not; she had never felt the need for it and didn't want to go around searching for it like she was hunting for diamonds in a dark, dank cave. Ivy always turned off those TV shows. She thought sex was better when it was kind of a naughty little secret, a nighttime mystery that occurred when the lights were out and the covers pulled up, and you didn't go around boasting about it. You just thought about it now and then and smiled to yourself about how wonderful it had made you feel. But did anyone else need to know about it? No.

Ivy also had no urge to imagine what other people did in bed or how often they did it. In fact, she preferred not to think about it. It wasn't any of her business. She was especially annoyed by most of the Hollywood movies these days, where the actors were so swept away by passion that they copulated on kitchen tables and on the floors. Ivy had felt very passionate many, many times in her life (Joanie would be surprised and shocked if she knew just how many times!), but she would never have considered having sexual intercourse in the kitchen. She was old-fashioned enough to believe that each room in a house had a purpose—and the kitchen was expressly designed for cooking. After you had been married for several years, in particular, there was no excuse for kitchen sex. You could always manage to walk to your bedroom, however quickly.

What Ivy had loved about sex, beyond the physical pleasure, was that it was the only time she could be sure she had John's complete attention. He was wide awake and he was concentrating on her. Outside the bedroom, this hadn't happened often. He had always been so quiet and preoccupied with—well, *what*? She had never known. Men and women, in those days, didn't talk as much as they seemed to now. Maybe that was why the divorce rate had been so much lower then. Constant communication, especially between men and women, was overrated in Ivy's opinion. A marriage could be very quiet, but good and strong. Still, it would have been nice to have a husband who had talked to her more, who had thought she was more interesting than whatever happened to be on TV that evening. That hadn't happened, though. It hadn't been Ivy's life or her marriage. She had made her peace with it, all those long, silent years she spent with John. What else could she have done?

She still had the lustrous blue pills in her palm. She rolled them around and watched them slide and bump up against one another. According to the Internet, you could overdose on them and die. People did things like that. They always had. Ivy could understand why, since she'd been sad in her own life. She'd once known a woman at her church, Helen Moriarty, who had committed suicide. Helen Moriarty looked like a pioneer woman—a frail pioneer woman, the kind who always died before the wagon train got to California and got buried in a lonely, makeshift grave on the prairie. Her hair was a faded blond and her eyes light blue. She always wore cotton dresses with dainty, faint floral prints that looked as if they'd been washed too many times.

Once, Ivy had shared a hymnal with Helen. They had both stared straight ahead, singing. Ivy couldn't remember much about Helen's voice—just that it was as tremulous as the hand that shared the hymnal with her. Finally, the hymnal was shaking so much that Ivy used her second hand to steady it.

Helen's eyes had stared downward and she never said anything. She never looked at Ivy after the hymn was over; just bowed her head and acted like she was praying.

About a month later, Ivy heard Helen had hanged herself. Everyone—especially everyone at their church—had been deeply shocked and very excited by the suicide. Too excited, Ivy had thought, too eager for any kind of information or speculation. It had been unseemly and distressing. Helen had attracted far more attention in her death than in her life. Where had those people who were now gossiping about her been when her hands shook so badly they could hardly hold a hymnal? What had they noticed or cared about then?

But, but, but. That was beside the point. The point, to Ivy, was that she was not like Helen, even though she felt horrible and hopeless right now. Ivy would always finish what she had begun—her marriage, her life, all her earthly obligations. She would see it through somehow, no matter how much it hurt. She would take the pills if that was what the doctor and Joanie wanted her to do.

"I should go back to my novel," Bruce said. "I feel like a failure—not finishing it."

"But you're still known for your ads," Joanie protested. She hated it when Bruce's self-deprecation turned to bitterness like this. "They're highly regarded by everyone in the industry."

They were eating lunch at a Greek restaurant close to their office. Joanie was currently jamming a giant chicken sandwich in a pita halfway inside her mouth. If she ever got any money, she would go to Greece immediately and eat like this three meals a day.

"Yeah, but I'd like to be known for something else, too," Bruce said. "I'd like to go back and dig the novel out of a drawer—wherever it is. Finish it. Make it better. Take a chance."

"So, do it," Joanie said. "Or don't. You're the one who's always jumping on me about complaining too much."

"That's different."

"Yes, I know," Joanie said. "Women take criticism better than men." She lay her sandwich down so she could clean the sauce off her chin. "Besides, most people live and die without leaving much behind. Isn't it how you live your life that counts?"

"Spoken like someone who's younger than I am," Bruce said.

"Spoken like someone who's about to turn fifty," Joanie said.

Her birthday was next week, as a matter of fact. She still hadn't decided on anything. Mary Margaret had been bugging her about a party or a dinner out. Caroline, despite many obvious hints from Joanie, had failed to react much. Ivy—well, Ivy had continued to be quiet and leaden, her eyes barely open, as if she didn't want to see the world around her. But recently, Joanie had to admit, her mother seemed a little more like herself. Maybe there was hope after all. Her mother might even stop stealing in the future.

"Maybe you're right," Bruce said.

"Of course I'm right."

"I don't—" Bruce began.

"Well, hello there!"

The voice was familiar, even if Joanie hadn't heard it in person for a few months. It was Richard, standing over their table. His face was fixed into a megawatt smile. He'd lost a few pounds since Joanie had last seen him and his skin glowed with a light tan. He looked annoyingly good. If Joanie had constructed any dreams about how unhappy he was after the fatal mistake he had made in leaving her, they expired quickly.

"Richard Pilcher," Richard said, extending his right hand to Bruce.

Bruce stood up and shook Richard's hand, introducing himself. He was taller than Richard. Richard looked down at Joanie, then up at Bruce, and smiled even more brilliantly. "Are you two friends?"

"Yes," Joanie said quickly. "It's so lovely to run into you, Richard. What a nice surprise."

"I'm sorry if I interrupted you," Richard said. His eyes searched Joanie's face, looking for something.

"Not at all," Joanie said.

Richard nodded pleasantly. "Nice to meet you, Bruce," he said. He took a couple of steps back, then walked off, his face still glowing with that surreal smile.

"God," Joanie said. She put her fork down.

"The ex-husband," Bruce said. With two ex-wives, he was more practiced at these meetings than she was. "How was it for you?"

Good question. How was it for her? It had been surprising, really. Joanie had looked up at Richard's face and—after her initial surprise—had felt very little. No drama, no fury, no heartbreak, no rejection, no unrequited love. Just a view of someone she had finally started to forget.

When, at what precise point, she wondered, had she begun to fall out of love with Richard? It had happened so gradually and subtly, she had hardly been aware of it.

Once, many years ago, when she first met Richard, her heart had hammered wildly when she saw him. Over the seventeen years of their marriage, that wild beating had been replaced with something as steady and regular as a metronome. Then, after he left her, she'd thought her heart had been ripped from her chest and squeezed into a vise of agony; if it beat or not, she didn't care, couldn't tell. But now, *finally*, it was steady once again. The pain had muted to something small and manageable—an annoyance, a trifle, a memory. When had that happened? Why hadn't she noticed it till today?

"It was all right," she said to Bruce. She cocked her head and looked down at the floor, where an answer was presumably lurking. "It was surprisingly all right."

"That's the way it happens," Bruce said.

"Hello?"

"Joanie!"

"Yes, Richard. Hello." Joanie eyed the scene in the dining room, where Caroline was lightheartedly dancing around, depositing plates at the table for dinner. What on earth had happened to her today? Joanie hadn't seen her this happy in decades. Was she on Ecstasy or something?

Oh, no. Of course not. She was in love. How could Joanie have been so blind and dumb?

"It was wonderful to run into you today," Richard said. "And to meet your new beau."

"What do you mean, *beau*?"

"You know exactly what I mean, Joanie. Your new boy-friend."

"We're friends, Richard. Good friends."

Richard laughed heartily. A little too heartily, in Joanie's estimation. She continued to watch the dining room scene, with her whirling dervish daughter with either the personality transplant or the drug addiction or the possible loss of virgin-ity. In the meantime, Ivy had planted herself in her usual seat at the table and was hardly moving. She looked better, almost cheerful, though. Maybe her antidepressants were starting to kick in. Good grief, was Joanie the only person in this house-hold who wasn't on mind-altering drugs? Evidently so. Even if Caroline were "only" in love, though, Joanie considered that to be one of the more powerful, potentially fatal natural phar-maceuticals around.

"You can't fool me, Joanie. I know you too well. I saw the way you were looking at each other."

This was too much. Joanie's eyes zoomed to the ceiling, where she saw the usual number of cobwebs.

"Don't be silly, Richard. We're friends. Coworkers."

Richard laughed with some kind of odd hilarity. Joanie got it. The more she protested and told the truth, the more con-vinced he became that she was lying and carrying on a torrid affair, with lengthy morning trysts followed by tzatziki at the Greek restaurant. Well, fine. Let him think that if he wanted. And he did seem to want it.

"I saw your face, Joanie. You looked like a woman in love."

"I have to go, Richard. We're about to start dinner."

"Can I talk to Caroline for a minute? She's not answering her phone."

Joanie shoved the phone in Caroline's direction, mouthing the words, *it's your father.*

"You're not answering your phone?" Joanie asked Caroline after she hung up the landline.

Caroline shrugged. "I'm trying to keep the line open." The corners of her mouth turned up into what most people would call an irrepressible grin. Very strange. Caroline had never had much of a grin, much less anything you could call *irrepressible.* Truth was, she probably hadn't smiled in a couple of years. Joanie was thrilled her facial muscles had a memory of a happy expression.

"Was it anything important?" Joanie asked. "From your father, I mean."

"Nope." Caroline sat down at the table across from her grandmother. "He just wanted to tell me he was going to be out of town next week."

"Why?" Joanie sat down, too.

Caroline rolled her eyes, with the same cheery, devil-may-care effervescence she was bringing to every gesture and expression tonight. "He just wanted me to watch out for B.J. She gets really nervous when he's out of town."

Caroline paced around her room.

She hung up some of her clothes, like Joanie was always nagging her to do.

She lowered the shade.

She stared in the mirror to see if she looked different. She did. She looked better than usual. She had color in her face and, for once, she was smiling without forcing herself to try to look happy.

She peeked down the front of her blouse to see if her breasts had grown. They had, just a little.

She emptied out her backpack on the floor and sat down beside it.

She put her head between her legs, since she was feeling a little faint.

She opened a textbook. Algebra. Boring. She slammed it shut. She couldn't concentrate. Not now.

She bit her nails.

She jumped up and looked in the mirror again. She screwed her face up to look surprised. She turned her face left and right to see which was her good side. They both looked the same. She didn't have a good side.

She flopped on her bed.

She pulled a pillow over her head and imagined Henry's face as he spoke to her.

She opened her phone to see if the battery was dead. It wasn't.

She tried to read another textbook. It was even more boring than the first.

She took deep breaths. She tried to relax. She imagined she was on a tropical island, lying on the sand, getting warm and tanned from the sun.

She checked her cell phone for the time. It was eight forty-one.

Her phone rang—*finally*. But it was the little beeping noise it made when Sondra called.

"Yeah?" Caroline answered.

"Has he called yet? Or texted you?" Sondra asked.

"No." Caroline fell back on her bed.

"It's still early. He probably stays up really late."

"Gotta get off," Caroline said. "I need to keep the line clear."

"Call me the second after you talk to him. The very *second*."

"Yeah, sure. Bye."

Caroline hung up, feeling deflated. For some reason, she knew he wouldn't call. Not tonight. She'd misjudged something, everything. She finally understood that.

"I ran into my ex-husband today," Joanie announced. "At lunch."

Everybody in the divorcée support group sat up a little straighter. News of chance sightings of exes was always treated with minute attention and clenched faces.

"How did you feel about that, Joanie?" Denise asked, furrowing her brow and leaning forward.

"Not bad," Joanie said. Around the circle, faces relaxed a little. Maybe it wasn't the time for lit torches and an impromptu lynch mob. "It didn't affect me the way I thought it would. It didn't really affect me much at all."

"You're healing," Denise said in her best Mother Earth voice, which always made Joanie squirm. "It's happening finally."

"How did he look?" Lori asked.

"A little too tan. A little too cheerful," Joanie said. (On the whole, the group always preferred to hear news of ex-husbands who were emaciated and haunted by the grave, life-wrecking mistakes they'd made by ending their marriages. Too tan and too cheerful weren't qualities they looked for.)

"Creep," someone said.

"What a dick," someone else said. She was new to the group, but already had lots of opinions. Such as all ex-husbands were dicks.

"Was he by himself?" Lori wanted to know.

"I think so," Joanie said. "But *I* wasn't. I was with a friend from work. A man."

"Just a friend?" Sharon asked.

"Just a friend." Joanie could feel herself smiling. "But Richard didn't think so. He called me up later to talk about my new boyfriend. He kept saying he could tell I was in love again." It was odd how much it pleased her, in spite of herself. She liked the fact that Richard was thinking about her. It served him right—after all the months she'd sobbed and taken to her bed about him. Even if it wasn't true about her and Bruce. Especially if it wasn't true.

"Men always see what they want to see," Denise said.

"And women don't?" Joanie asked crossly. Denise and her New Age babble were starting to get on her nerves. What did she think she was? An oracle?

"Women are more reality based than men," Denise said. "More grounded. It has to do with our monthly cycles."

"I don't have any more monthly cycles," Lori said. "Does that mean I'm not grounded?"

"You know what I mean," Denise said, sounding irritated.

"Did you tell him you were just friends?" Sharon said.

"Twice, three times." Joanie shrugged. "The more I denied it, the more he thought it was true."

"Keep denying it," Lori advised. "It'll drive him nuts."

"As long as you're at it, why don't you deny you're sleeping with the yard guy and the postman?" Sharon said. "He'll think you're fucking all three of them."

"I don't think this discussion is very productive," Denise said.

"That's what makes it fun," Lori said.

"Who else are you not fucking?" Sharon asked.

"Everybody," Joanie said. "The whole world."

"Then *maybe*," Denise said a little more loudly, "we should talk about why you've shied away from dating, Joanie." She sat up straighter, raising her eyebrows dramatically. "We come to these groups so we can heal. Seeing other people is a part of that."

"I'm happier not seeing anybody right now," Joanie said. "I've already told you that a million times. I thought I was supposed to listen to myself."

"Have you decided how long you'll remain celibate?" Denise asked.

"*Celibate?*" Joanie snapped. "I'm not a priest. I'm just not having sex at the moment."

"Which is the definition of celibate," Denise said. "Sexual intimacy is one of life's great joys."

Spare me, Joanie thought. "According to whom?" she asked.

"According to Denise," Sharon said.

"Not me," Denise said. "I'm just *suggesting* that Joanie is missing something truly wonderful. Because she's afraid she's going to get hurt again."

"Of *course* she's afraid she's going to get hurt again," Lori said. "We're all afraid of that."

"Well," Denise said. "It's just that Joanie seems stuck to me."

"That's funny," Joanie said, shrugging. "I don't feel stuck. I'm just trying to figure things out."

"What's wrong with that?" Sharon asked.

"There's no right and wrong," Denise said wearily. "We're talking about making healthier lives for ourselves." She paused, making sure everyone was listening. "I just feel that Joanie is resisting change."

"I hate change," Sharon said. "Why shouldn't Joanie resist it?"

"Because life is change," Denise said. "We don't have any control over—"

"I've got to go," Lori said. "The babysitter can only stay till nine." She stood up. "But I still think Joanie is right. She's trying to do what's best for her." She stared at Denise calmly, almost daring her to answer. "Isn't that why we're here?"

Caroline's phone buzzed. It must be a text. A text! Her heart promptly stopped beating.

She opened the text, her hands clammy. It was from B.J. Wait till you see my new surprise! she'd written.

chapter 15

"This may cheer you up, Mother," Joanie said.

She and Ivy were driving back from an early-morning doctor's office visit. Joanie had phoned Zoe to let her know she was coming in late, but she'd only reached Zoe's voice mail. She hoped it was all right. Zoe had seemed so deranged and out of control recently, like a marionette being jerked around by a drunken puppeteer.

"What?" Ivy was staring out of the passenger's seat window. The world whizzed by, fast and relentlessly. Where were all these people going? Why did they have to get there so quickly? Who were they? Didn't they realize life was a bitter charade and they'd all be dead soon? Ivy scowled. She was feeling very put out these days. But put out, she told herself, was better than depressed.

"David," Joanie said, gripping the steering wheel and making a half-turn toward her mother. "David may be coming here to visit us. To visit *you*, I mean."

"Why?" Ivy's voice was like a karate chop, quick and flat.

"Why?" Joanie botched a right turn, almost grazing the curb, and glanced at her mother's profile. No information there. Ivy just stared straight ahead. "What do you mean, *why?*"

"He never comes here," Ivy said. "He never calls or writes. Why should he be coming now?"

"I thought you'd be excited," Joanie said, deciding to skip the bald-faced, feel-good lies that were clamoring to be spoken. A subtle accusation might work better. A little guilt. Yes.

"He doesn't want to come. Does he?"

"Well, yes, of course he does!" So much for the subtle accusations. Joanie was now embracing the lie. The big lie. "It was *his* idea to come. He called me about it."

Ivy sniffed audibly, but didn't answer. Finally, after several long seconds, she answered. "He doesn't want to come. He hasn't been in touch with me for weeks. You can't fool me, Joanie. You've always been a terrible liar."

Joanie pulled into the garage and stopped the car. Ivy was right. Joanie couldn't have bluffed Helen Keller in a game of poker. She'd always been like this—a little too open and honest. She sighed. "You're right. I'm sorry. I just wanted to help."

"It's all right." Ivy shrugged her shoulders. "I'm feeling a little better these days. Maybe the medication's helping. But I'm going to be all right. David doesn't need to come for my sake."

Men, Joanie thought spitefully. Right now, she wanted to

kill the lot of them. Everywhere she looked, they were hurting women, disappointing women, wiping their feet on women. Sons, lovers, ex-husbands—it didn't matter. They were all the same.

"There's a Dorothy Parker poem about this," she told her mother. "Something about how men will flick you from their sleeve."

Ivy looked at her, the corners of her mouth turning up in an expression that resembled amusement. "You've got the quote wrong," she said.

She sat up straight and began to recite:

> *He will leave you white with woe,*
> *If you go the way you go.*
> *If your dreams were thread to weave*
> *He will pluck them from his sleeve.*
> *If your heart had come to rest,*
> *He will flick it from his breast.*

"I've always loved that poem," Ivy said. "I memorized it when I was just a girl. Do you know the title? It's 'To a Much Too Unfortunate Lady.'"

"I'd forgotten that," Joanie said.

Dear David, Ivy wrote at the computer, Joanie tells me you may be planning to come to Texas to see us.

Ivy looked at that sentence. For just a minute, her eyes filled with tears. She pulled out a handkerchief and dabbed her face. Then she went on.

When she told me that, I realized you were thinking about coming because she had urged you. Because I had been "depressed," as the doctor said, and because I engaged in some regrettable behavior. If you are really thinking about coming here, it is only out of a sense of duty and guilt.

So, please, do not come.

I am on antidepressants and am feeling much better.

Again, Ivy paused. She searched her mind for what she wanted to say to her son, the person she had always loved more than anyone else in the world. She could never say what she really felt—that, in spite of all her love for him, he had abandoned her and didn't really care about her. And he'd broken her heart.

No, she could never say that. She had never chosen to love David as much as she did. Similarly, he had never chosen to be loved so much by her. It had simply happened—one of those odd facts of life that visited themselves on you. No one was at fault or they were all at fault.

Love, Mom

She pressed the SEND button and watched the email disappear from her screen. There. She had set him free. It was the right thing to do.

Ivy placed her chin in her hands. Then she pulled her hands out and looked at them closely. Her veins were ropy and blue and her skin was mottled with freckles and age spots. They were the hands of an old woman, still vaguely unfamiliar to her. The body withered on its own schedule. The mind, she had been noticing, did, too.

But Ivy still had some faith in the heart; that neglected organ. Her heart, she felt, had aged in a different way from the rest of her. It had finally rid itself of some kind of silliness and baseless hopes. Once it finally got stripped of youth and high spirits and recklessness about love, it began to see life more clearly. Too bad you had to be this old for that to happen.

It had taken her all these years to see her two children more clearly, to understand them both better than she once had. She had overly esteemed one while consistently underestimating the other. She had done some damage, she knew. She had amends she needed to make.

"Did you hear?" Bruce asked. He leaned into Joanie's doorway a few minutes after she'd gotten to work.

Joanie looked up from the website she'd found—*Depression and the Elderly: What to Do When Your Loved One Doesn't Want to Go On.* "It's very confusing to be an older person in our youth-obsessed society," the website had begun. "No wonder so many of our elders feel left out and distraught." No shit, Joanie had thought. Try being almost fifty in this youth-obsessed society. That sucks, too.

She closed the computer window. "Hear what?"

"We didn't get the car account. And Zoe's been fired."

"Fired?" Joanie echoed. "That's awful." The car account wasn't that big a deal. But Zoe! Her career was her life. She loved her job, even if it drove her crazy, made her drive everybody else crazy. "What will Zoe do?"

Bruce shrugged. "Find another job, work insane hours, have another nervous breakdown."

"During a recession?"

"Zoe's the type who always survives. She's like a cockroach."

"Oh." Well, Bruce certainly sounded very matter-of-fact about the whole thing. All this ad agency cynicism got a little distressing sometimes. Joanie should go to work for a nonprofit, she often thought. Try to save the world or the whales or some other endangered species or something. Anything noble. A car dealership wasn't noble. "What will happen—well, to *us*?"

"We'll worry about that later," Bruce said. "Some new creative director is already coming in from Dallas."

"Already?"

"They don't wait for the body to cool off, Joanie." Bruce opened her door and stepped halfway out. "Anyway, the whole creative staff is going out for lunch and drinks together."

"Why—after something like this just happened?"

"Tradition. Kind of like a wake."

"Did he call?" Sondra asked. Her eyes were wide and avid.

"No," Caroline said miserably. "He didn't call. He didn't text." She slumped against her locker and rubbed her head against the cold metal. After being so excited for so many hours, she hadn't been able to sleep much.

Wasn't it odd, she'd been thinking over and over that morning, that you could focus so much on another person—and he didn't think of you at all, barely noticed you? She'd relived the hallway scene over and over in her mind in the past twenty-four hours. Had Henry even thought of it once? How could two people walk away from the same experience with such different reactions?

Answer: Because they hadn't had the same experience. They didn't even live on the same planet or inhabit the same universe. Caroline hated that answer. It made her sick to her stomach—just like her demoralizing therapy session with Karen Abrams. All because she knew it was probably correct. She hated the truth.

Sondra heaved a gigantic sigh. She clutched Caroline's arm, giving it a friendly, sympathetic squeeze. "He probably just got busy. I bet he'll apologize when you see him."

"No, he won't," Caroline said in a small voice. "It will never even occur to him."

She closed the locker door quietly and slipped down the hall to her next class. She slid into her seat and closed her eyes. She wished she could sleep right now, instead of waiting.

The class was American History. Boring.

Caroline glared and crossed her arms in front of her chest. In the row ahead of her, a pretty blond girl named Emily passed a note to a boy, then she turned to smile at him and toss her hair back like she was a model or movie star. The back of the guy's neck got red. He liked Emily. Caroline could tell, just by looking at his neck. Emily, Caroline knew, would never carry her cell phone around for hours, waiting for it to ring or buzz. Her parents probably made her turn it off while she studied since it was always ringing. If the boy she'd passed the note to didn't like her, Emily would find someone else by next period. It wouldn't be a big deal. It wouldn't be like her life was over—the way Caroline's life was over. Girls like Emily had no idea what it was like to be a girl like Caroline or Sondra. They never would. It was as distant an existence to them as Jane Eyre's—assuming they ever read *Jane Eyre*, which they probably didn't. Popular girls didn't have time to read books.

"This happens all the time in the advertising business," Bruce said. "You lose accounts. Creative directors come and go. People get fired. They—"

"*Fired?*" Rachel's face crumpled and turned ashen. "Fired?"

"Well . . . sometimes," Bruce said.

He looked around the table at all the young faces from the agency. For once, they didn't seem as cocksure or casual as they'd been before. They looked troubled and nervous and so terribly young that Joanie wanted to gather them up and hug them as she often tried to with Caroline.

"It can be a tough business," Bruce added gently. He'd been talking to the group for the past few minutes, trying to buoy their spirits—and they'd been listening to him. Oddly, with Zoe's departure, it was as if their roles had been suddenly reversed. Maybe being old wasn't quite the stigma it had been two hours earlier. Maybe people as ancient as Joanie and Bruce might have a little wisdom to offer.

Rachel upended her glass of beer into her mouth, then wiped away the foam with her wrist. "If I get fired . . . I'm going to have to move home with my *parents*."

"Me, too," one of the designers said. His name was Brad.

"Can you imagine?" Horror spread over Rachel's face. It was as if she were contemplating being adopted by rabid wolves or a coven of witches. "I'll die if I have to live with my parents again."

Bruce's eyes shifted to Joanie's briefly. Imagine, they agreed silently, how thrilled these recently liberated, middle-aged parents would be to have their adult children descending on them, schlepping months of accumulation of attitude and posters and beat-up futons in with them. Did that ever occur to the young people around the table? No, of course it didn't. They were young. You never learned things like this until you had to.

Just wait, Joanie thought a little sourly, wait till your elderly parents move in with you and you still have kids at home. Wait till you find out how much fun that is. You'll see. You'll learn. You'll find out what responsibility and self-sacrifice are like someday when you're middle-aged.

She thought about Ivy's set face and slumping shoulders, her stubbornness and her inflexibility. Life had definitely altered for her and Caroline when Ivy moved in with them.

Then she felt an odd, unexpected pang. For the first time, it occurred to her how hard it must have been for her mother to accept Joanie's offer to move to Austin. If going back to your parents' house was hard for twentysomethings—how tough must it be to move in with your own child when you were elderly? How could it be that Joanie had never thought of that before?

"This is an exciting business," Bruce told the group. "It can be great fun—and I've enjoyed it. But you have to expect upheavals like this from time to time."

Around the table, shoulders shrugged. Most of their younger colleagues were on their third or fourth drinks. Joanie was feeling woozy halfway into her second Bloody Mary. She'd never learned to drink on an empty stomach.

Bruce looked at her again and they both smiled. It was a

brief moment, warm and rueful. They were both remembering, she somehow knew, what it was like when you had your first great and jarring disappointment in life, how it felt when you learned the world was unfair and it cracked your heart open and you were sure you would never recover or be happy again.

Joanie missed a few things about being young. But so much—like this—she had no longing for. She was happier where she was now.

The bell rang. Finally. Caroline gathered up her books and walked as slowly as she could to Spanish. Dragging her feet, bumping up against the walls, stopping to let other people go past her. What was she going to do now? Pretend nothing had happened? Accept her destiny as one of life's biggest losers who had fading pink hair and a flat chest and a terminally morose (but not clinically diagnosed) personality?

Henry was already there as she slid into her seat. He was wearing a yellow shirt today, made of a creamy, soft cotton, his head bent over his book. He didn't even notice she was there.

Fuck it, Caroline thought. She might as well self-incinerate, instead of withering away. She reached in front of her and touched Henry on the arm. After a few motionless seconds, he turned slowly around to look at her.

Caroline stared up at him in what she hoped was a come-hither look. She would have even batted her eyelashes, if she had any.

"Have you started that Spanish paper yet?" she asked. She tried to lower her voice so it sounded husky. Men liked husky voices on women. She had read that on some Internet site about being popular.

Henry shook his head. A lock of his hair spilled onto his forehead and he pushed it back. He looked friendly, but vague. Like he kind of knew her, but not really. If she stopped now, Caroline knew, it would never get any better than this. An occasional exchange of words. A semiflirtation that existed mostly in Caroline's mind. Nothing more. Not ever.

Caroline tilted her head at what she hoped was an attractive angle. She smiled, like she knew something, like she was mysterious, like she had something more to give him than tutoring.

"Would you like some help with it?" she asked in her husky voice.

Henry raised his eyebrows. It was like he was seeing her for the first time today. He smiled. "Yeah? That would be great."

Push it, Caroline told herself. Do not, under any circumstances, do what you really want to do—to shrink back into your shell and keep on dreaming. For once in your life, do something. Have a little guts.

"How about tomorrow night?" she asked raspingly. It was hard to keep that husky voice going. She now sounded like a car grinding its gearshift. "At my house?" She pulled her mouth into what she hoped was a little mysterious smile. "We could get a lot of things done."

Henry stared off into the distance, calculating his schedule. "Tomorrow night?" He nodded. "Yeah. Sure. That could work."

Caroline touched him on the arm and smiled. Senora Schmidt was already screaming something in Spanish from the front of the room. People had stopped talking and were swiveling around in their seats toward their teacher. Henry smiled back, briefly, then turned around.

Caroline half-fell back into her seat, her heart thumping wildly. What had she done? She didn't know. But it must have been good.

Back at the office, Joanie stumbled through her door.

"Careful," Bruce said. He grabbed her elbow and left his hand there while Joanie wobbled a little.

"I'm all right," Joanie said. She smiled at him, thinking of how caring and sweet he'd been to their younger colleagues. He was a good guy. She was glad they were friends.

She reached out and, for some reason, pulled him toward her. Bruce kicked the door shut.

Joanie could feel his lips against hers. She could feel her head roll back, as if her body were warm and melting. She put her arms around his neck and kissed him back.

Nerve endings in her breasts and between her legs awakened like a blast furnace. *Damn!* she thought to herself, drawing a quick breath and plunging back in, *I'd forgotten how much I like this.*

"I can tell by your face that something happened," Sondra said.

Caroline flung herself into the car. "Give me a cigarette. Fast." She threw her head back against the torn seat, like a soap-opera actress who's just been ravished by the hero and felt the earth move.

Sondra shook the almost empty pack till it yielded a bent cigarette. "Here."

Caroline sat up to light the cigarette. Her hair got caught in the torn upholstery and she had to pull it out, strand by strand, while Sondra watched. Definitely deflating. People like her just could never get dramatic gestures right.

"Well," Caroline said, inhaling and not even coughing for once, "he's coming over to my house tomorrow night." She emitted a tall white plume of smoke.

"No! Oh, my God!" Sondra fumbled with the limp pack and extracted a cigarette for herself. She lit it, her hands trembling with excitement. "What are you going to do?"

What was she going to do? What was he going to do? What were they going to do together? Caroline hated technical questions like that. They revealed the total lack of romance in her plan. She was going to write a paper for Henry. That was why he was coming. Well, it was, wasn't it? She'd seduced him by promising to do his homework. How romantic was that?

"Oh, I think we'll just study together," Caroline said airily. No need to drown their celebration.

"I could never study with a guy there," Sondra said solemnly. "Especially with somebody as hot as Henry. It would take up all my attention."

"I know." Caroline sat and smoked and contemplated her new life. Or at least she thought it was her new life, since it wasn't quite as boring as her old one. At least something was happening now.

Maybe it wasn't nearly as great as Sondra thought it was. But maybe something good would come of it. Maybe Henry would look at her over the Spanish paper and see her for the first time and fall madly in love with her. Romance can be very circuitous, especially at first.

Caroline stamped out her cigarette in the ashtray. She eased her head back onto the upholstery, taking care so her hair wouldn't get caught again. Maybe she'd just bought a little happiness for a few hours. Well, that was okay. What was wrong with that?

A soft noise. Joanie could hear it just barely, as if it were happening miles and years away. She might as well have been in the middle of Niagara Falls, floodgates open, with a roaring in her ears, a powerful rush surging through her, sending her twirling and spiraling and reeling in ecstasy and—

A louder noise. Joanie turned just as the door opened and fluorescent light poured into the room. She saw a tall, bald man in a three-piece suit standing at the threshold. Behind him, all the youthful faces she and Bruce had just gone drinking with crowded around. In the slowest of slow motion, she could see all their faces turning from anticipation to something she could only describe as horror. Then the door closed as quickly as it had opened.

Joanie fell back on her desk and banged her elbows. She smoothed her hair, which was standing up straight (almost erect, she would have called it). As Bruce stood up, quickly pulling up his pants and fastening his belt, she hoisted up her pantyhose and smoothed her skirt down.

"I—" she started.

"How—" he said at the same time.

They stopped, facing each other in the darkness. They both laughed nervously. Hearing the laughter, Joanie relaxed. It was going to be okay, however it turned out. Somehow, she believed that.

"Who was that bald guy?" she asked.

"Ed Blankensmith. Our new creative director, I'm assuming."

"You know him?"

"I worked with him once. A few years ago."

So Bruce, obviously, needed no introduction to their new boss. Come to think of it, Joanie realized, neither did she.

"Hello?"

"Caroline?"

Great. Just what she needed. B.J.

"Hi," Caroline said, trying to be polite, trying not to be impatient. It was a struggle. She had many, many other important things to think about.

"How are you?"

"Fine." Caroline examined her cuticles. They looked shitty. She wished she could afford to get a professional manicure, like other girls at school. It would help her self-esteem.

"I—I just thought—that maybe we could get together sometime," B.J. said. "Maybe . . . tomorrow night? I could take you out for dinner."

Her voice was uncertain, almost shaky. Listening, Caroline could feel the sadness and desperation. She drew in a long breath and released it quietly.

"I'd really like to, B.J.," she said, "but I've got plans tomorrow night."

"Oh, I just thought— I'm sorry, I—"

"I'd really like to get together," Caroline said. "Another time would be great. It's just that I've got something going on to-morrow night." She felt a weird surge through her body, just thinking about it. Yes, for one time in her life, she actually had plans. Fun, exciting plans! "How are you doing? I know Dad's out of town this week."

"I'm fine," B.J. said a little too quickly.

"What have you been doing?"

"Well . . . lots of things. Going shopping for the baby. Get-ting wedding invitations out. Have you gotten yours yet?"

She had. Caroline had seen the creamy envelope addressed in B.J.'s fat, loopy handwriting, but she hadn't bothered to open it yet. She knew what it was, when the wedding was. Why bother? "No," she lied. "I don't think so."

"Really? Oh, my God. I wonder if it got lost."

"Probably not. Maybe it's just late. You know I'm coming, anyway."

"But everybody else—"

"How many people are you inviting?"

"Twenty-five. Richard—your dad—wanted to keep it small."

Caroline could see B.J., sitting in the kitchen, drinking some kind of health drink for the baby. Just wandering around the big apartment, polishing here and there, reminding her-self how lucky she was. But what did she do all the time, all those hours in the day when Richard was working or out of town? Caroline had never understood. B.J. didn't seem to do much of anything, didn't have that many friends. She was just waiting, seemingly happy, almost floating, in a way Caroline couldn't understand. Didn't she want more? Work, friends, interests? But no, she didn't. She'd told Caroline that. She had everything she'd ever wanted.

"Small weddings are nicer," Caroline said.

"Richard says they're much more tasteful," B.J. agreed.

A lot less expensive, too, Caroline thought. Her father had always been a cheapskate. "How are you feeling?" she asked.

"Oh, bigger. I think I can feel the baby moving now. I'm pretty sure."

B.J. talked on, her featherlight voice lilting over the colors she was putting in the nursery, the china and flatware patterns she'd picked out at the swanky department store in the mall. "I've been so busy," she said. "I haven't even minded being here alone." She cleared her throat. "Did you get my text last night?"

"What text?"

"The text about my big surprise."

Caroline moved guiltily. That's right. She'd wanted to smash her cell phone when she realized it was B.J.—and not Henry— texting her. "Oh—I'm sorry. I didn't answer you, did I?"

Silence. B.J. was pouting, evidently.

"What's your surprise?" Caroline prompted her.

"Can you hear that?" B.J. said.

Caroline could hear something making a noise in the background. "What is it?"

"Just the sweetest, cutest, most adorable thing you've ever seen. Aren't you?"

Oh, no. B.J. was speaking in baby talk. There was nothing Caroline loathed more than baby talk. She hated baby talk more than terrorists, even. "What is it?"

"You're sweet! Yes, you are!" More baby talk. Caroline again considered destroying her phone, the instrument of so much pain in her life. Finally, B.J. quit. "It's my new puppy," she said in her normal voice. "Sir Elvis."

Caroline kept examining her cuticles, listening to B.J. chatter about how Sir Elvis was some kind of rare, very intelligent dog, even smaller than a Chihuahua. The same kind of dog Paris Hilton had before it was kidnapped and held for ransom.

Caroline made occasional sounds when the conversation lagged. "Why don't I call you," she said maybe ten minutes or ten hours later, "after tomorrow night?"

"That would be fine," B.J. said. She and Caroline would have so much to talk about then, when they finally had the time to be together. She knew Caroline was going to love Sir Elvis.

The left rear side of the car screeched as Joanie pulled into the garage. Great. She must have scraped it again. She'd investigate it tomorrow.

She turned off the car and sat there for several minutes, with her head lolling on the headrest, her seat belt unbuckled, her hands idling on the steering wheel. She looked upward, through the moonroof, and noticed that the garage roof had a hole in it. She could see a couple of stars through the hole, twinkling and insistent.

She supposed that she'd just done the dumbest, most irresponsible thing she could have done. Having sex with a colleague. Getting caught in flagrante. Putting on an X-rated exhibition for a group of kids, for God's sake.

As she'd left the office, most of her coworkers had looked

down at their desks. Only Rachel had flashed her a big, mischievous grin—as if she'd finally noticed Joanie for the first time.

Yes, dumb, irresponsible, ridiculous, humiliating, unprofessional, unforgivable, shameful. All of that and more. So why had she been looking up at those two flickering points of light through that hole in her roof, laughing till her stomach began to ache?

chapter 16

No, Joanie had insisted earlier in the week. She didn't want a big party for her fiftieth birthday. She had finally agreed to meet Mary Margaret and Nadine for dinner that night, though. That would be enough celebration for her.

"Happy birthday, hon," Nadine said, when Joanie joined her at the restaurant the next night. "We're gonna get smashed tonight."

"Speak for yourself," Joanie said, easing into a chair. "I'm working tomorrow."

"You can call in sick," Nadine said, slurping her margarita. "Like I'm planning to."

They were at a loud, festive restaurant that served classic Mexican food. Around them, waiters spun and pivoted, delivering red and green salsas and big tropical drinks, and customers at the tables had to scream to hear one another.

"Where's Mary Margaret?" Nadine wanted to know.

"She's always late," Joanie said. She smiled at Nadine, who had dressed up tonight in a fuzzy black miniskirt and a sequined tank top that could have been painted on. She looked thinner and paler, her freckles darker against her whitened skin, circles under her large eyes. There was a whiff of sadness about her that Joanie couldn't quite pinpoint.

But Nadine was happy, she'd assured Joanie. Very happy. Everything with Roy was fine. Well, not exactly fine, but pretty good. She'd explain later. Right now, she didn't want to talk about it.

Joanie understood. She'd hugged Nadine's thin shoulders and given her an extra squeeze. A small birthday celebration at a swanky restaurant wasn't the time to go into details that weren't happy. They'd have plenty of time to talk about it later, as Joanie forged into her fifties. Years and decades to talk about it. Just not tonight. Nobody needed introspection when you had to scream about it.

"Goddamn! I'm sorry I'm late!" Mary Margaret arrived in a thick cloud of perfume and with the clatter of her stilettos, carrying a bouquet of flowers. "Can you put this in some water, hon?" she asked the waiter. "And bring me whatever these girls are having."

She looped an arm around Joanie's neck and planted a kiss on her cheek. "Shit, I got lipstick on you," she said, picking up a napkin and rubbing Joanie's face. "You're looking gorgeous," she announced. "And you must be Nadine," she said, smiling across the table and blowing a big red kiss.

Mary Margaret and Nadine had never met before to-night. But, through Joanie, they knew everything about each other—the shiftless Roy, the handsome married boyfriend, the unsatisfying job at the day care center, the divorcée support group, the heartbreak, the spoiled and messy children at the day care, Mary Margaret's dead but still-domineering mother. Women's friendships were always a buffet of personal details and histories, Joanie had observed. You came to the feast and brought your own contributions. Funny how the offerings never ran out.

"Here you are, miss," the waiter said, easing a margarita in front of Mary Margaret.

"How about a toast?" Nadine said. "To Joanie on her fiftieth birthday—"

"Your best year ever!" Mary Margaret said.

"Your best decade," Nadine said.

They smashed their glasses together, spilling a little liquid and knocking some salt off the rims.

Ivy hoped Joanie didn't expect her to police Caroline and the boy who had just shown up at their front door. Caroline had raced to the door, moving faster than Ivy had ever seen her move, and the two of them had quickly disappeared down the hall. Caroline's bedroom door was shut now and Ivy couldn't hear anything, no matter how patiently she lingered in the hall, pretending to be straightening a framed photograph that hung on the wall.

Well. Joanie hadn't told her Caroline was expecting company. Of course, maybe Joanie didn't know. It wasn't as if

Caroline had lots of friends coming by the house. Just that girl with the purple hair whose name Ivy could never remember. Cassandra or something like that. The plump one. People named their children such odd things these days. How could she be expected to remember?

Ivy hoped that Joanie had already told Caroline the facts of life. Would it be out of line for her, as Caroline's grandmother, to knock on the door and talk to the child? She certainly hoped she wouldn't have to. As a veteran mother, Ivy had already talked to her own two children about sex. Surely that was enough for any one person. She couldn't be expected to enlighten a new generation, could she?

A year or two ago, she would have been enormously shocked that a teenage boy and girl were in the same room together—a bedroom!—with the door closed. But now, as an avid reader of several advice columns on the Internet, she knew this had become a common situation in most households.

Boys and girls even had slumber parties together these days! Ivy shook her head, wondering what her neighbor Myra would have said about that. "What are their parents thinking?" she and Myra would have murmured to each other. "Have they gone insane?" But Myra was dead and Ivy didn't have any longtime friends to discuss the terrible state of the world with. Death and moves had left her alone, wandering through that facsimile of life and companionship on the Internet. It wasn't enough, it wasn't the same thing. Still, it was something.

She quietly positioned herself at the computer, which was about ten yards away from Caroline's room. If anything untoward were going on—if the girl screamed, for instance—Ivy would be ready to force the door open and, if necessary, call the police. She could always throw something at the boy—a book, perhaps, or a vase—in an emergency.

In the meantime, she needed to look busy and preoccupied. Ivy typed in her email address, then her password. The computer made its usual whirring noises, then jumped to Ivy's in-box.

There was nothing in it. Not even one of those nasty emails about growing a big, hard penis. Or somebody from Nigeria begging for her help to transfer a fortune. Just—nothing.

David hadn't replied. Was he angry? Or just relieved he didn't have to come to visit her?

She moved quickly to another site. There was always something else to read, stories about someone whose problems were far worse than her own.

"So, where do we start?" Henry asked. He turned and smiled at Caroline.

It was amazing. There he was, sitting on her bed in her newly cleaned room. He'd never have any idea how long she'd worked on the bed to make it look neat, how hard she yanked on the bedspread so it would conceal all the papers and books and dirty clothes she'd stashed under the bed. Half her belongings were under that bed. It was amazing it wasn't floating.

Caroline angled her head so her freshly washed hair moved over her shoulder in what she hoped was a seductive ripple. *Where do we start?* Why didn't he grab her and kiss her? Wasn't that what was supposed to happen? They were in her bedroom, weren't they?

She looked up at him out of the corner of her eye. His jeans fit him perfectly and his bronze shirt made him look more handsome than she'd ever seen him. Too bad she didn't have candlelight in her room. Joanie always acted like candles were a big fire hazard, but what did she know? Candlelight would have improved the atmosphere of her room, with its frayed posters and garage-sale lamp and stupid lavender walls (why on earth had Joanie let her paint it that awful color when Caroline was just eight? Weren't mothers supposed to protect you from mistakes like that?).

Caroline smiled in a way she thought might be described as either bewitching or mysterious or deranged, and waited for several seconds. Henry didn't move. She had put on eye makeup—tawny shadow, eyeliner, and black-brown mascara—and he didn't even notice that she looked different. And what about that perfume she'd borrowed from Joanie's cosmetics drawer? Didn't she smell better than she usually did? She guessed not. Maybe she just smelled like her mother.

"We need to get that paper written," Henry said. "It's due next week. And I haven't started it." He smiled again. But he shifted on the bed, a little impatiently, it seemed to Caroline.

"Oh, yeah," Caroline said, as if she'd forgotten all about the assignment. Which she had of course. Why would she be thinking about some stupid Spanish assignment she could whip out in twenty minutes when Henry was going to be coming to her house?

"I thought that we were going to be working on it," Henry said. "That's why I came over."

That's why I came over. Caroline drew in a shaky breath and let the words rattle around in her mind. *That's why I came over*.

Henry might as well have taken a sledgehammer and bludgeoned Caroline's rabbity little heart with it. She could feel it crack with sudden, unexpected pain.

For just an instant, she tried, desperately, to concentrate on the tiny spurt of hope from his using the first person plural. *We* were going to be working on it. The two of them. They were a couple, a team.

But, no. She knew better than that.

Caroline straightened her posture and looked Henry straight in the eye for the first time that evening. He had such a handsome face. She had memorized his features, going over them lovingly at night, when she was alone and the room was dark. What she had never memorized or noticed before was this expression on his face—the partly curled lip, the eyes flintier than she'd seen them before. There was a hardness there that never came in her dreams. It was unexpected.

Caroline could feel a few silly tears rushing into her eyes. She blinked them away. Grow up, she told herself. Just grow up. Stop being such a baby.

"You're right," she said, standing up and lurching toward her textbook and laptop. "We don't have that much time. We need to get started."

Maybe her eyes were a little pink and moist. Maybe her carefully applied eye makeup would begin to run. But she knew Henry wouldn't notice. Had he ever even looked at her, seen her at all?

She couldn't think about that now. All she could do was to do what he wanted. Talk about the paper. Explain it to him. Get him started. Write it for him. Try to salvage a small bit of dignity by not whimpering and sobbing in front of him. She could cry later and scream into her pillow, if she felt like it. She just had to get through the next hour or so.

"He's never going to leave his fucking wife," Mary Margaret said. "I know that." She pulled her chin up and stared at the ceiling, like some kind of personal message might be printed there. "Hell, I've known that for years."

"Goddamn men," Nadine said. "Goddamn fucking men." She pointed to her drink and asked the waiter for another. Her third.

Nadine and Mary Margaret were getting along famously. How strange, Joanie thought. They inhabited opposite sides of the dilemma—with Nadine having been cheated on and Mary Margaret sleeping with a cheater. But that seemed to be a minor detail tonight. As long as the margaritas flowed, they could agree that it was all men's fault. Blame men for everything!

"I haven't had this much fun in a year," Mary Margaret proclaimed. "Hell, in *years*."

"Fuckin' A," Nadine said. That seemed to be her answer to everything.

Joanie, the birthday girl, the honoree, the cause of all this fun and drinking and repeated *Fuckin' A*s, had had better nights. Lots of them. Right now, she'd rather be home washing her hair, curled up in a bathrobe, contemplating her life, falling asleep on the couch. She hated being a boring, stick-in-the-mud third wheel to all this fun and these raucous high jinks, these whispered intimacies about men and heartbreak and threats of wrenching testicles off and shooting penises with AK-47s. Hated it.

"*You* aren't saying very much, Joanie," either Nadine or Mary Margaret would observe every few minutes. They would stop their chatter and their sloppy, moronic toasts and turn to her guiltily. "My God! We've been doing all the talking! Let's talk about you!"

Joanie hated that even worse—the forced concentration on her from two women she normally liked so much. But not right now, not tonight, not in the shape they were in. Was there anything worse than being the only one who wasn't having any fun? The only one who wasn't drunk on her ass and throwing her head back to howl with laughter at something that wasn't remotely funny?

She could have grabbed the center stage of course. She could have announced that she'd just become the office tramp, caught in the act with a colleague. Caught with Bruce—who was what to her? She didn't know. He was sweet and funny and she was fond of him. He was also in really good shape, with a sculpted butt and powerful legs, she'd noticed. He'd been a lot sexier with his clothes almost off; she'd never noticed before.

So, her years of no sex appeared to be over. But now what? She needed to think. She needed some time to herself. She needed to talk to Bruce and say—well, she had no earthly idea what she would say. But they were good enough friends to be able to talk, weren't they? What did he want? What did she?

If she could have vanished from her birthday celebration, she would have. Just like that, disappearing into the cosmos. Instead, she had to stay, because this was her birthday and these were her best friends. She had to paste an insincere grin on her face and pretend to chortle whenever Mary Margaret or Nadine unleashed a new, fresh diatribe about Roy or Marc or the women their lovers really loved and how life was bearing down on lonely middle-aged women like the two of them, creasing their faces with crepe-paper wrinkles and plummeting their breasts and butts, now pockmarked with cellulite and neon blue veins, directly toward the earth, like a runaway elevator. God, it was so unfair.

"Shouldn't we think about ordering?" Joanie asked. She sounded tentative and that irritated her. Why should she be tentative at her own fiftieth birthday? "I'm hungry."

"I'm gonna drink my dinner," Nadine said. "But let's order for you, hon. You look a little peaked."

"What's that sound?" Henry asked.

"Nothing," Caroline said.

"Isn't it your cell?"

Of course it was her cell. Sondra, probably, unable to resist calling to find out whether Caroline was still a virgin and whether she'd used the whole fresh, unused package of condoms Sondra had gotten from her cousin. Sondra calling to know what sex was really like. Was it better than weed?

"I'm not answering it," Caroline said. "We need to finish this paper."

"Suit yourself," Henry said. He crossed his legs and fell back on the bed. He looked happy. How nice that one person in the room was happy. Caroline leaned in closer to the computer and started to write. For once, Henry was going to turn in a stellar paper.

~~~~~~~

"What about Richard?" Mary Margaret asked.

"What about him?" Joanie countered, tearing into her crab-meat enchiladas. She was starving. At least the enchiladas gave her something to focus on.

"Well—how is he?" Nadine said. "Him and that girlfriend of his—"

"The albino," Mary Margaret said.

"She's an albino?" Nadine turned to Joanie, frowning and trying to focus. "You never told me that."

Joanie shrugged, refusing to stop eating. "They're getting married. Having a baby. Same thing. Nothing new."

"I've never seen an albino. Except on the Internet." Nadine shook her head disapprovingly. "I thought they were kind of like unicorns. You know, not real."

"She has pink eyes," Mary Margaret said. "That's how you can tell she's an albino."

"Pink eyes?" Nadine turned to Joanie. "He left you for someone with pink eyes?"

Joanie could feel her jaw start to lock. This was just exactly, precisely how she didn't want to spend her fiftieth birthday—talking about Richard and B.J. Working on a sense of outrage and hurt she no longer felt. Dredging it up, shoveling it all over the table, ruining Joanie's hearty appetite, and spoiling her million dollar crabmeat enchiladas.

"Richard didn't leave me for anybody," she said flatly. "He just left."

"I think that's worse," Nadine said. "You mean he just didn't want *you*?"

"He didn't want to be married to anybody," Joanie said. And he still doesn't, she knew. Not that it mattered. She could have brought that up, could have shown that B.J. wasn't really a threat to her, pink eyes or not. But why bother? Besides, the more Joanie had heard from Caroline's occasional comments, the less ill will she felt toward B.J. The more she heard, the more she'd begun to feel sorry for B.J. And Richard. The whole world, really.

"No, it's better," Mary Margaret insisted. "This way, you don't end up comparing yourself to somebody else—wondering what's wrong with you. What's so great about her. Why he chose her, instead of you."

"I'd rather be left for somebody else," Nadine said stubbornly. "That way, you have two people to blame."

They began to argue the point, loudly and enthusiastically. Joanie returned to her enchiladas and tried to glance at her watch without being noticed. It was still early. Way too early.

The phone in the kitchen rang. It awakened Ivy, who had fallen asleep in her chair, with her head on her folded arms over the keyboard.

She looked around. The girl never answered the phone in the kitchen. That was because it was never for her, Joanie said. Most kids just cared about calls on their own cell phones. They didn't want to answer the "landline."

Ivy pushed down on the table and rose to her feet. When she was younger, she had never taken naps. Now that she was past seventy-five, though, she noticed she fell asleep everywhere. Sometimes she woke herself up by her loud snoring.

"Hello. Pilcher residence."

A long silence. Ivy was about to hang up, since it was clearly one of those awful sales calls asking her to buy land in some place she'd never go to. But then she heard a muffled sound in the background. It sounded like someone crying.

"Hello?" Ivy said again.

"Yes—hello. May I speak to Caroline, please?" The voice was young and uncertain. It must be one of Caroline's friends. The girl with the purple hair. Why would she be crying?

"Are you all right, dear?" Ivy asked.

Another silence. More muffled sounds in the background. Finally, the girl began to talk again. "I—no, I'm not all right. I just need to speak to Caroline, please." A great, tremulous sigh at the other end of the phone. *"Please."*

Ivy held the phone at arm's length and stared at it. The girl with the purple hair sounded terrible. It must be an emergency of some sort. Ivy stepped away from the kitchen and carried the phone to Caroline's door, where she knocked loudly.

"What?" Caroline's voice was surly. Ivy didn't know why Joanie didn't teach her better manners. She didn't even bother to open the door as a polite young woman should have been taught.

"Telephone for you," Ivy told the closed door.

A great exhalation of breath from behind the door. "I'm busy now," Caroline said. "Can't it wait?"

Ivy turned the knob and opened the door, sticking her head in. "No, it cannot." She stared at the two teenagers inside the bedroom. The boy was surprisingly good-looking, with smooth, full brown hair and a deep tan. He looked annoyed. So did

Caroline, who was sitting at her desk, using her laptop computer.

Ivy covered the receiver. "I'm afraid whoever is on the line is very distressed. I don't believe this can wait, Caroline."

Caroline heaved herself out of her chair and marched up to Ivy. "All right, all right." She yanked the receiver up to her ear. "Yeah?"

Ivy stepped back a little, watching her granddaughter. Caroline's face paled almost immediately as she listened. "Oh, my God," she said. "What? Are you—are you—does it hurt?"

More noises from the other end of the line—a voice that rose and fell in anguish. Then, sobs.

"Lie down," Caroline said. "Just lie down. But—but, wait. Leave the door unlocked. We'll be there in a minute." She looked at Ivy, her face twisted in an odd, painful way. "Just lie down. Please. Just be still. Okay?"

Caroline pushed the hang-up button, then pressed in a new number. Ivy watched her granddaughter's face while the phone rang. In the background, she could see the young man get up and stretch, then pop his knuckles one by one.

"Mom!" Caroline shouted. "Mom, you've got to come home immediately. B.J.'s bleeding. She's scared to death. We need to go over there."

chapter 17

By the time Joanie arrived home, her brakes screeching in the driveway, Henry was already gone. He had nodded politely enough to Ivy, then waved at Caroline. Caroline had hardly looked at him, hardly noticed he was leaving. That was strange, Ivy thought. But she didn't say anything. She just watched Caroline's face, surprised by how emotional and haunted it seemed.

B.J.—she was Richard's girlfriend, Ivy knew. His fiancée, rather. She was pregnant—and due when? Around August. Ivy didn't want to ask Caroline, who already seemed overcome with the responsibility of it all. But yes, that would make her four months pregnant. Just about the same length Ivy had carried her first baby before she lost it. "You'll have another one," they had all told her, when they bothered to say anything. "You'll forget all about this." But she hadn't. She'd never forgotten that horrible feeling of life slipping out, bloody and formless, between her legs. She had lain down to try to stop it, but she couldn't. It had leaked out in a painful rush that buckled her knees and left her sobbing and clutching her stomach. "Good thing you weren't any further along," John had said. It had been the only thing he had ever said to her about the miscarriage.

Oh, John. He had never understood much of anything.

As the horn honked—was Joanie sitting on it or something?—Caroline grabbed Ivy's elbow and propelled her outside, into the soft night air. Ivy had no idea why she was going, since she had never laid eyes on this B.J. But Caroline seemed to want her to come. For once. Besides, Ivy felt alert and ready for anything after her brief nap.

"Caroline, you scared me to death!" Joanie shouted the minute they opened the car door. "Don't ever scare me like that again! I thought something had happened to you—or to Grandma!"

Caroline slipped into the car and burst into loud tears. "I didn't know what to do. B.J.'s scared to death of blood." She wiped her nose with her hand. "She was all alone—and she doesn't have any friends. Just us."

Oh, well, that explains it, Joanie thought grimly, backing the car out of the driveway and leaving a layer of rubber on the pavement. What did Caroline mean, B.J. didn't have any friends? Everybody had friends. Why did B.J. have to call her almost stepdaughter and her almost husband's ex-wife when she got into a mess? Joanie was beginning to suspect she had the worst karma of anyone on earth. She'd just had a perfectly horrible time at her own birthday dinner (had they even noticed when she'd rushed out?), only to get wrenched away for some kind of emotional crisis her ex-husband's pregnant fiancée was having. Something about something bleeding, she'd heard Caroline say over the roar of the restaurant and Nadine and Mary Margaret's bright and drunken chatter.

"What's wrong with B.J.? Why is she so upset?" Joanie asked. "I couldn't hear you in the restaurant. It was too loud."

"She's bleeding! A lot!" Caroline yelled. "She doesn't know what to do."

"She's miscarrying," Ivy chimed in from the backseat.

"Oh, my God," Caroline said. She had understood the blood, the hysteria, the fear. But she hadn't quite understood that B.J. could be losing her baby. "She wanted that baby so much!" She burst into tears again.

Joanie stopped at a light. Bleeding? A miscarriage? She reached over to touch Caroline, who slumped against her and sobbed. In the rearview mirror, she could see Ivy's sad face staring out the car window.

Joanie drew a long, deep breath. Well. Somebody was going to have to take charge of this situation. She guessed she knew who it would have to be.

"It's going to be all right," she said in a low voice to Caroline. "We'll be there in just a few minutes. We'll take care of her. I promise." Caroline nodded and sniffed.

They pulled into the condominium complex a few minutes later. Caroline had straightened up and was staring anxiously out the windshield. No one had spoken for blocks. From the backseat, Ivy sighed and hummed a tune Joanie didn't recognize. Then she sighed again.

Joanie eased the car into a parking space, then pushed the gear into park. The car shuddered and died. They all exited quickly, but Caroline raced ahead, her skinny legs pumping.

"B.J.! B.J.! We're here!" Caroline pushed in the front door. Silence. "B.J.! Where are you?"

A dog barked. A faint voice answered. "In the bathroom." Caroline raced down the hall.

Joanie stopped at the door, frozen for an instant. She had never been inside Richard's condo before. She'd always dreaded seeing the place where he lived with his new girlfriend. It was different from what she had imagined. His taste had changed, evidently, going from classic traditional to some kind of angular modern, with lots of sharp edges and hard, shiny surfaces.

She looked around quickly. Everything was polished and spotless, with thick, fluffy white carpeting. Stepping on it was like walking on a cloud. Joanie walked across the feathery surface quickly, waiting to be walloped by a storm of emotion and pain. She could feel her heart beating a little more quickly. But that was all. She didn't feel much of anything but the softness of the carpet.

They could hear B.J. sobbing in the bathroom down the hall. There she was, sitting on the toilet, her face clutched to her knees. Her long, tangled hair fell almost to the floor, where a tiny dog lay next to her.

Caroline knelt beside her, coiling a tentative arm around her neck. "Are you okay?" she asked.

B.J. pulled her face out of her hands. Her face was streaked with tears and makeup. "I think I lost it," she said. "I think I lost the baby." Her shoulders began to shake. "Oh, my God," she wailed. "What am I going to do?"

Caroline could feel tears swelling in her own eyes. She squeezed B.J.'s icy hands.

"What happened? Are you all right?" It was Joanie, standing in the doorway. Behind her, Ivy peered over her shoulder, straining to look in.

Joanie stepped into the room and knelt down on the floor next to Caroline. She looked up into B.J.'s tearstained face. "What happened, B.J.?"

The tiny dog sat up and yelped a high-pitched bark. B.J. began to cry harder, till she almost gagged. Joanie grabbed a wad of toilet paper and handed it to her. B.J. mopped her face and rubbed her eyes. Her sobs subsided, growing quieter and farther apart. She pulled the dog up onto her lap.

"B.J.," Joanie said, "you need to tell me what's happened—"

"Mom, she can't talk," Caroline protested. "She's too upset."

"Shhhh," Joanie said. "Hush, Caroline." She leaned in toward B.J. and stared at her intently. "B.J., we have to know what happened to you."

B.J. ran her hand under her nose and sniffed loudly. "I was bleeding."

"Bleeding? Very much? Did you pass anything . . . very big?" Joanie peered into B.J.'s narrow face.

B.J. lowered her eyes. "No," she whispered. "I just bled. That's all."

"A little? A lot? Tell me what happened."

Caroline fell back, sitting on the cold tile floor. She still watched B.J., but not as intently.

"Are you all right, little fella? Sir Elvis?" B.J. picked up her dog and cooed to him. He nuzzled her face.

"Tell me exactly what happened, B.J.," Joanie said again. "I know you're upset. And scared. But you've got to tell me exactly what happened."

B.J. reluctantly lowered the dog to her lap. "Well," she said. "I just bled . . ."

"A little? A lot?" Joanie persisted.

"Mom, stop it," Caroline whispered.

Joanie put her hand on Caroline's knee and squeezed it. "Hush," she said again.

"Well . . . I guess you'd say . . . a little." B.J. sniffed loudly and wrapped her arms in front of her, enfolding Sir Elvis in a hug.

"So, it was kind of . . . wouldn't you say . . . spotting?" Joanie said quietly.

B.J. nodded. "Yes. Spotting."

"A little spotting," Joanie said, trying to keep her voice even and unemotional. B.J. wasn't much older than Caroline, she reminded herself. She was hysterical and frightened and hormonal. She probably hadn't intended to throw such a scare into the rest of them.

Or had she?

No, that was harsh, Joanie told herself. Surely not.

"A little spotting," B.J. echoed.

"So you didn't have a miscarriage," Ivy announced from the doorway.

"Mother," Joanie said warningly.

"I guess not." B.J. looked up at Ivy and shook her head.

"You bleed a lot when you have a miscarriage," Ivy continued. "I had one before R—before *Joanie*—was born. It was terrible. Very painful."

"Maybe we should get you up, B.J.," Joanie said. She stood up and extended her hand.

"I cried for days," Ivy said. "Nobody understood. Nobody said anything."

Caroline stood up, too, and she and Joanie pulled B.J. to her feet, while Sir Elvis barked at them. "Spotting is very common in many pregnancies," Joanie told B.J. She had learned that when she volunteered at the local hospital for several months, before she got bored and quit to pursue her new-found interest in sculpting. Her sculpting phase had lasted how long? Three months? "It usually doesn't mean anything."

"People have no idea how painful a miscarriage is," Ivy said. "Especially men."

"Mother," Joanie said, "will you see if you can find a bath-robe for B.J.?"

Outside, the temperature had cooled and feathery clouds surrounded the moon. Joanie rolled down her car window and felt the breeze on her flushed face as she drove. It felt soothing.

"People will tell you you'll get over a miscarriage," Ivy said to B.J. The two of them were huddled in the backseat of Joanie's car. "But you don't. You never really forget."

"Mother, I don't think that's helpful," Joanie said. Did she have to drive and control her mother at the same time? "B.J. didn't have a miscarriage. She just spotted a little. That's all. She's going to be fine."

"Men never understand," Ivy continued, undeterred. "Even the best ones can be very stupid and insensitive. My husband never understood."

"Yeah," B.J. said. "I know."

Oh, hell, Joanie thought. I give up.

Next to her, Caroline sat very still. Joanie knew Caroline was overwhelmed by the drama and the emotional whiplash. That's why she had begged Joanie to take B.J. and Sir Elvis back to their house to stay till Richard returned the next day. "B.J. can't stay alone," she had insisted. "She's too upset. Too weak. Please, Mom, *please*. Just for tonight and tomorrow morning."

And Joanie had relented. What else could she have done?

In the backseat, Sir Elvis stirred and barked a couple of yappy barks. B.J. leaned over to kiss his little mop of a head. "Shhhhh, baby dog," she said. "Shhhhh."

Sir Elvis whimpered and B.J. kissed him again. She loved taking care of small creatures. It had taken her years to figure this out about herself, but now she finally understood, knew her true purpose in life. It was so good to have a purpose after all these years.

"Nobody else knows this," B.J. said into the darkness and the shadowy faces ahead of her, beside her. "But I'm going to have a little girl. A daughter." She smiled in the dark. "So we're going to be very close. Like best friends."

She waited for someone to answer her, to squeal with pleasure. But, for a few long seconds, the car was enclosed in a polite silence. All she could hear was Sir Elvis's sloppy breathing.

"You're lucky to be having a daughter," Ivy said in a low voice, as if she were speaking to herself. "A lot of women prefer sons. But it's your daughter who'll take care of you."

"That's what I've always heard," B.J. said.

Caroline leaned back against the seat. She was glad no one was talking now. Even Ivy had given up her little miscarriage lecture in the backseat. And B.J. appeared to have fallen asleep.

"I know this was upsetting for you," her mother had said, as they were waiting for B.J. to pack an overnight case. "I wish you hadn't had to be here."

But, no. Joanie didn't understand, couldn't understand what Caroline had seen, what had really upset her. She had sat on that cold bathroom tile and watched her mother gently and matter-of-factly question B.J. Caroline had been surprised by Joanie's quiet authority and her kindness to B.J. She had calmed B.J.'s hysteria, which had finally relaxed into an exhausted silence. B.J. had stopped crying. She had become docile and agreeable.

Ivy had wrapped her into a warm bathrobe and patted her on the back. B.J. should just go to bed and get some sleep, they had all urged her. But, no. B.J. hadn't wanted to be left alone. So she had come with them, at Caroline's urging. Joanie had been reluctant, Caroline knew. But, once Caroline asked her, she'd nodded with that same calmness she'd shown all evening. Unlike everybody else in the car, Joanie actually seemed to know what she was doing. She'd been stronger and more reassuring than Caroline had seen her in years.

Now, sitting in the front seat next to her mother, Caroline turned around and gazed at B.J.'s face. It looked calm and satisfied in repose, streaked and momentarily illuminated by passing streetlights.

Something about that satisfaction, that utter peacefulness, unsettled Caroline. It was strange. She had always felt oddly sympathetic toward B.J. after all. She had seen so much of herself in B.J.—the wistfulness, the striving, the crazy, irrational hopes for something better.

Caroline hadn't approved of B.J.'s lying—well, wasn't that what it was? Lying?—about her getting pregnant. But she had understood why B.J. had done it. B.J. had simply wanted something so badly that she would have done anything to secure it. Was she so different from Caroline, who had been willing to cheat for a boy she'd fallen in love with?

Still. Peering around, Caroline watched B.J.'s narrow face, saw her chest rise and fall with sleep. She had lied to Caroline's father about her pregnancy. Then she had been perfectly willing to hint at a miscarriage tonight when she was scared to stay by herself. Had she even spotted, shown any blood? Or had it been another convenience to say so? Caroline would never breathe a word of it to Joanie, but she wondered.

At some juncture, it seemed to Caroline, you could pass a point. You could lie and cheat for just so long before it caught up with you. Not that anyone else would ever know. But wouldn't you eventually start doubting yourself, failing to appreciate what was honest and what wasn't? And who would you be then? What would you have left of yourself?

~~~~~

Tomorrow, Ivy thought, she would make some hot tea from a recipe she'd seen on the Internet. It was a "healing" tea, full of antioxidants and herbs. Probably, it tasted like swill, but that was acceptable if it was healing enough. Healing substances often tasted foul.

Then she'd take that steaming cup of tea to B.J. She would sit down and they would talk. She would tell B.J. more about her own miscarriage. Since B.J. was pregnant and had had her own scare, she would doubtless be interested in hearing about Ivy's experience.

Ivy didn't know the girl, B.J., that well. She didn't even know why she called herself B.J. or what it stood for. But Ivy could tell she needed help. The same way she had known Lupe needed help that first day in the restaurant.

Maybe B.J. just needed a friend. Ivy could understand that. You needed to gather people to you, even if it wasn't easy, even if it was something you didn't do naturally.

Caroline thought of Henry's handsome face, of his lean and muscular body. She thought of how much she'd wanted him, how much she wanted him to like her, how she ached for him. She would have done anything to please him. It was only B.J.'s phone call that had stopped her.

Caroline could see what had really happened in her bedroom. She could see the impatience, the expectations that Henry had brought with him. She could see that skinny girl with the fading pink hair who was so eager to please. She knew her too well. It was her, but it wasn't who she wanted to be.

She was going to change. She promised herself that, leaning over her knees and squeezing them in the darkened car. She needed a new life for herself, since the old one sure as hell wasn't working.

She was through with Henry, disgusted with him, finished with her desperate, foolish dreams about him. Next year, she'd take French instead of Spanish. French was much more exotic and artistic—like Caroline herself.

Yes, over the summer, she would change her life. She could hardly wait to leave the desperate, pink-haired girl and her dreams of that handsome, careless boy behind her. She would have three long months to think about what she would do with her life. That should be enough time to change, to become a different person. Maybe she could learn to like herself a little more, as Joanie had once urged her. Maybe she could learn to be a kinder, better person. Maybe she would dye her hair a new color.

Caroline threw her head back and stared in front of her, watching the dark night flood past her as the car raced forward. She felt that same overwhelming sense of longing rise up in her. She couldn't have said what it was she wanted so badly. She just knew it made her ache, almost pleasurably, and feel alive with possibility. She could feel her heart expanding till it was almost too big for her. For just a moment, she recognized that feeling, that silly, irrepressible gust of joy.

B.J. slept on. Joanie could see her in the rearview mirror, curled up with that yappy little dog of hers. She looked comfortable and cared for, seemingly unaware of all the trouble everyone else had gone to for her. Some women, Joanie thought, had the expectation they would always be cared for, that breathtaking thoughtlessness.

She supposed she herself had had those same qualities when she was younger. To some degree, anyway. But B.J. seemed to be a different kind of person. She had a steely tenacity to her that Joanie had lacked, a definite knack for getting her own way. Did Richard have any idea what he was in for?

"What does Richard think about the dog?" Joanie had asked B.J. as they loaded her into the backseat.

"He doesn't know about Sir Elvis yet," B.J. had said over the dog's barks. "It's a surprise."

Joanie had thought about mentioning Richard's allergies. But, no. She wouldn't want to spoil B.J.'s latest surprise.

Besides, Joanie had enough on her mind these days. She had a semiromantic relationship with a friend that needed to be resolved. A job she didn't like—and wanted to quit—in the middle of a crippling recession. A family to support. A new decade of challenges. Plenty to think about. More than enough.

Why was it, though, that—driving through the dark, with her fractious little half-asleep family and the jumbled complexities of her life—she felt so content and calm, as if she, or all of them together, could handle everything? Where had this eerie confidence come from? What had changed—and when?

Driving, Joanie could hear her friends now—Nadine and Mary Margaret and most of her soon-to-be-disbanded divorcée group. "You did *what*?" they would chorus. "You went to your ex's house and helped his girlfriend after her faked miscarriage? Then you brought her—and her ratty little dog—back to your house to stay till he got back? Oh, my God! You have *got* to be kidding! Like you didn't have enough problems already with your mother and daughter!"

And Roxanne Joan Horton Pilcher—age fifty, harried mother and reluctantly doting daughter, nobody's wife, and of late, nobody's fool, middle-aged office libertine, more buoyant than she would have ever believed, more demanding and expectant of herself than she'd ever been before—would listen to them and nod. Maybe she would say something. She didn't know yet. Or maybe she would stay silent and let them think whatever they wanted.

readers guide

for

women

on the

verge of a

nervous

breakthrough

Discussion Questions

1. Why does Joanie feel the need to tell Caroline that Richard and B.J. are expecting a baby instead of letting Richard tell her himself? How does Richard react when he discovers that Joanie has already shared the news with their daughter instead of letting him do so? Is his reaction justified?

2. Ivy knows it's wrong to have a favorite child, yet she admits to herself that she (secretly) prefers her son to her daughter. She feels this way despite the fact that she barely ever sees or even speaks to him. Given that Joanie is the one who took Ivy in when her finances plummeted, why is David still her favorite child? What does this say about Ivy's ideas on who has status or value in the world?

3. Joanie tells her friend Nadine that Richard once bought his mom a particularly large bouquet for Mother's Day right after his father had left her for a more exciting life. Years later, he leaves Joanie in much the same way. Why does it take her so long to realize that her husband had turned into his father?

Why is she so shocked when he behaves the same way his father did?

4. How does Ivy feel when the woman in the clothing store makes rude comments to her? In what ways does the salesperson's behavior perpetuate Ivy's feelings of uselessness and irrelevance? Is their interaction an accurate reflection of how we treat older women in society?

5. When Joanie blows up at Ivy during an argument at dinner, each of them behaves very differently. Do their ways of handling disagreements reflect a generational shift in the way they reveal their feelings? If so, how?

6. What does Joanie's reaction to Caroline and Sondra's decision to dye their hair reflect about her understanding of Caroline's state of mind? Is she in touch with her daughter's feelings? Is she surprised at her own reaction to Caroline's hot pink hair? If so, why?

7. Joanie offers many reasons for not getting out and dating after her divorce. What are they? Do they seem like they are really meant to help her heal from her sadness, loss, and anger, or are they just excuses for not wanting to risk being hurt?

8. Why does Ivy start acting out in strange ways—lying to the church receptionist about Myra and Francine hating flowers, shoplifting, getting thrown out of the diner? Why is she suddenly behaving so uncharacteristically?

9. What is going through Ivy's mind when she breaks down in the doctor's office? She hasn't cried like that in years, maybe ever. What is it about being in that situation, and having the

doctor behave so tenderly toward her, that makes her dissolve in tears?

10. When B.J. calls Caroline's house, so obviously in need, why does Caroline respond with such sympathy? She even interrupts her mom's fiftieth birthday celebration to get her to help take care of B.J. Why does Caroline care so much all of a sudden about her father's girlfriend? Is her behavior surprising?

11. Caroline finally realizes that Henry is just pretending to be interested in her because she is smart and will help him in school. Surprisingly, she isn't especially sad or even crushed. Instead, she realizes that she needs to change and looks forward to it. What do you think has made Caroline so insightful? Have we seen her grow and change over the course of the novel?

12. The author deals humorously with some fairly serious subjects—aging, economic hardship, divorce, adolescent rebellion, unrequited love (or at least infatuation). Do you think the humor in the book diminishes the importance of the subject matter or enhances it? Why?